DEVICE
FREE
WEEKEND

Previous Works by Sean Doolittle

DEVICE FREE WEEKEND

SEAN DOOLITTLE

GRAND
CENTRAL
NEW YORK   BOSTON

Grand Central Publishing
Hachette Book Group
1290 Avenue of the Americas, New York, NY 10104
grandcentralpublishing.com
twitter.com/grandcentralpub

First Edition: February 2023

Grand Central Publishing is a division of Hachette Book Group, Inc. The Grand Central Publishing name and logo is a trademark of Hachette Book Group, Inc.

The publisher is not responsible for websites (or their content) that are not owned by the publisher.

The Hachette Speakers Bureau provides a wide range of authors for speaking events. To find out more, go to www.hachettespeakersbureau.com or call (866) 376-6591.

Library of Congress Cataloging-in-Publication Data
Names: Doolittle, Sean, 1971- author.
Title: Device free weekend / Sean Doolittle.
Description: First edition. | New York : Grand Central Publishing, 2023.
Identifiers: LCCN 2022042076 | ISBN 9781538706596 (hardcover) | ISBN 9781538706633 (ebook)
Subjects: LCGFT: Thrillers (Fiction) | Novels.
Classification: LCC PS3604.O568 D48 2023 | DDC 813/.6—dc23/eng/20220909
LC record available at https://lccn.loc.gov/2022042076

ISBNs: 9781538706596 (hardcover), 9781538706633 (ebook)

Printed in the United States of America

LSC-C

Printing 1, 2022

For David Hale Smith
Champion and Friend

DEVICE
FREE
WEEKEND

THE PLEASURE OF YOUR COMPANY

CHAPTER 1

I<small>T HADN'T OCCURRED</small> to Stephen Rollins that buying an island was something that anybody, even your old college roommate, could go out and do.

Beau and Lainie said sure, why not? It's just real estate. There were websites. Will and Perry claimed to know a couple who'd bought their own ghost town, and those people weren't even all that wealthy. Not Ryan Cloverhill wealthy, certainly. Not cover-of-*Time*-magazine people, just regular ones.

If he was honest, Stephen supposed he'd never quite fully grasped, even after all these years, that Ryan *was* cover-of-*Time*, own-your-own-island people. This was the same Ryan Cloverhill who'd mistakenly filled their apartment dishwasher with regular Dawn and flooded the kitchenette with suds.

But that was a long time ago. Ryan Cloverhill—their Ryan Cloverhill—golfed with presidents now.

And he'd invited them all for Labor Day weekend: Beau and Lainie, known internally as Blainey; Will and Perry, known as Will and Perry; Emma, of course.

And Stephen, who'd spent the last month gravitating between opposing poles of delight and terror. He loved them all, his oldest and dearest friends. But when had they last spent any real time together in person, in the same place, all seven of them? A decade ago?

Closer to two.

Would they survive?

"It's a fair question," Will said on the phone. "But worth the risk."

Perry agreed: "Get your ass on that plane, Rollie. The pleasure of your company is cordially required."

Blainey—predictably—seemed fixated on the numbers. "What did Will and Perry get?"

"A four and a five," Stephen told them. "I don't remember who got which."

"Huh," Beau said. "We got three and six."

"I got three," Lainie joked from the other line. "*You* got six."

They'd been referring to their invitations, delivered earlier that week by private courier: heavy linen cardstock, clean Neutraface lettering, the geometric four-leaf insignia Ryan Cloverhill now used as a personal colophon. On the back of Stephen's, in a splash of glitz that didn't quite fit the minimalist design: a large numeral 2 stamped in silver foil.

"I'm sure it's not a personal ranking," Stephen told them.

Beau laughed. "Easy for you to say, number two."

"Anyway," Lainie said, "I guess we know who number one is."

Emma, of course.

Stephen never did manage to connect with her, somehow.

At least not until Denver International, a dozen weeks later, when they found themselves hopping the same connecting flight to Seattle. It was Friday morning, thirty minutes before takeoff. Stephen had completed the list of tasks required to leave his entire life and business in Chicago behind for four days, which consisted primarily of setting out extra food and water for the cat and locking the door to his apartment. The big weekend had arrived.

He saw Emma before she saw him. Stephen waited until she came within earshot, then said, "Of all the boarding gates in all the airports."

Emma Grant looked up, locking immediately on the sound of his voice. She'd been in hustle mode, joining the queue a touch on the late side, fighting with the zipper of her carry-on with coffee in one hand, her phone in the other.

The sudden wattage of her smile hit Stephen with enough force to make his heart stutter; she laughed and headed straight for him, arms outstretched. It looked almost as though she were offering him coffee and an iPhone. "Do you really see yourself as the Humphrey Bogart of this airport?"

"Good point." He stepped out of line to meet her, buzzing with adrenaline. He wasn't prepared yet. "Ryan probably owns it already."

"Come here," she said, and they were hugging tightly, awkwardly, all shoulder bags and elbows and handheld accessories. She smelled like Cinnabon and felt just like Emma; Stephen's head swam a little as she planted a fat kiss on his cheek. "It's so good to see your face. You asshole."

"You, too, Em. Please don't spill that on me."

"I should dump it on your head. Let me look at you."

"Then let me hold something."

She handed him the coffee, finished situating her bag, then laid her free palm on his cheek, shaking her head in wonderment that seemed to border on anthropological. The guy at the counter called the first group onto the plane, and people around them started to move. "Stephen Adelaide Rollins." She scratched at his temple. "The gray looks good."

"Bullshit. I look like my dad."

"I always had a thing for your dad."

Same old Emma. "You haven't aged a single damned day."

"Speaking of bullshit."

"Speaking of Ryan," he said, "obviously we have our illustrious host to thank for this meet-up. I'm 3C. Where are you?"

Emma swiped up her boarding pass, grinned, showed him her phone. "3D. Wanna switch?"

"I guess we should have known." Ryan had taken care of everybody's travel arrangements. Or had an assistant book it, more likely, but there must have been specific instructions involved. Leave it all to him, he'd said. You guys just do the getting here.

"We *would* have known," Emma noted, "if you'd returned any of my calls."

"I know. You're right. I'm an asshole."

"Or texts."

"Sorry, Em."

"Or emails."

"Shall we?" he said, gesturing toward the first-class line already trundling into the jet bridge.

They joined the procession, boarded the craft, and stowed their bags in the overhead bins. After settling in to their nice wide seats with extra padding and plenty of legroom, Emma looked over and said, "Hey. What number did you have on the back of your invite, anyway?"

They touched down at Sea-Tac at 12:37 p.m., already swapping stories like a pair of old thieves, perhaps the teensiest bit loopy from the in-flight transition from coffee to Bloody Marys somewhere over the Idaho Rockies.

Emma had relocated back to the Twin Cities after her divorce, which Stephen had known; she'd taken a new job last winter—general counsel to a midsize biotech firm in Minneapolis—which he should have known but didn't. Her son had started his freshman year at Vassar this fall. It was no Bardsley, haha, go Badger Hounds.

Stephen was still doing his thing in Chicago. Never married, no kids, which she already knew; not seeing anybody seriously at the moment, which she pretended not to know (though he felt reasonably certain that Will and/or Perry had probably been keeping her updated). It didn't seem important to observe the sad truth aloud: a six-hour drive, or a cheap ninety-minute flight, was really all that had stood between the two of them and a visit these past few years. But they'd always been good with unspoken agreements, him and Emma. Why lament missed opportunities when here they were now?

At baggage claim they were met by a lean, densely muscled fellow in a black T-shirt and aviator sunglasses holding up a sign that read "1 & 2" in sparkly silver glitter.

"Seriously, what's the deal with the numbers?" Stephen asked him. "Do you know?"

The guy grinned. "You must be two."

"We call him the Deuce." The Bloody Marys had been Emma's idea.

"Mr. Cloverhill asked me to play this for you." The guy tapped the screen of his own phone and held it out for Stephen and Emma to see. On the screen, an animated green Wicked Witch of the West croaked *All in good time, my little pretty*, flipped him a double bird, blew a raspberry for good measure, then dissipated in a puff of cartoon smoke.

Emma giggled merrily. Stephen said, "That sounds like Mr. Cloverhill."

"My name's Junipero. Call me Jud. The others should be on-site any time now. Barring the unexpected, you'll be joining them right on schedule." He took their suitcases, one in each hand, his sign tucked under one arm. "All set, then?"

The schedule, as Stephen understood it, began with a 2:00 p.m. muster at

Link Village, Ryan's waterfront office complex in South Lake Union. A light lunch, followed by a one-hour campus tour, ending in a ferry ride to Sham Rock, which was—of course—what Ryan Cloverhill would name his personal island.

He'd be awaiting their arrival, great-and-powerful-style, at the weekend home he'd built himself there. There would be preparatory cocktails, followed by a sunset cruise around the island aboard Ryan's VanDutch 55, piloted by Ryan himself. Then a chef-prepared meal, at which point, Stephen presumed, they would work together as a group to become properly shit-faced. It was to be a long, lazy, device free weekend: a chance to unplug, catch up, and enjoy one another's company for the first time in far too many years, free from the kinds of digital distractions that had purchased all of this in the first place.

"We're all yours, Your Judness." Emma looped her arm through Stephen's. "Show us the yellow brick road."

CHAPTER 2

THEY FOLLOWED THEIR chaperone out of the terminal into a bright blue September day. A parking valet met them outside the terminal in a gleaming black Lincoln Navigator. Jud binned his sign, handed the valet some glitter-flecked cash, and loaded their bags into the back himself. Before long, they were gliding north on I-5 through midday traffic with seemingly preternatural ease.

Alone up front, Jud displayed the aptitude of a practiced executive transpo man, scanning far ahead, anticipating gaps, rarely so much as brushing the brake pedal until it was time to join the crush of downtown traffic. Though his impressive physique could have been acquired at any local gym, his personal carriage—a certain efficiency of movement, a certain relaxed alertness—suggested something more than standard-grade limo driver to Stephen. If he'd been forced to guess, based on a few of the people he'd encountered in his line of work over the years, he'd have guessed ex-military.

"So how long have you known Ryan?" he asked.

"You mean Mr. Cloverhill? About ten years," Jud said pleasantly. "Started out driving, but I may be rusty. Sorry for the bumps back there."

Stephen hadn't noticed any; they might as well have been riding on a cloud. "What do you do now?"

"Most of the time, physical security on campus," Jud said. "For travel and big events, I head up Mr. Cloverhill's personal protection team."

"My, my," Emma said, nudging Stephen. "Mr. Cloverhill has a team."

Jud chuckled. "Usually it's just me. But we live in troubling times."

"Ain't that the truth." She continued to engage Jud Bernal in friendly chatter while Stephen drifted, watching the world pass beyond his window, focusing on nothing in particular. As Jud took an exit, Stephen spotted the top of the Space Needle up ahead, hovering just over the tops of the buildings like a flying saucer in broad daylight. Something about the image gave him an odd feeling he couldn't quite name. Then the off-ramp dumped them onto tree-lined Mercer Street, and the buildings closed ranks around them.

Link Village—Ryan's aforementioned corporate campus—occupied a thirty-acre strip of shorefront just east of Lake Union Park. It consisted of a four-story headquarters building designed by Rem Koolhass, along with six other main structures, all roughly ring-shaped, laid out in a greater oval. Viewed aerially— which was the only way Stephen had ever viewed the place before now, using internet satellite maps like everybody else—the buildings appeared to form links in a chain, with solar rooftops and winding footpaths and a parklike green space in the middle.

Jud left their bags in the car and led them from the parking facility through a series of badged entrances, still brushing glitter from his dark clothing. They took an elevator to the lobby level. There, he bid them a good lunch, transferring custody to a young woman in a sharp skirt and blouse who introduced herself as Kai.

"Welcome to the Pacific Northwest," she said, greeting them with handshakes and a pleasant smile. "How was your flight? Everything smooth?"

"A little too smooth," Emma said. "I should know better than to start tipping this early in a vacation. And on an empty stomach no less."

Kai laughed. "I think we can help with that. Follow me."

She took them through the bright, soaring lobby, all glass and steel and bamboo accent panels, her heels clicking along the polished concrete floor. She asked if either one of them had ever been to Seattle before.

"Not since Kurt Cobain was alive," Stephen said, thinking back to the Sub Pop store he'd spotted in the airport on their way to baggage claim. God, they were all ancient now. "With Ryan, if you can believe it. Sorry. I mean Mr. Cloverhill."

"Not to worry. He mostly goes by Ryan around here. So! Full circle for you, then."

"Like links in a chain."

"God, that road trip," Emma said. "It was the first time any of us had latte. Do you remember he took that cab to wherever Starbucks had their headquarters and tried to convince somebody to give him a meeting? They didn't even have a website yet, and here's this longhair stoner kid from Minnesota talking franchise. What was his idea? The online ordering thing. This was way before anybody felt comfortable using..."

Stephen said, "Star bucks."

"Star bucks! That was it." She snorted at the memory. "Poor Ryan. He was so outraged when they sent him packing. He griped about that for fifteen hundred miles."

"And he was never heard from again," Stephen said, nodding generally at the sleek, ultrahip space around them.

"That," Kai said, "is hilarious. I've never heard that story before."

Stephen chuckled. "Stick with us. We got all kinds."

They passed through another badged door and out into unfiltered sunlight again, following a path through a small sculpture garden and into the sprawling, vibrantly landscaped central courtyard.

"Wow," Emma said, breathing in a deep dose of fresh inland air. "Get a lungful of that, why don't you?"

"We've got the right breeze today," Kai told them. "The lake can smell a little funky sometimes. The whole town, really, if the marine layer gets weird. Ah—there they are."

Stephen saw four figures grouped together near a freestanding water wall. The feature—a vertical slab of salt-and-pepper granite curtained in what looked like stainless-steel chain mail—lent a cinematic shimmer to the sight of them.

Will. Perry. Beau. Lainie. Immediately, Stephen felt that strange parallax he always felt when seeing someone intimately familiar from a distance—the same thing he'd felt when he'd first spotted Emma at the airport in Denver. Had that really been just four hours ago?

Then the distance was gone, and everybody was hooting and cackling. Kai stood well aside, respectfully granting the others full access so that Stephen and Emma could be appropriately mauled.

"God, it's really you!" Will said, clapping Stephen on the back, shaking him by the shoulders, then giving long, tall Perry a crack at him, while Emma and Lainie hugged and squeezed hands. Beau stood around grinning with his too-white teeth against his too-tan face, his too-blond mane ruffling in the breeze, until Emma grabbed him by the shirt and they all coalesced into one big hugging huddle. A huggle.

"I hope nobody's watching this from the windows," Stephen said.

Beau said, "Are you kidding? I hope they're Linking it!"

Will and Perry groaned. Lainie said, "Lay off, haters. Going viral is better than sex."

"Sex with him, maybe," Perry said, making a play for Beau's hairdo. Beau swatted, everybody laughed.

"I think it's sweet," Kai called, somewhere outside the circle. "Two o'clock, gang; who's ready to eat?"

Lunch was mixed greens and swordfish sliders in the employee food court. The tour, led by Kai, was impressive and informative and featured lots of productive-looking young people in flip-flops, T-shirts, and wireless earbuds. Finally, when it was time, the ferry to Sham Rock, out beyond the Sound, turned out to be a Sikorsky S-76 executive helicopter.

"Holy shit," Beau said, appraising the bird with unmasked covetousness. He pulled out his phone again and immediately started shooting video. "Now this is how you live."

Perry said, "Will you put that away?"

"Are you kidding? If we're going dark all weekend, you better believe I'm getting this while I can."

The tour had ended on the roof of the main building, which the Linksters referred to simply as "One." Kai introduced them to their pilot, who turned out to be none other than Junipero "Jud" Bernal. Same shades, same black T-shirt. Much less glitter.

Will looked around, glanced out at the lake, then said, perhaps a little nervously, "Is it even legal to fly this low?"

"Of course it's legal," Beau said. "They wouldn't have a helicopter up here if it wasn't legal."

Lainie nodded. "All the bigwigs have helicopters."

"Sure, bigwigs with skyscrapers. We're only four floors up. Aren't there, like, ordinances or something?"

"Mr. Cloverhill's pretty good with ordinances," Jud said. "Anyway, down-wash radius on this honey is 132 feet, and we're well clear of the park and the nearest marina. Flight conditions are perfect, I've got over five hundred PIC hours, no worries."

"No worries!" Emma said, patting Jud on the shoulder. "He's a really good driver."

"I'll bet he is," Lainie said.

Beau said, "Hey!"

Jud seemed to take it all in stride. "All set, then?"

They all thanked Kai and loaded in, one by one. Beau and Perry squabbled over the forward-facing window seats like grade-schoolers. Will looked more than happy to take the middle between them. The cabin smelled like leather and, after Jud buttoned them up, seemed almost hermetically sealed. They could carry on yakking at normal volume even as the main rotor began its howling windup directly over their heads. Even beanpole Perry seemed to have enough room for all his limbs.

"Oh, come on, admit it, you grump." Emma elbowed Stephen lightly in the ribs as they slowly lifted, climbed, then tilted forward over the rippling lake. "This is pretty amazing."

"Our little Ryan," Will said. He sounded fine but appeared to be white-knuckling Perry's knee. He'd never been a great flier.

Perry patted his hand. "I'm so damn proud of him." Then he glanced at Stephen. "You there. Everything okay?"

Why did everybody keep looking at him? "Who's grumpy?" Stephen said. "I'm proud of him too."

It was the honest truth.

Although, looking out his window, he was pretty sure, based on arm gestures, that the tiny guy on the miniature sailboat two hundred feet below was inviting them to cram it as they ascended, up and away.

CHAPTER 3

THEY FOLLOWED A narrow channel west from the north end of the lake, out over Salmon Bay, then Puget Sound, Jud occasionally narrating from the cockpit over the onboard sound system: *Whidbey Island starboard—that's off to our right. Marrowstone coming up port. We're tracking right along Admiralty Inlet.* Then the landmasses drifted away beneath them, and the view from the cabin windows was nothing but shimmering water, calm for miles. *Strait of Juan de Fuca, eastern edge. San Juan Islands to the north; Olympic Peninsula to the south. Any fishermen onboard, the halibut run pretty good out here.*

"You know, we should get out there and try that...," Beau started.

Will, Perry, and Lainie, in unison: "Please don't say it."

"...just for the halibut."

Perry grimaced. "Can somebody please reach over and murder him?"

Emma said, "What about fisherwomen?"

Jud, over the speakers: *Nice blue water today.*

Beau said, "That's because it's reflecting the sky. I saw that on the Discovery Channel."

A lot of people think the water reflects the sky. It's really the sun. The water eats up the longwave light and sends back the shortwave. That's the blue.

Beau kept looking out his window as if he hadn't heard anything, but he casually lowered his phone and placed it facedown on his knee. He wouldn't be using that take, it seemed. Perry bit back a grin and turned toward the window. Emma said, "I think I'm crushing on Jud a little." Stephen wondered if the guy could actually hear them up there in the cockpit.

"Ooh!" Lainie said. "*I think I see it.*"

Jud: *Coming right up. Everybody hang tight, we'll put down in a bit. I'll fly over first, give us all a good look; then we'll come back around.*

Beau's phone came right back up again in video mode. Stephen nudged Emma in the middle seat next to him, asked her if she wanted to switch places. It really was quite a view.

"Thanks, but I'm with him," Emma said, pointing at Will in the seat directly across from her. "I don't like looking down from up here."

Will batted his eyes at her, covering his heart with his palm. Stephen knew she was lying through her teeth, and Will probably did, too, but that was Emma: always aiming for solidarity.

As for the view, it more or less matched the overhead shots he'd already seen in *Dwell* last year. Sham Rock was shaped approximately like a jagged boot print, fatter at the heel, narrower at the toe. There was an upcurved spit at the narrow end, a navigation light tower perched at its tip. A smaller spit jutted out like a cleat near the inside arch of the boot. Lots of evergreen-type trees on top. Rocky cliffs down to the water below.

The main house occupied the fat end of the island: a big L-shape nestled into a clearing, near the cleat, overlooking a dock and boathouse. Stephen saw a rooftop pool and tennis court. Across the island, a smaller, simpler house sat at the narrow end—some kind of guest or caretaker cottage, Stephen presumed. He saw a narrow track of road winding through the trees between the two. A few other miscellaneous outbuildings here and there.

"If I were a Bond villain," Perry said, "this is exactly where I'd put my lair."

Emma liked that. She steepled her fingertips and adopted her idea of a villain voice: "Come, come, Mr. Bond. We both know you'll never leave this island alive."

"You guys," Lainie sighed. She'd always felt left out when people started riffing.

They passed over the helipad: a big white square set off from the house, with a high-viz geometric clover in the center. Then over the cottage, then the light tower, then out over the water again. Will looked a little green as they banked and came around, just as Jud had promised. Perry casually took Will's hand without taking his eyes from the window.

Then they were descending, slow and easy, treetops waving in the rotor wash as if welcoming them back to solid ground.

The first time Stephen Rollins ever laid eyes on Ryan Mitchell Cloverhill had been the week before the start of fall semester, freshman year, at Bardsley College in Stillwater, Minnesota. They'd been assigned as roommates on the second floor of Anders Hall, the campus honors dorm. This had been long before incoming freshmen had the ability to meet and select their future bunkmates through an online portal. In those days, at least at Bardsley, you showed up, saw who you'd gotten stuck with, and went from there.

Who Stephen saw, upon first entering room 205 on move-in day, was a knobby rope of a kid with long, wavy blond hair, a hearty soul patch, and a Fugazi T-shirt that looked at least a size too large for his frame. The first thing he'd thought, seeing the milk crates full of music CDs already taking up valuable square footage, was: *We're gonna get along juuust fine.*

The Ryan Cloverhill waiting for them at the edge of the helipad had matured nicely, even photogenically. He cut a sturdy-looking figure in the late-afternoon light, outdoorsy-casual, yet perceptibly well-heeled. He'd dressed for the occasion in hard denim jeans, oiled leather Chelsea boots, and a light canvas jacket appropriate to the air, which smelled like salt and cedar and seemed about fifteen degrees cooler out here than it had back at Link Village. The long hair was gone, but he still had a full head of it. The soul patch was gone, but his face had squared up with age. Overall, he passed convincingly, Stephen thought, for what he was: a middle-aged megabillionaire social media CEO on holiday.

But the moment he saw them all, his face lit up, and the old Ryan resurfaced in a snap. He shot out his arms, shimmied his hips, and dance-walked toward them, grinning like a lunatic.

Emma cried out joyfully, sprinted toward him. Ryan laughed and swung her around, and then it was bear hugs and kisses and feinted gut punches for everybody, individually and in batches.

Stephen brought up the rear, and Ryan saw him coming. More than anything else in his life just then, Stephen did *not* want to do that thing from the movies where the two estranged old friends stare each other down like gunslingers, then suddenly grab each other in a big, manly, backslapping hug, but goddammit that's exactly what happened. Because it was Ryan.

Their Ryan. He felt a little bonier under the jacket than he looked from a

distance. Like a longhaired cat that was mostly fur. Stephen couldn't help thinking of that too-big Fugazi T-shirt. Same old Ryan under there.

"Jesus, man," Ryan said, a warm hand on Stephen's neck. "Just…Jesus." His
eyes flickered up. "The gray looks good."

"Ow," Stephen said, rubbing a spot on his sternum where something hard
and sharp had poked him during the clinch.

Ryan grinned. "Oh, yeah."

He reached inside the jacket and pulled out a CD: Jane's Addiction's first
album, liner insert faded, jewel case clouded with age.

He handed it to Stephen and said, "You left that in my car."

They determined, on the tarmac path leading from the helipad down to the
house, that it really had been approaching twenty years now since they'd all
breathed the same air at the same time: Cape Cod, 2004, Will and Perry's wedding, the same day the marriage law took effect in Massachusetts. This had still
been a couple of years before the rise of Ryan Cloverhill and Link Labs, starting
with that first humble social networking website and taking over the world from
there. The inevitable after-college drift had started a while before that, of course.
But their own little postsecondary Pangaea had yet to break apart into wholly
separated continents, connected primarily by technology.

"I don't even know where to start!" Lainie said. "I feel like I want to eat you
all up."

Will said, "Yikes."

Ryan chuckled. "Well, we've got all weekend. Plus there's lamb chops for dinner, so save some room. Come on, let me show you around."

Down the path they went, as Jud stayed behind and unloaded their bags: the
Stillwater Seven, reunited.

The house at the end of the path was a showpiece, no question, yet somehow—
apart from its location—not overly ostentatious, by mansion standards: sixty-five
hundred tasteful square feet in the perennially sought-after "midcentury modern"
style. Two stories of clean angles and cantilevered planes, constructed of smooth

concrete, with entire walls made of windows to capture the stunning 360-degree views.

At the mahogany front door, Ryan said, "I'll show you your rooms and you can get settled in." He opened the door, then turned and said, "But first things first."

"God, it smells good in there," Emma said.

"You just wait," Ryan told her. "Luna's risotto will put you in a coma." He reached into the warm, golden mystery of the interior entryway behind him and produced a small wicker basket. "Now, my good friends, we come to the uncomfortable matter of...your devices."

"Aw, come on," Beau said. "Are we really doing that?"

"The sat-fi's encrypted, and you probably won't get a regular signal out here anyway, but still: the rules *were* clearly stated."

"Yeah, but think of our feed!" Beau laughed, hooking an arm around Lainie, though Stephen could tell he wasn't completely kidding. "This shit *definitely* puts us over the top with the people at Netflix."

"Don't mind him," Lainie said, patting Beau's midriff. "Our agent made us promise to ask."

Stephen still had trouble getting his mind around it. Lainie and Beau Hemford: bona fide, self-made celebrity Linkstreamers. Having owned and operated a real estate agency in Laguna Beach for many years, they'd been old hands at producing their own local television spots by the time UpLink and Linkstamat came along. Like everyone else, they'd embraced the platforms as a cheaper, easier way to accomplish what had cost them an arm and a leg to accomplish before. But then a funny thing happened: little by little, the Hemfords became more popular as Link personalities than they'd ever been as Realtors.

Three or four years ago, they'd finally gone all in on building their online brand. They now traveled the world, ate a lot of food, wore a lot of clothing, and remodeled a lot of "life spaces" for increasingly well-to-do clients, which they packaged as half-hour episodes for their own UpLink series: *(I)n (R)eal (L)ife with Lainie and Beau*. Their million-plus followers seemed to love their bantering luxury-couple dolce vita routine: Lainie starring as the long-suffering, sun-bleached, surf-milf shotcaller; Beau as the overconfident, equally sun-bleached, know-it-all dunce who couldn't seem to help falling ass-backward into flowers.

"I'll make some calls later if it helps," Ryan said. "This weekend's just for us. Fork 'em over."

Will and Perry laughed and dropped their phones into the basket. Emma followed, then Stephen.

Ryan narrated as they passed the basket around: "Transport yourselves, if you will, to a time before. A time when hashtags were pound symbols. When computer screens, for those lucky enough to possess their own, had nothing but words on them. Bardsley College circa 1991, let's say."

The basket finally made its way to Blainey, collectively named Gleen.com's "Linkstamat Lifestyle Power Couple" for June. Beau dropped his phone into the basket, handed the basket back to Ryan.

"And the watches."

Beau sighed, trading the basket back and forth with Lainie as they each removed their smartwatches and dropped them in. Again, he extended the basket to Ryan.

Again, Ryan made no move to accept. "And the backup piece."

Beau stared blankly, then rolled his eyes. "Oh, fine." He pulled a second phone from his back pocket and dropped that in too. "Happy?"

"Jubilant," Ryan said. He looked sternly at Lainie.

Lainie showed her palms. "I'm clean!"

"Very well. You may enter."

"All this from the Man Who Linked the World," Beau said. "Incredible."

"We'll handle tablets and laptops after Jud brings up the luggage."

Emma said, "He can search me if you think it's the wisest course."

"Me too," Will said.

"Somebody's feeling better," Perry said. "Good grief, when did this crew get so slutty?"

Emma laughed. "Not to worry. Something tells me Jud only has eyes for Kai anyway."

Ryan said, "Oh? What makes you say that?"

"Just a hunch. But we definitely caught a vibe when he handed us off for the tour."

Stephen said, "We did?"

"Ooh," Lainie said. "Workplace romance. I love it."

Ryan chuckled, tucking the basket full of smart devices under one arm. "I'm sure they'll self-report to HR when appropriate. Meanwhile, I appreciate you being such good sports. I still can't believe you're all really here."

Emma stepped in and gave him another squeeze. Ryan roped her in with his free arm and squeezed back. Then he stood to one side, opening the threshold for business.

"Welcome to Sham Rock," he said.

CHAPTER 4

THEY'D STARTED LIKE this: Ryan and Stephen in room 205, Lainie and Emma down the hall in 209, Will and Beau next door to them in 211.

Ryan and Emma had known each other well already—had in fact been close friends since childhood, having grown up together on the same street in south Minneapolis, in a picturesque neighborhood of dense winding streets then called Fuller, now known as Tangletown. Lainie Goss hailed from the funky, well-to-do shadow of Mount Tamalpais in Marin County, California. Beau Hemford came from Dallas, where his family owned a group of luxury car dealerships. Will and Stephen both came from more working-class backgrounds: Will Shrader's a farming community in rural Nebraska; Stephen's in Carbondale, Illinois, where his mother worked occasional temp jobs and his father fixed trucks in the USPS motor pool.

In those days, at Bardsley, all honor students were automatically enrolled in the requisite Introduction to Philosophy seminar their first year on campus. The six of them wound up in Professor Mendota's section together, fall semester; it was here that they'd first met Perry Therkle—the long, slender guy Stephen had seen lounging in the common or loping across the quad, shaggy hair in his eyes. Perry, from quote-unquote Back East, inhabited one of Anders' coveted solo rooms up on the third floor. While his bone-dry slyness garnered him a quick reputation as something of a smug assface amongst others in class, Stephen had thought he was hilarious; he'd been first to invite the guy into their study group, formed naturally around the gravitational hub of Ryan and Emma's preexisting friendship (along with the nearly instant chemical reaction that had yielded the new compound known as Blainey).

They'd been young strangers traversing a strange new land, moored together on this quaint wooded campus on the banks of the St. Croix River. But by that first winter break, they'd all learned something valuable about one another: for every clear gulf that existed between them as individuals—in personalities, in politics, in their tastes around such basic compatibility indicators as movies and music and television—they could all, at any time, intentionally or unintentionally, make each other laugh out loud.

Thus they became seven, practically inseperable from that point on. Second year, they'd pooled their dough and rented a creaky converted duplex off campus together: four of the guys crammed into one apartment, with Emma, Lainie, and Perry luxuriating in the other. It was a group that ultimately had produced, in total, countless good times, two cross-country road trips, two long-term households, and an uncomfortable romantic triangle that had, for a few stupid years at least, become a wedge.

But now, on the ample foredeck of Ryan's fifty-five-foot motor yacht, even Stephen had to admit that they felt hardly wedged at all.

They described a smooth, easy ring around the island, the view from water level consisting mostly of cliff faces topped with trees. Douglas fir and western red cedar, according to Ryan.

"How do you get electricity way out here?" That was Will's question. Ever the farmboy, always interested in the nuts and bolts.

"Ninety percent solar when it's sunny," Ryan called back from the wheel, hair ruffling in the breeze. "Twenty when it's pissing rain for weeks on end. The generators fill in. Mags and Luna stay year-round in the house up there." Ryan pointed up toward the narrow end of the island, silhouetted in the long light of the setting sun. "They'll head back to the mainland with Jud for this weekend. Otherwise, they look after things when I'm not here."

Beau called, "What about flyovers?"

Perry rolled his eyes. "Flyovers."

"What?" Beau said. "You don't think tourists flock to this place? It was on *60 Minutes*."

"That's true," Ryan conceded. "The tour companies are out here all the time. Paparazzi too. It's a strange world when even a private island isn't private."

"What about boats?" Beau said, casting a smug look toward Perry. "Ever get hop-ons?"

But Ryan had tired of the topic of island security if Stephen were any judge of his old pal's body language. Always that slight raise of the shoulders. His method of changing the subject was literally to point with his finger, like a father distracting young children—out to the open water, away from Sham Rock. "There's been a pod of orcas hanging out all summer. I hope we get to see them."

"I'm going to be dreaming about that," Emma said. "Orcas, please."

"Hey, Beauregard." Perry reached out a leg and kicked Beau playfully in the shoe. "Give us the lowdown on orcas."

"Why would I know anything about orcas?"

"I thought you watched Discovery Channel."

"Oh, that's funny. What's it like being a professional comedian? Is there health insurance? Do people ever push you off boats when you least expect it?"

"Christ almighty, will you two knock it off already?" Lainie shook her head. "I swear, you're worse than the boys."

Freshmen at Arizona State, Beau and Lainie's twins. Stephen had met them when they were toddlers, at Will and Perry's wedding, but he hadn't seen them since. Not outside a Christmas card or Blainey's UpLink, at least. He wondered if they were still maniacs.

He also wondered why Captain Cloverhill kept massaging his right side when he thought the rest of them weren't looking.

＊＊＊

Back at the house, as promised, everybody met Mags and Luna. The two women were already on their way to the helipad, hand in hand, weekend duffels slung over their shoulders. They looked to Stephen like a May-September pair: Luna younger and brunette; Mags a little taller and silvery blond. Both were dressed in joggers and fleece pullovers.

"This is like meeting royalty," Luna told them on the tarmac path, greeting them each by name, on sight, apparently needing no formal introductions. "We've heard so much about all of you."

Emma laughed. "Loyal subjects, more like."

"Lucky for him," said Mags, patting Ryan's cheek. Stephen guessed she was closer to their own age than Luna's—somebody they might conceivably have encountered at Bardsley, once upon a time. He supposed that made all of them Septembers. An appropriate time of year for this trip, now that he thought of it. "This weekend is literally all he's been talking about."

"Well," Ryan said, "I've made some grandiose claims about the risotto. What do I need to do?"

"Not a thing," Luna said. "Except eat it."

What was the glance that had passed between her and Mags just then? Stephen had no way of deciphering it. He noticed the comfortable way Ryan embraced them both. He noticed the platonic affection in the way Mags looked him in the eyes as they separated—affection and something else he couldn't decipher. In fact, there seemed to be a whole unspoken conversation going on between just the three of them.

But none of it was any of his business. A clear thought came to him in that moment: *These are the people in Ryan's life now.*

Then the two women wished them all a good weekend and hiked along up the path.

At the helicopter, silhouetted in the dusky distance, Jud took their bags and helped them load in. Everybody stood around watching from the path until they finally lifted off, *whop-whop-whopping* into the purple twilight. Soon the Sikorsky became a fixed triangle of location lights beneath a flashing red collision beacon, floating off to join the faint constellation of nighttime lights already forming on the far-distant mainland.

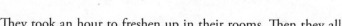

They took an hour to freshen up in their rooms. Then they all rejoined around Ryan's dining room table, an oblong slab hewn entirely from the Washington State gemstone: petrified wood.

There they ate themselves silly, stuffing their faces with tomahawk lamb chops, fresh grilled vegetables, Luna's now-infamous lemongrass risotto, and lots of good red wine. There were rich, tangy persimmon tarts for dessert, which nobody could eat, but everybody ate anyway. By the time the meal was over they could barely speak, let alone move.

But somehow they made their way to the living area, where they deposited themselves into the furniture. Their host—over Emma's strenuous objections, and everybody else's not-so-strenuous ones—insisted on clearing the dishes himself as they convalesced.

Meanwhile, the booze kept flowing, a full range of digestif options: there was port wine, or cognac, or a selection of rare whiskeys and tequilas. And they all had plenty to digest.

Ryan joined them in no time. He'd taken the liberty of gathering about a month's worth of early-'90s MTV, which he called up over the in-house streaming system. A massive flatscreen rose up like a servo-driven monolith from the sustainable hardwood floor. "Okay, okay," he said. "*Some* devices."

They chilled and laughed at the clothes, the hair, the old music videos that had played on an ever-present loop back then. At that size, the old broadcasts looked so pixelated that it felt easy to glide right through them, slipping back in time. They gorged on nostalgia, flowing naturally into a running game of *Remember that time when...?* Everybody laughed until their faces were rubber. Lainie held her head in her hands, and Perry consoled her, as Will and Beau fell back into their Beavis and Butt-Head routine.

Around midnight, just as it was time to really get the party started, the wild-and-crazy lot of them had mostly fallen asleep where they sat.

Stephen wasn't far from it himself. He was slouched in one of two available Corbu sofas—legs sprawled, Emma's stocking feet in his lap, looking at the TV through his eyelashes—when he sensed movement. He mustered the energy to hoist his eyelids open and turn his head.

Ryan was there, grinning. He shifted his eyes in an upward motion, indicating some unspecified area above them. Quietly, he said, "Cigar?"

CHAPTER 5

STEPHEN ROLLINS HAD always been pretty good at reading people. Or so he'd believed. Then came the day he'd first met Ryan Cloverhill: a work of dense literature hidden inside an open comic book.

From that day to this, it remained the fastest friendship he'd ever formed. Stephen had come to Stillwater a retired semi-jock after a summer spent shedding his high school skin. Ryan, back then, was still a mystery even unto himself: three parts puppy to one part gremlin, with more brain than he knew what to do with and the social grace of a writhing power line. Six months prior to meeting each other, neither might have spared the other a glance. Five minutes after meeting each other, it was as if they'd been best friends for years.

They'd eventually fallen out hard over Emma, of course; this was as central a plot point in the legend of the Stillwater Seven as Stillwater itself. Somehow, back then, Stephen truly hadn't seen either twist coming—the romance *or* Ryan's reaction to it. After nearly three years spent riding shotgun in each other's lives, he'd honestly expected Ryan Cloverhill to be happier for the two of them than anybody. So much for reading people.

But they were middle-aged men now. Those hatchets were buried, rusting underground.

Meanwhile, he had a few questions.

So he eased off the couch and followed their illustrious host up the central floating staircase, past the upper bedroom level, all the way to the rooftop of the house.

Outside, in the chilly dark, Ryan led the way to a bunch of laid-back seating around the illuminated infinity pool. They sat facing west, looking across the pool, across the clearing, in the general direction of Vancouver Island, somewhere in the much bigger water out there. Ryan produced a strictly prohibited smartphone, tapped the screen a few times, and killed the pool lights. In the silvery moonlight, their little man-made puddle became part of the twinkling ocean beyond.

"Be honest," Stephen said. "You have no intention of following your own no-device rule this weekend, do you?"

Ryan winked, dipping his fingers into his shirt pocket. "It's good to be the king."

He came out of the pocket holding a nice fat joint. He sparked up the twist of end paper with a butane lighter, took a hit to get it going, and passed the joint to Stephen.

Stephen chuckled. "I thought you said cigars."

Tight voice: "Good to be the king." Exhale.

What the hell. Stephen pinched the number from between Ryan's fingers, trying to remember the last time he'd gotten high. He coughed like a rookie.

"Attaboy." Ryan settled back and looked at the vast, inky, star-crusted sky. "Riding a bike."

They passed the joint between them for a few minutes, enjoying the brisk sea air. It felt like breathing pure oxygen out here. Oxygen and Lemon Diesel, anyway.

In the far distance, above the jagged horizon formed by the dark treetops, Stephen could see the regular pulsing of a bright white light. It took him a moment to understand what he was seeing: the automated navigation tower out on the spit. Something about it made him think back to the sight of the Space Needle hovering over the buildings in town.

"This really is something," he said.

"I know," Ryan croaked. "I got a guy down-coast, does his own crossbreeding. One-thousand-percent completely organic."

"I mean this." Stephen gestured all around. The sky seemed otherworldly out here. The whole world seemed otherworldly out here. Or maybe it was partly the weed; three hits in, his arm movements already felt exaggerated. "It's like... I don't even know what it's like."

"A fantasy?" Ryan nodded. "Yeah. Prospero's Island without the tempest, I know."

"I thought you were going to say *Fantasy Island*. Without Hervé Villechaize."

They fell into giggles. Ridiculous. "Damn," Stephen said. "I am very stoned."

"Lightweight."

"Riding a bike, my ass. This bike's got jet engines." Stephen took one last baby puff, then left Ryan to finish off the herb by himself.

"Part of me wondered if you'd make it out here," Ryan said.

"Really?"

"A little."

Stephen felt utterly placid. Not quite true, but he felt pretty good. "Turn down an expense-paid invitation to spend four days on Prospero's fantasy island with the world-famous billionaire himself?"

"Don't even start with that shit, man. Not you. Seriously."

"Kidding. Couldn't wait to see everybody." He cocked a finger Ryan's way. "You most of all, Scarecrow."

"I don't hear much from you anymore."

"I don't hear much from you either."

"I guess that's true."

"It's just life. Everybody's doing their thing." *You most of all*, he thought. "But rest assured, the Rollins-Cloverhill cosmic tether stretches light-years and crosses many moons."

Tight voice: "You really are stoned." Exhale. "Still, I'm glad to hear you say that."

"But I *would* like to know why you invited us in the first place."

Ryan gave him a look, but he didn't bother playing coy. It may have been an unfair question, or at least an impolite one, but that didn't make it any less legitimate. The invitations truly had come straight out of the blue. "You're really going to make me go through the whole cliché?"

"I'm a guest. Humor me."

Ryan sighed. "I'm staring down the other side of fifty. Married twice, divorced twice, no kids. Almost nobody in my life who doesn't work for me. Definitely nobody who knew me before I had more dough than any one asshole needs." He blew lightly on the end of the joint to keep the ember going. "Recently, I had a moment of clarity, during which I realized that I had a choice: I could start the long, slow process of Charles Foster Kane–ing myself out here alone...or I could make a real effort to reconnect—actually reconnect—with the people I love. And hope they still love me." Here he paused for a beat, gazing out across the water. He seemed ready to add something more, but then he shrugged. "Does all that satisfy?"

"No...," Stephen started to say.

"Jesus, dude. You always were a tough room."

"No, I mean: Why now?"

"I don't understand the question."

Stephen sat up, tried to focus. His brain seemed to be trailing his eyeballs now. "You hardly ate anything at dinner. You made a big show, cutting up your food and clinking your silverware together and moving shit around on your plate, but you didn't really eat much. And you were sweating bullets the whole time. You keep making these faces when you think nobody's paying attention. You stand funny sometimes. And on the boat. Don't even try telling me whatever's going on with you wasn't flaring up then."

He finally gave himself an ulcer. That's what he'd been thinking at first. Stephen knew it had been a challenging couple of years for Link Labs; for a while there, it seemed like every time he turned around, there was Ryan's face beneath a high-strung headline. Or on the news, testifying before one congressional subcommittee or another. But nobody called an elaborate reunion over an ulcer.

Ryan said nothing for a long moment.

Then: "Okay."

"Okay what?"

"I won't tell you that."

Stephen felt his heart sinking. "But it's nothing too serious."

"I guess I won't tell you that either." He chuckled a little, shook his head. "Goddammit, Rollie. You're ruining my surprise. Leave it to you, man."

Even though he'd known the answer before he'd asked the question, the answer still packed a wallop. "Where?"

"Pancreas," Ryan said. "For starters."

"Shit."

Ryan nodded. "Yep."

Stephen felt numb. And the weed was finally getting the better of him. The rooftop seemed to be tilting, making it impossible to properly process this kind of information. "But you've got, like, the best doctors, and all the experimental drugs, and everything normal people don't have, right?"

"Oh, I've got 'em," Ryan said. "The docs are the only people on planet Earth who know about this so far. Probably because I'm paying them more to keep a lid on it than anybody would give them for leaking."

"And?"

"And...so far this thing appears to be intent on demonstrating who's boss."

"I don't even know what to..."

"You don't have to say anything. In fact, please don't."

Stephen tried to stabilize. "Scale of one to ten. How much pain are you in?"

"This helps." Ryan raised the joint. "Less than it used to, but it helps."

Which wasn't quite an answer. To look at him the way most people did, you wouldn't even know he was sick. Stephen had so many more questions. *How far has it spread? What's the prognosis?* But it didn't seem like the time to ask. Also, the rooftop had tilted back the other way, and now it was starting to spin. He closed his eyes.

"Look, don't spill to the others," Ryan said. "Not even Emma. Not yet, okay? Let me tell them my way, when I'm ready. It's fair to say I've been planning this awhile."

"She'll know something's up." Stephen kept his eyes closed. Mayday. "If I noticed, she noticed."

"Either way, this weekend's about to get weird. And as long as you're skipping ahead, I could use your help."

"What can I do?"

"Just go with the program," Ryan said. "The others will look to you and Em. If you two set the tone, you know they'll follow your lead. Keep everybody together: that's my one dying request. Please tell me you'll grant it."

Stephen found that he had no choice but to grip the arms of his lounge chair to keep it from spinning off the roof with him in it. What was he supposed to say to this? "I promise I'll try."

"Thanks. You don't look so good, by the way."

"Said the guy with cancer."

Ryan laughed. Stephen heard him get up out of his chair. "Okay, Cheech. Time for beddy-bye. It's getting cold out here anyway."

"I'm really sorry, man."

"I know." Ryan took his arm gently. "Come on, I'll steer your weak ass back inside."

CHAPTER 6

SATURDAY MORNING, STEPHEN woke with early sunlight flooding his room. He sat up on the edge of the bed and held his head in his hands. The wiring that connected the lobes of his brain felt disconnected; Ryan's thousand-percent completely organic turbo weed, on top of all that wine and whiskey, had been a thousand-percent completely terrible idea.

It was the last thing he remembered: sitting up on the roof, passing the joint back and forth like old times.

Then their conversation all came back at once.

Shit.

It was the only way to describe starting a day this gorgeous having learned what he'd learned. It was also what his mouth tasted like. Stephen noticed a glass of water waiting for him on the nightstand. A glass of water and a packet of Alka-Seltzer.

Nice touch.

As day carried on breaking outside the crystal-clear, floor-to-ceiling windows, he tore open the tablets, got the plopping and fizzing started. He shambled into the bathroom and relieved his aching bladder, then stood at the east-facing window and drank his medicine. There was a light mist over the water, clear pale sky above. He could just make out the faint outline of the Whidbey in the far distance, a low silhouette along the horizon. They were miles from anything out here.

He chased the bicarb with a glass of flat water, splashed some more on his face, then wandered down the hall in his socks, toward the stairs.

The others were still down below, sacked out where they'd fallen. Beau was snoring like a one-man logging operation. Emma was beginning to stir. He saw her head lift, register his presence, then slowly sink below upholstery level again.

"Morning, sunshine," he whispered on his way past her couch, following his nose toward the smell of coffee brewing in the kitchen.

"Mmmph," she said, flopping an arm over her face. "Sooo...much...wine."

Stephen scared up a pair of mugs and filled them both: black for him, a shot of milk for her. She padded in while he was doing that, yawning and blinking, hair afly. "Too good to sleep in a pile like the rest of us, huh?"

"I got abducted," he told her. "Cigars on the roof. Sort of."

"With Ry?" She slumped onto a stool, yawned wide enough to swallow her own face. "I'm glad. You two needed some one-on-one time."

Already he felt guilty, desperately wanting to tell her everything he knew. How could he not?

Instead, he deposited the café au lait on the breakfast bar in front of her. "I guess he's up early. Getting the worm and so forth."

Another big yawn. "I haven't heard anybody moving around yet but you."

"Somebody made the coffee."

"I think it's on a timer. The beeps woke me up."

"Over that?" Stephen jerked his thumb back toward the sound of Beau, still cycling away with circadian regularity. His snore pattern ranged from not-intolerable at the low end to comically extreme at the peak.

"You stop hearing it after a while." She encircled the mug in both hands, placed her face directly over the steam, and breathed in deeply through her nose. "Sweet baby Jesus, that smells good."

Stephen leaned against the counter as Emma took a careful sip, sighed, and sat with her head on a hand. "So, what's on the roof?"

"An elevated view of all creation. And a pretty nice pool."

"You guys talk about anything interesting, or just puff stogies like strong silent types?"

"I dunno. This and that." *You gave your word*, the voice in his head advised. But the voice in his head was making his stomach hurt. He could already feel himself cracking. "Just catching up."

"How did he seem to you?"

Stephen sipped his coffee. "How do you mean?"

"I don't know," Emma said. "He looks thin to me. A little dark under the eyes."

"He was never a sleeper."

"That's true. Still, he doesn't quite seem to have that Hi-Pro Glow. Do you think?"

"I don't know, Em. It's been years since I saw him. He seemed to be having fun."

Will wandered in then, scratching his chest with one hand, his ass with the other. "I smell coffee."

"Coming right up." Stephen found another mug and filled it black, grateful for the rescue. Maybe a little disappointed—it was nice having coffee alone with Emma first thing in the morning again. But mostly grateful. "How'd that chair sleep?"

"Didn't notice. Mornin', Em." Will kissed her on the head and plunked down on the stool beside her. "Where'd Ryan go?"

Stephen handed him his coffee. "Go?"

"I thought I heard the boat."

"When?"

"Dunno. Early." He yawned. "Coulda been Beau, I guess. Man, that guy can snore."

Before too much longer the others began to straggle in, one at a time. Everybody looked about the same: deeply hungover. Except Beau, who seemed almost chipper. "Anything to eat in this joint? I'm starved."

Emma said, "How is that possible?"

Beau shrugged, plucking a fresh pear from the bowl on the bar. He polished the fruit on his shirt, took a bite. "Clean living?"

"Well, don't eat anything else," Lainie said. "I'm sure Ryan's got something big planned." She stretched like a cat, then made a shampooing motion with her fingertips, bunching up her hair. "Somebody come out on the balcony with me, I want to smell the ocean. Clean the cobwebs out of my brain."

It was still chilly out, so they all grabbed jackets and took their coffees through the big sliding glass door off the living room. There were chairs out there, so they sat and woke up a little, enjoying the view, nobody saying much of anything important. Morning sun glinted on the wavelets. A hundred yards out, a group of seabirds took turns dive-bombing the water, also looking for breakfast.

After a while, they came back inside and spent the next hour getting ready for the day, whatever it might hold. Everybody showered, put on fresh clothes, generally put themselves back together. Stephen dressed in jeans and a pullover and headed back down for one more cup of joe.

Still no Ryan.

A search of the house found the master suite empty upstairs, bed neatly made. When nine o'clock rolled around and their host still hadn't shown himself, they took a trek outside to the eastern bluff. They followed the footpath all the way to a set of heavy iron stairs leading down to the boathouse. Here they discovered that Will had been right: the VanDutch was gone.

"Maybe he went for donuts," Perry said.

Just go with the program. Stephen was starting to get annoyed. Whatever Ryan was up to, it was almost ten o'clock in the morning. By the time they got back to the house, his annoyance had turned into a bad feeling. *Screw it*, he thought. "Guys, I'm probably overreacting, but there's a chance..."

But no, that didn't really make sense. As soon as he'd opened his mouth, logic kicked it in. Why was that always how it worked?

Emma said, "A chance of what?"

Stephen sighed. "Like I said, probably overreacting. But there's a chance he could be having some kind of medical issue."

This caused a stir: *What do you mean, medical issue? What are you... Where did you... What?* Emma seemed especially irked to learn he'd been holding out on her. He could hardly blame her.

"This is stupid," Will said. "Maybe we should call his cell."

Beau said, "With what?"

"Oh. Right."

"Where did he put the phones?" Lainie said. "Did anybody see?"

"Living room," Beau answered. "That little Danish-looking cabinet thing. I watched him do it."

They all went back inside.

The cabinet was locked.

"Stand aside," Beau said.

Lainie looked horrified. "No! Don't you dare harm this man's furniture."

"It's a medical emergency. You heard Rollie."

"No, no." Stephen shook his head emphatically. "No. I said he could be having an issue, and I shouldn't have said even that. He wouldn't just…"

"Stephen, what's going on?" Emma said. "What did he say to you up there?"

"Up where?" Lainie wanted to know.

Stephen retreated to the kitchen, but they followed him like pigeons. He tried to find his way into an explanation without betraying his promise, but now that he'd dropped a crumb, everybody wanted more. They stood around squabbling for a minute. *You had one job*, he thought to himself. So much for keeping everybody together.

Then Will said, "Guys?"

They all looked.

He'd stayed behind at the cabinet. The doors were now open.

Lainie said, "How'd you do that?"

"The drawer locks the doors," Will said. "You just push it in a little, and the mechanism gives. My grandparents had one like it. We have it now."

"Why didn't you say so?" Beau was already heading back toward the cabinet. "Let's call him."

"I agree," Emma said. "If we can. He said there might not be a signal."

"There's a signal somewhere," Beau assured her. "There's always a signal somewhere."

But when they all regrouped around Will, they found him holding an empty wicker basket.

Well, no. Not empty. Just no phones.

In their place: a touchscreen tablet of unknown make, cased in some kind of rubberized, shock-resistant frame.

At the sight of it, Stephen's bad feeling dissipated immediately. The annoyance came back. Will removed the tablet from the basket, returning the basket to the spot where he'd found it. He turned the device around so they all could see the screen.

"It just came on when I picked it up," he said.

On the charcoal-colored screen: six blank white entry squares above a numbered keypad. Below that, a geometric clover insignia. Below that, two words:

Unlock Me!

CHAPTER 7

It's a game," Lainie said, clapping her hands. "Ha! Wily devil. Leave it to him, right?"

"Unbelievable," Stephen muttered. Yes, leave it to Ryan Cloverhill. This was his big plan? To disappear and leave them solving puzzles?

"Oh, come on, it's fun. Now." Lainie leaned forward to better scrutinize the tablet screen. "How do we start?"

Will used his pointer finger to indicate the instructions a foot from her nose: *Unlock Me!*

"Obviously," Beau said, "but what's the code?"

Perry had already caught on. "You mean you don't know?"

"Try his birthday," Lainie said. "No, wait. Too easy. Try *our* birthdays. Start with Emma's."

"Nope."

"Well, what then? Wait: 827828. Either that or 828827."

Will said, "What's that?"

"Our addresses. From the duplex: you guys were 827; we were 828."

"Oh, yeah," Will said. "Nice pull, Lainie."

"Wait, don't enter it," Beau said. "Is this thing going to lock us out if we guess wrong too many times?"

"He *wants* us to get in," Perry said. "But you're still ice cold."

"Then warm us up!"

"Just think a minute. Even you can get this one, Beauregard."

"In support of Beau," Will said to Perry, "you're being extremely annoying right now."

This earned Will a fist bump from his old dorm-mate. "*Thank* you."

Even Emma looked stumped.

Stephen couldn't believe it. She was smarter than any of them. Except maybe Ryan, the self-absorbed prick. He almost chided himself for being so harsh, but no: The guy had always been this way. Even before he was dying. Utterly, willfully deluded.

Then her eyes brightened. She'd tipped to it.

Lainie saw this, too, and stamped her foot in frustration. "I give up! What is it?"

"The invitations," Stephen said impatiently, stealing Perry's thunder, hearing Ryan's voice in his head: *I've been planning this awhile.* He pointed around the room: first at Emma, then himself, then the rest of them in order. "One two three four five six."

Faces bloomed with sudden understanding. "Ahhhh," Beau said. "He *is* a wily devil."

Lainie said, "Right?"

"Punch it in. One two three four five six."

"It can't be *that* easy."

"Never know 'til we try…"

"Last time you said wait don't enter it!"

"I have an idea," Will said. "Anybody mind?"

Perry looked at Emma, then Lainie. Emma shrugged. Lainie shrugged.

Beau said, "Go for it." Then, just as Will began tapping away, Beau said, "Wait, what number are you entering?"

It didn't matter. The tablet responded by playing a game show fail horn.

Will looked up, his face gone scarlet. He turned the tablet again. The screen had gone dead black, reflecting their faces in the glass.

"Well, shit," Beau said. "Even our Link account gives you three tries."

"Wait a minute." Emma pointed. "Something's happening."

Even as she said it, the screen popped back to life, showing them a readout of their results. The graphic on-screen appeared to be a progress meter, shaped like none other than…

"Barksley!" Lainie cried.

Indeed. Barksley the Badger Hound. Stephen had no idea how their alma mater had ended up with a floppy-eared dachshund for a school mascot. A founder's loyal companion, maybe? The institutional literature revealed only that *dachshund* translated from German as "badger dog," hence, Badger Hound. The joke banner that had gone up on campus every homecoming weekend read: "Welcome Back to Bardsley College—Home of the Fighting Wiener Dogs."

The hound on-screen was an empty white outline. The words above said:

0% Correct—Try again!

"Oof," Will said. "Sorry, everybody. I guess I was way off."

Perry said, "Now what?"

Will tapped the screen. Nothing happened. He tried swiping right, tried swiping left. Still nothing.

"Try the collar," Emma said.

Stephen had already noticed what she was talking about. The collar's clasp was the same clover insignia they'd seen before: on their invitations, on the helipad outside, on the home screen of this very tablet.

Will followed her suggestion and tapped the clover. Sure enough, the tablet played a happy success chime as the clover turned green.

The next screen showed a faded photograph of the seven of them, all crammed together on one of the futons in room 205, Anders Hall. Stephen hadn't seen this photo in at least twenty-five years, but he recognized it immediately; they were mugging like idiots, half on each other's laps, their limbs tangled like knobby vines.

"Oh my God," Lainie gasped, covering her mouth with one hand. "Look at us."

Perry covered his eyes instead. "We look like the fucking cast of *Friends*."

Will laughed. "Why are our clothes so baggy?"

"I remember taking this picture," Emma said. "We balanced that little camera of Will's on those milk crates you guys kept all your CDs in, and it kept falling over right as the timer went off. We had half a dozen pictures of blurry CD spines when the prints came back. Do you remember?"

The text above the photo said:

Hmm. That was piss-poor.
Perhaps you are not the people in this photograph after all.
To continue, prove yourselves.

Beneath the photo, Stephen saw six white ovals in a row.

"I know this one," Beau said. Before anyone could respond, he reached out and pressed the pad of his right thumb to the first oval.

Success chime. The white oval turned into a green clover.

"Yes! Way to go, honey." Lainie reached out and copied him. Now there were two green clovers. "Everybody get in here."

One by one, Emma, Perry, and Will entered their thumbprints, until a single white oval remained. Stephen's turn. Everybody looked at him.

He sighed. Pressed his thumb to the screen.

"For Pete's sake," Emma said. "What's with you this morning? If you know more about this than you're telling us, spit it out already."

How the hell had he managed to put himself in this position? Stephen didn't know what to say or not say. He only knew that if Ryan were here, instead of wherever the hell he was, he might be tempted to wring his neck.

"I need some air," he said.

He turned and headed for the front door. Behind him, he heard a beat of awkward silence. Then more squabbling. Then Beau saying, probably to Perry: "Okay, genius. So what order do they go in, then?"

CHAPTER 8

Emma shook her head as she watched Stephen go. He'd put her at a loss.

What on earth? He'd always been a little moody. Not like Ryan—not even close, really—but Stephen Rollins definitely had that brooding-male gear when he wanted to find it. And, boy, had he found it this morning.

She'd known this weekend was going to present challenges. No matter what they said, those two had never truly put the past behind them. And though he was too rational ever to admit it, she suspected that Stephen—on some far less rational level—still resented Ryan for having the gall to become a spectacular success while they, as a romantic couple, had ended in garden-variety failure.

She felt a hand at her waist. Perry. He spoke without speaking: *I'll go talk to him.*

Emma gave him a squeeze.

Perry slipped away toward the door.

Meanwhile, the others were still occupied with the tablet. A little group drama, that was all. Tempest in a teapot. Nothing new.

Fine. In fact, something about Stephen's agitated departure had given her a flash of inspiration. So she left him in Dr. Therkle's capable hands and rejoined the others, where there was still a fun vacation going on.

"No," Beau was saying. "That can't be it. There's not a seven in the invites."

"Exactly!" Lainie said. "The seven is Ryan! It's implied."

"An implied seven." Will seemed doubtful. "He'd be number one, wouldn't he? Probably?"

"He could be zero," Beau suggested. "That seems like his idea of funny."

"It also leaves out Stephen. He wouldn't have left out the two."

Beau and Lainie exchanged glances. *Are we all completely sure about that?*

"I might have an idea," Emma said. She twiddled her fingers at Will, who still held the tablet. "Anybody mind if I give it a go?"

Stephen heard the front door open behind him. He assumed it was Emma, but the late-morning shadow that joined his own on the walkway was far too lengthy. In a moment, Perry unbuckled his knee joints and folded himself into a sitting position beside Stephen on the low, sun-drenched front stoop.

"Rollie."

"Perrier."

Perry leaned back on his hands, drawing a deep breath through the nose. "I," he pronounced, "am a hurting unit."

"Tell me about it."

"I mean, I know we drank a lot, but I didn't think we drank *that* much. It's possible we're not twenty anymore."

"You know you're not twenty when you're drinking Lalique 62 instead of Rolling Rock."

"Generally true," Perry agreed. "Now. Tell Uncle Perry what's crawled up your ass."

Stephen sighed. "Do you think it's occurred to anybody that we're literally stranded on a deserted island right now? Mags and Luna are gone. Ryan's off looking at orcas for all we know. Nobody has a phone. Nobody knows how anything in that house works. We don't even know where to find the Band-Aids. He could sink that boat of his, and then what?"

"I...guess that's all true?"

"But I'm overreacting."

Perry patted the concrete riser upon which they sat. A solid, civilized structure. "We're not exactly the crew of the SS *Minnow* here. Nobody's hunting for coconuts."

"Suppose Will went hyperglycemic or something. All that shit we ate and drank last night?"

"He's got his insulin," Perry said. "And we *are* grown-ups. We've been managing his diabetes for years. We've even been to dinner parties before."

"Sorry," Stephen said. "I'm just saying: If Ryan wanted to jerk us around, why bring us all the way here to do it?"

"Maybe he's just going a little overboard trying to show us a good time," Perry said. "But I feel like you're still not telling me what's really eating you."

Stephen looked out across the clearing. *Just wait for Ryan*, he thought. He followed the main path across the island with his eyes until it went meandering off into the trees. He looked at Perry.

Perry wore an easy expression. "Maybe this will help." He stretched out a leg and dug into his front trouser pocket, grinning as he produced yet another blast from the past: a yellow pack of American Spirit cigarettes, still wrapped in cellophane.

"Oh, God," Stephen said, chuckling. "I *know* you don't still smoke those."

"Picked 'em up at the airport," Perry said. He flashed a mischievous wink as he tore open the wrapper and pulled the foil, shoving the scraps back into his pocket. "Will was in the bathroom."

"But *why*?"

"Old time's sake," Perry said, pulling two cigarettes from the fresh pack, handing one to Stephen. "Why else are we here?"

None of them had ever been serious smokers, but Perry and Stephen had always carried a pack of these stupid things with them when they went out to the bars. It was the early '90s. Stephen looked at the cigarette in his fingers, then glanced skeptically at Perry. "Are you sure? What about your lungs?"

He'd had a terrifying bout of COVID not so long ago. Will said it had left him with scar tissue. Apparently, he was part of an ongoing study at Mount Sinai.

"One won't kill me."

As Perry hung the cigarette from his lips and dug back into his pocket for a lighter, Stephen said, "Let it be entered into the record that smoking is bad for you, and you should not, under any circumstances, be doing this."

"I promise I won't inhale, Mother."

What the hell. He was probably right; one couldn't be fatal. They lit up. Coughed. Laughed.

"This is so dumb," Stephen said.

"Moronic. Now, then, where were we?" Perry leaned back again, squinting one eye at Stephen through the swirling smoke. "Something about a medical issue, you were saying?"

Emma tried the number she had in mind: 453612.

Fail horn.

"Nuts," she said.

Lainie said, "Hang on, hang on. What does Barksley say?"

Plenty, it turned out. This time, the tablet had filled the dog's outline with green from tail to collar. Only his head was still empty. The words above said:

83% Correct—Try Again!

"Oh man!" Will said. "That was really close, Em. You're on to something."

"But now I'm confused," Emma said. "I was sure I had it. Will, you were number five, right?"

"I had four."

"Crap. Right, what am I thinking? Sorry. Brain lock."

"What *are* you thinking?"

"When did Perry get accepted into grad school? Ninety-four?"

"Ninety-five."

"Right. Okay, I know what to do."

"Wait wait wait," Beau said. "That's two wrong answers. Don't lock us out."

"It's not going to lock us out!" Will insisted. "I don't think."

"Em, just tell us," Lainie said. "What's the play here?"

"I think he assigned us our numbers in the order he met us," Emma said. "I'm entering them in the order we all left. Stillwater, I mean."

Beau shook his head. "That can't be right."

"She got eighty-three percent, didn't she?"

"Yeah, but Perry would be six, not me. I knew you guys before he did."

"Ah. That's the wrinkle. He's trying to throw us off track." Emma tapped her noggin. "But we're too clever for him."

Beau said, "Are we?"

"You used to have a little catchphrase," she told him. "Do you remember?"

He crinkled his brow. "What did I say?"

"Nice guys finish last."

Will snapped his fingers. "Oh, man, that's right! You *did* always used to say that."

"I didn't either."

"Anytime we played a game," Emma reminded him, "if one of us got over on you, you'd sort of sigh and say that. 'Nice guys finish last.' "

Will said, "Whenever GPAs came out."

"If a waiter gives you the wrong plate." Lainie laughed. "Honey, the *boys* even say it. Have you really never noticed that before?"

"Yeah, okay, great, fine." Beau's suntan had darkened. Was he blushing a little? "I'll take your word for it."

"Okay, eighty-three percent," Emma said. "We're only one number off. That has to be the mistake: I got Will and Perry switched around. Here we go."

"Wait wait wait," Beau said.

Everybody stood around impatiently.

"Ryan left before you two," he said. "When he went off to Cal Poly."

Lainie kicked him in the shoe.

"What? It's not awkward. We're strategizing."

"He's right," Emma said. "But I don't think Ryan put himself in the mix. Sorry, Beau; sorry, Lainie. I think we just have to switch the four and the five around. Everybody agree it's at least worth a shot?"

"Switch away," Lainie said. "This is exciting!"

Emma tapped the clover on Barksley's collar.

But once again, the tablet blocked them with a new challenge screen. This one showed a different old photo: all seven of them at the duplex, crowded around a truly pathetic-looking Christmas tree. They'd decorated its sparse, spindly boughs with empty mini-bottles of Fireball, toilet paper for garland. The text above said:

Much improved!
But I remain unconvinced.
Thumb a ride home for the holidays.

"Oh, come on," Beau said. "We can look at old pictures later!"

"And now we're missing two thumbs," Lainie said.

Emma said, "I'm sure they'll be back in a minute."

"Screw that," Will said. He took the tablet from her hands and headed for the door. "Two thumbs. Coming right up."

Perry looked at the ground for a long time.

Finally, he said, "How long?"

Stephen shrugged. "He didn't say. He found out a year ago, maybe more. That was my impression."

"I meant, how long do these doctors say he has left?"

"Oh." Stephen picked up a stray pebble, gave it a toss. "I didn't know how to ask. He wanted to tell us all together, made me promise I wouldn't say anything before he did. I figured we could count on Beau to blurt that one out."

"Well reasoned." Perry thought for a minute, then pulled out two more cigarettes.

"No way," Stephen said. "I already feel like an ashtray."

"Special circumstances," Perry counseled. "We'll spend the rest of the day recuperating."

"You talked me into it." Stephen put the damned thing in his mouth and leaned forward. The first cigarette had tasted like shit and left him feeling queasy, and he wished he weren't already looking forward to this one.

Perry lit him up, then touched the flame to his own. It was during this process that the front door opened, and Will emerged, saying, "Sorry to interrupt, but we need your— Are you guys *smoking*?"

They both turned like twelve-year-olds caught in the middle school boys' room. Will stood behind them, tablet in his hands, the look of utter shock on his face slowly transforming to glaring rage.

"Shit," Perry muttered, tossing his newly lit cigarette to the steps and grinding it out with his shoe. He stood and raised his hands. "I can explain."

"Bullshit," Will said. "I can't believe this. *Jesus*, Pear! Are you—"

"It's my fault," Stephen said quickly, tossing his own cigarette away. "I talked him into it."

"Bullshit again," Will said. "Stay out of this, Rollie."

Stephen faced front. He felt one inch tall.

Behind him, he heard quiet murmuring: Perry trying to defuse the situation, Will refusing to be defused. Finally, he heard Will say, "Just give me your damn thumbprint and enjoy your coffin nails. Smoke the whole pack while you're out here. We'll talk about this later."

He heard Perry's heavy sigh.

There came a moment of silence.

Then: "It's not working."

"What do you mean, it's not working? What did you do?"

"I didn't do anything," Perry said. "It's just not working."

Stephen snuck a glance over his shoulder to see Will swiping at the tablet screen. He finally sighed and stalked back into the house without another word.

But just inside the doorway, he stopped, looking down at the tablet.

After a moment, he stepped out onto the stoop again.

Then back into the house.

Back out onto the stoop.

Perry said, "What are you doing?"

Stone-faced, without speaking, Will turned the tablet so they could see the dead black screen.

Then he took one step backward into the house. The screen flickered to life: another old photo on a charcoal background, six white ovals beneath.

He took one step forward, back out onto the stoop again. The screen went black.

"Huh," Perry said. "Look at that."

Without changing his facial expression, Will stepped back into the house. The screen turned back on. Will stood there, tablet extended, silently waiting.

Perry sighed again, hanging his shoulders. He trudged toward Will, stopping short of the doorway. Standing on the stoop, with Will still a foot inside the house, he reached out, pressed his thumb to the screen, and pleaded his case no further.

"Your turn," he said to Stephen, returning to his place on the stoop.

Stephen got to his feet, gave Will his thumbprint, and said, "I'm really sorry. We're almost done out here."

Will nodded. Took one more step farther back into the house.

Then he said, "You both reek," and shut the door.

Emma could see the look on Will's face from ten feet away. She said, "What was that all about?"

"My husband's a shithead, that's what. And your ex isn't much better." Will handed the tablet back to her with a scowl. "And this thing only works inside the house, apparently. Hang on, I almost forgot."

He pressed his thumb to the screen.

"There," he said. "Next?"

Clearly, he wanted to move on. Emma, Beau, and Lainie all reentered their thumbprints. When they were finished, the tablet redisplayed the keypad screen once again, ready for their next guess. Emma paused with her index finger poised.

Lainie said, "What are you waiting for?"

"I'm almost positive this next one is going to work," Emma said.

"Right. Switch the four and the five, you said. Go."

"Will, what did you mean when you said this thing only works inside the house?"

"It goes dead as soon as you step outside. The second you come back in..." Will snapped his fingers. "Back on again."

"And every time we guess wrong," Emma said, "we're stuck until we give it our prints."

"Yeah," Beau said. "It's getting annoying. What's your point?"

"My point," Emma said, "is that Ryan obviously went to some lengths to make sure we were all in the same room for this. Whatever happens next, he means for us to see it together. So maybe we should play ball?" She surveyed the others. "Wait for Perry and Stephen?"

Beau looked at Lainie. Lainie looked at Will.

Will said, "Punch it in."

"Well," Perry said. "That was unfortunate."

"I told you smoking was bad for you."

After they'd picked up their discarded cigarettes and shoved everything back into the pack, Perry said, "Shall I tell you what I think, so we can go back inside, and I can take my medicine like a man?"

"Please do."

"First: I think this is Ryan we're talking about. He's always been a little... enigmatic."

"If by enigmatic you mean living on his own planet."

"Another way to phrase it, perhaps. The man literally bought himself an island."

"And here we are."

"Exactly," Perry said. "I think he invited us here to tell us about the cancer, but being Ryan, he doesn't really know how. Doesn't know how to deal with the reaction. Or maybe he just doesn't want to. Whatever. Under the circumstances, it's sort of his prerogative, no?"

Stephen could hardly argue the point.

"So he steps out, leaves us that tablet. We unlock it, there's a video, we watch, everybody cries. He lets us get a grip, gives the dust a chance to settle, then he steps back in. On we go."

In fact, it was starting to bother Stephen that this reasoning seemed so obvious. All Perry had done was attempt to put himself in Ryan's shoes, which was something Stephen had to admit he'd not made a very good effort to do on his own. Which forced him to consider another possibility: that he himself was, in fact, the asshole.

Just go with the program. Let me do it my way. It's my dying request. Stephen had promised he'd try.

But had he, really?

How hard had he tried?

Perry sensed his reaction. He gave Stephen a nudge.

"Sure," Stephen said. "Dunk on me, why don't you."

"Don't be so sheepish. I get it."

"I'm a dick."

"You *are* a dick, but that's not what I'm saying. I'm just saying…he's our friend. And he's been going through this without us so far. Maybe his job is to figure out how to let us back into his life while there's still time. And our job is to let him."

Stephen sighed. Of the group, he was the one who was supposed to understand these things. He'd been the psych major.

"Come on," Perry said. "Let's go back in, let it play out. See what happens."

"Do we tell them?"

"Nope. But I hope he does it soon. This shit is way too heavy for just you and me to carry around all weekend."

"We agree." Stephen got up, brushed himself off. "Thanks, Perrier."

"Indubitably, dear Rollie. After you."

"But I insist."

Perry hadn't quite reached the front door when they heard the first strange sound.

Emma didn't need to be told twice. She was as curious as the rest of them. So she punched in the number: 543612.

The tablet screen flared success, playing a happy chime over a glowing green Cloverhill clover.

"That's it!" Lainie said. "Go, Emma!"

Then, almost instantly, the entire house seemed to come alive on its own.

From the front door came the unmistakable sound of multiple bolts locking. The heavy triple-*thunk* touched off a sequence that spiraled around the house like dominoes falling, winding and climbing from the bottom level up: *thunka-thunka-thunka-thunka-thunk*. Meanwhile, a motorized whine seemed to emanate from everywhere at once. Shadows played around the floor as massive automated panels began sliding closed over the big windows, slowly squeezing out the daylight.

It was a symphony of mechanical noises as the house locked itself down around them. Everybody gasped, turned in circles, stood staring: at the floor, the ceiling, the darkening windows. Even as night replaced day inside the house, the interior lighting came up like stage lights opening a new scene.

As suddenly as it all began, the racket ceased.

Total silence.

Then, everywhere, the world outside quietly winked back to life again. Now in ultrahigh definition.

Emma felt completely disoriented. Slowly, she came to understand what she was seeing:

Inside each window shield, just beyond the original glass, was a digital screen as large as the window itself. Every screen displayed camera-fed versions of the same views that had been real only moments ago.

Emma looked at Will. He gaped back at her, eyes wide, mouth hanging. Lainie was actually panting.

Beau stood like a living statue: head back, eyes staring straight up, arms limp at his sides. "Whaaaaat..."

"...the fuck?" Perry said.

He turned to Stephen.

Stephen stood staring at the front door.

Rather, at the heavy security panel now covering the front door. It had emerged from an unseen pocket, driven by hidden motors, sealing off reentry right in front of their faces.

He looked back at Perry, but he was damned if he could think of a reply.

QUEEN OF THE INSIDE

CHAPTER 9

Somehow, emma managed to hang on to the tablet without dropping it. But she didn't know the screen had changed again until she heard Ryan's small, muffled voice somewhere down by her leg.

The others mobilized instantly, gathering behind her. Emma held the tablet at arm's length so everyone could see. It was a video call.

"Morning, guys," Ryan said from their screen. "And well done, Beau! I knew you were paying attention when I put up the phones."

"Will unlocked the cabinet," Beau said absently. He still hadn't completely recovered his wits. Emma knew just how he felt.

"Just like Grandma's, right, Will? You showed me when I was in New York that time. Couldn't find one quite like it, so I had one made. Anyway, bravo to everybody: I knew you'd crack the code, but I didn't expect you to nail it on the third try. Without clues, even. I worked hard on those too."

Ryan wore a high-collared, waterproof offshore coat and polarized sunglasses. His hair ruffled in an otherwise invisible breeze. Blue water in the background. He was coming to them live from the deck of his boat somewhere.

Emma said, "Ryan, what is this?"

"Satellite connection," he said over the breeze raking across his microphone. "Make sure you leave the tablet inside the case, okay? It doubles as an antenna."

"I mean what *is* this? What's going on?"

"First things first, you're all safe. Emma, do me a favor, will you? Tap the upper left corner of that screen."

Emma raised a finger, then hesitated.

"It's not another trap, I promise. Go ahead. Right there in the corner."

She did as instructed. Lainie and Will nearly jumped out of their skins at the sound of new motors whirring, but it was just the big television rising up from the floor. When it reached position, the set turned on and paired with the tablet. The tablet screen automatically mirrored to the much larger flat panel.

Ryan waved. "Perfect. I can see you all better. Well. Almost all of you."

"Rollie and Therkle got locked out," Beau said. He pointed to one of the window displays, where everybody could see Stephen and Perry outside, wandering into the frame. "There they are right now."

"I'm aware," Ryan sighed. "I swear, I spend months building fail-safes, and Rollie manages to break the system in half an hour. I should have hired him to run my quality assurance division."

Emma said, "Ryan..."

"Just hang tight, guys. Make yourselves at home. I need to make a few quick arrangements, and then we'll get started. We've got a lot to go over."

Stephen and Perry hiked around to every part of the house they could access without free-climbing the exterior walls.

The whole place was plated up like an armadillo on defense. The stone-colored security panels now covering every access point and egress seemed to be made of some kind of heavy-duty composite material that might as well have been solid concrete. The big house on Sham Rock had become, from all outward indications, a 6,500-square-foot safe room.

"Okay," Perry said. "Now *I'm* annoyed with him."

The panels barricading the windows featured rows of beady, hooded eyes. Camera lenses. Hooked up to security monitors somewhere, Stephen presumed. Then he had a crazy thought: "Do you think they can see us in there?"

They took turns waving their arms, standing close and shouting to the others at the top of their lungs.

It was like yelling into the side of a mountain. Their voices bounced off every unyielding surface and carried away on the breeze. If anybody inside *could* hear them, Stephen and Perry couldn't hear them back.

"It's almost like he didn't think this all the way through," Perry said.

Stephen said, "He did say things were going to get weird."

It was all so surreal that it almost seemed funny. Maybe it really would be funny one day.

At the moment, however, the sense of absurdist humor he and Perry had always shared seemed mutually diminished. The sun was high overhead by now. Stephen stood at a hundred paces and looked up toward the flat roof, shielding his eyes from the glare. From what he could tell, the entry points up there had barricaded themselves just like the ones down here.

He came back to find Perry testing the exterior light sconces as if one of them might be a secret lever in disguise.

"Any theories?" Stephen's own best guess: some kind of escape room parlor game for extraordinarily wealthy people. Perhaps the kind of people who owned islands and had, somewhere along the line, utterly lost touch with reality.

"We're not going to be able to Scooby-Doo our way back in there, that's my theory." Perry looked up toward the roofline, shielding his eyes. "It's a work in progress."

They still had their jackets from their trip down to the dock. Perry had already tied his around his waist. The temperature had risen to somewhere in the seventies, Stephen guessed—quite comfortable as long as the few passing clouds dodged the sun. The noonday warmth seemed to activate the pleasant aroma of cedar and fir on the light ocean breeze. All in all, under any reasonable set of circumstances, it was a hell of a nice Saturday to be outdoors.

"So," Stephen said. "What should we do next?"

Perry looked sternly at the house. He shielded his eyes again, looked out toward the coastline. He turned back and looked toward the trees.

Finally, he shrugged. "I dunno. Go exploring?"

After Ryan cut the connection, they moved as a group around the lower level of the house, following Perry and Stephen from window to window—*monitor to monitor*, Emma thought—continuing to yell and wave their hands at them, even though the effort, clearly, was futile.

At one point they stood what must literally have been a matter of feet from their culled herd members as Perry and Stephen took turns cupping their hands around their mouths and bellowing directly into the outer window panels. Emma, Lainie, Will, and Beau made a chorus of shouting back to them. They might as well have been shouting at the contestants on a reality TV contest. With the volume muted.

It was strange to imagine that their friends on-screen were, literally, standing in real life on the other side. Ryan's camera system was able to reproduce what it saw at more or less a one-to-one ratio, so that Perry and Stephen appeared to them more or less actual size. But the screens filtered the real, made it seem unreal. The effect was disorienting.

"I love Ryan," Lainie said, "but I don't think I like this game."

"Welcome to the club," Will said. "Emma, what's happening?"

"Don't look at me, guys. I've got no clue."

Beau seemed suspicious of her. Emma didn't really blame him. She'd known Ryan the longest, and he'd always been apt to confide in her. It wasn't unreasonable for any of them to imagine she might have a little insider info, but she was, truly, as lost as they were.

They tried every door they could find. Nothing budged. They were at the far end of the lower level, at the corner windows of Ryan's home gym, when Beau straightened, raised a finger, and cocked his head. "Listen."

Emma heard it, too, somewhere near the center of the house. Again, Ryan's faint voice: "*Guuuuuuys?*"

They all hustled back to the television, where he'd reappeared on-screen, bobbing gently on an unseen current. They could hear the squawking of seagulls somewhere above him.

"Sorry about that," he said. "Let's start over."

CHAPTER 10

AND SO IT came to pass that two middle-aged white men with 401(k) plans found themselves at the edge of an ocean, traipsing around an island, looking for a way indoors.

Stephen and Perry wandered a little ways inland, just to the tree line, stopping to investigate the various outbuildings they encountered on the way. Each structure was built like the house in style and materials. Each, like the house, was locked fast.

The one that hummed from within must have been what Ryan called "the pump house." It had no windows, but it looked and sounded like a generator shed, considering the banks of solar panels mounted on the roof, with another crop of them planted in rows out back.

Perry said, "You don't suppose there's a switch in there labeled 'Unlock House,' do you?"

"Might be worth a look," Stephen said. "If you can figure out a way to get inside."

A larger building appeared to serve as toy storage. It was dark inside, and the windows had some kind of polarizing material baked into the glass, but peering in through cupped hands, Stephen could make out a few obvious shapes: a quartet of four-wheel ATVs, a pair of open-water kayaks, miscellaneous oars and paddles standing around. Fishing rods on horizontal racks along one wall.

"Well," Stephen said, "if worse comes to worst, I guess the two of us can paddle home."

Perry stood with his fists on his hips, surveying their acre of clearing like MacArthur at Inchon. "I wonder if Will misses me yet."

"I'm sure he's beside himself. Come on, let's see what's in that one."

They finished their tour of Ryan's locked buildings without discovering anything much of further use. For no good reason they wandered up to the helipad, which did not have a helicopter on it. The footpath meandered along the top edge of the dockside bluff, forty or fifty feet above the waterline. So they meandered it, listening to the seabirds overhead, the lap of the surf below. Eventually, Perry shielded his eyes, tilting his gaze up to the eastern sky. "We should probably look for some shade pretty soon. We're gonna be lobsters."

But Stephen had been looking the opposite direction. He pointed at a bank of dark clouds massing on the western horizon. "I was thinking shelter."

"Oof." Perry joined Stephen in looking out toward the west. Then he looked back toward the east. North, south, back up at the sky. "Two very wet, very handsome lobsters. By the way, I think I'm starting to get hungry. You?"

"I'd take a sandwich," Stephen said. "Maybe we should look for coconuts after all."

"Different kind of tree. Might have to settle for pine cones."

"Fir cones."

"What?"

"Pine cones are a different kind of tree too."

"Oh," Perry said. "Thank God you're here."

"Stick with me," Stephen told him, though he couldn't have said where they should go.

***

They forced themselves to sit, naturally following human habit, reclaiming the spots where they'd slept. Ryan sat down, too, fixing his tablet into a docking mount at the helm of the boat. He now wore a wireless headset with a shielded microphone. With one leg crossed over a knee, an elbow propped on the back of the pilot seat, he looked at ease. It pissed Emma off exceedingly.

"First, again, thank you all," he said. With the headset, his voice quality had improved. The wind and background noise had diminished. "There's nobody I'd rather spend my last Labor Day weekend with than you guys."

"Same here, but, Ryan," Lainie started, then stopped herself. "Wait a minute. What did you say?"

Beau said, "Last?"

Over the next few minutes, Ryan told them about a cancer diagnosis he'd received last year. He talked about a trip to Johns Hopkins. Other trips to see doctors in Europe and Mexico City. Months of treatments that made him feel like he'd died already, but hadn't done as much as anybody had hoped to forestall the actual event.

Lainie put a hand over her mouth. Beau pulled her close.

Emma felt like she'd been stabbed; she had no siblings, but she imagined this must be what it would feel like to hear your twin brother say he was dying. This was obviously why Stephen had been behaving so strangely—he'd had all this information already, no doubt sworn to secrecy. It must have been murder on him; Stephen Rollins had always been allergic to deception. As a romantic partner, it had made him both a dream and, occasionally, a nightmare.

Ryan told them he'd dialed back his treatments in July. Partially because he'd grown too weak and worked-over to hide his condition in public, and he'd already spent too much time playing Invisible Man where the company was concerned. Partially to get his strength back in time for their arrival.

"Please don't say that," Lainie said. "Not because of us. You need to keep fighting this. Promise you will."

Beau nodded. "She's right, buddy. Jesus. Keep throwing the kitchen sink at it, am I right?"

"Absolutely." Will nodded emphatically. "Abso*lutely* right."

"I appreciate that, guys," Ryan said. "But there comes a time when it's time to face facts, and the fact is, that time has come."

As calmly as she could manage, Emma said, "Ryan, where are you right now?"

"Not so far," he said. "But not within visual range either. Let's call my location undisclosed for now and move on."

"Why don't you just come back here? We want to be with you for this."

Everybody immediately signed on to that idea. But Ryan only sighed. "I'd like nothing more, guys. But no."

"Why not?"

"We're sort of already through the looking glass on this," he said. "I need the six of you to tell me what you find. One way or another, I'll know by Monday."

Will said, "Why is the house still locked? What about Perry? And Stephen?"

"Don't worry, they'll be fine. I've arranged to have them safely collected."

"Ryan," Emma said, "why is the house locked at all?"

"I'll explain everything," Ryan assured them. "In the meantime, try not to think of yourselves as hostages."

"Who said hostages?" Beau asked. The very word itself seemed to change his tune. "I thought this was a game."

"Game . . . yes and no," Ryan said. "Either way, come noon Monday, I promise, it will all be over."

"Monday!"

Emma stood. "Unlock the house, Ryan."

"You have my word."

"I mean right now," Emma said. "Whatever the game is, I don't want to play."

"Right now is more problematic."

"Then explain yourself."

Ryan nodded. "The easiest way is to show you."

With that he leaned toward them and unclipped his tablet. The big screen in front of them swirled with dizzying movement as he repositioned himself.

When things settled, they were facing the helm station pass-through to the cabin below deck. They watched Ryan's duck boots take two steps down. Then he sat and raised the screen again, showing them the view of the lower cabin from his perspective.

Emma saw six strangers crammed together in the lounge area. Three men and three women, all bedraggled in rumpled business casual attire. They were gagged. Their hands were zip-cuffed in their laps. Their feet were bound and daisy-chained with some kind of heavy, brightly colored marine cord. Above the gags, their eyes betrayed a variety of states: anger, confusion, indignation, fear.

Beau, Lainie, Will, and Emma sat around the television in stunned silence. Nobody made a sound.

Emma found her voice first. "Ryan, who are those people?"

"My board of directors," said Ryan off camera, waggling his fingers in the frame. "Everybody: nod hello to the Stillwater Seven. Well. Four of 'em, anyway."

CHAPTER 11

When Stephen was young, his mother used to say: *When you don't know where you're going, any road will get you there.*

Somehow, he never learned until Bardsley—filling out his core requirements with a survey section from the lit department called "The British Fantasists"—that this was actually Lewis Carroll's line and not his mom's. But in his mind, he still credited Jane Anne Rollins of Carbondale, Illinois. Frankly, he hadn't enjoyed *Alice in Wonderland* as much as he was supposed to, anyway.

Fortunately for him and Perry, they had an exact destination in mind. And even if they hadn't, Sham Rock had only so many roads to choose from.

"We could have taken a couple of those four-wheelers back there," Stephen said. "Assuming there's gas."

"And the doors weren't locked."

"That too. Although I'd be prepared to argue a broken window hardly seems out-of-bounds."

The secret truth was, as aggravated with their host as Stephen remained, it had been a long time since he and Perry had carried out a ludicrous misadventure together. He had to admit there was a certain amusement value to it all.

So they hoofed it, crunching along the oystershell track that led through the trees and across the island.

"Anyway," Perry said, "it's possible they'd count as devices."

"What would?"

"The four-wheelers."

"If you're Amish, maybe."

"Nah. I think even they use computers now."

"Is that true?"

"I have no idea. I'm sure we could look it up." Perry snapped his fingers. "Oh, wait."

They pointed at each other, spoke in unison: "No phones."

Such was the level of nonsense that passed for conversation as they strolled along through the trees, where the air smelled sweet and woody. It was shocking how quickly the cloudbank had rolled in across the strait. The darkening sky was beginning to look gnarly overhead. There wasn't much in the way of accessible overhangs from the ground level of the main house, and the pergola over the front entry wasn't apt to stop much rain, so they'd decided to try their luck at the empty cottage on the far end of the island until things blew over. Even if they couldn't get in, at least it had a porch.

The island, if Stephen remembered their tour boat patter, comprised close enough to a hundred acres to have been listed for sale as a one-hundred-acre island, spanning just under half a mile from one end to the other. Which put them, he estimated, maybe halfway across by now. The old-growth firs and cedars rose up around them like whispering sentinels. The wind had kicked up, and it was getting chillier. Stephen was glad for their jackets.

"At least we're not getting sunburned anymore."

"That's what I like about you, Rollie. Always looking on the bright side." Perry gazed off into the gloom-shrouded trees. "You don't think he's got wolves, do you?"

"Doubtful. Unless he made some in his laboratory."

"That *would* probably help with the hop-ons," Perry said, which got them both chuckling. Poor Beau. They really shouldn't give the guy so much shit all the time.

"I bet Will and Emma have their hands full in there," Stephen said. "I wonder what that scene looks like?"

"Ah, yes. Will. And...Emma."

"Why'd you say it like that?"

"Say what like what?"

Stephen shook his head. "You've got a lot of growing up to do, my friend."

"That's Will's position also." Perry whistled a brief melody, scuffing a heel casually through the crushed oyster shells underfoot. Then he said: "So... Emma."

"God, Perrier, what the hell about her?"

"I guess she got divorced, huh? That seems like a shame."

"It *was* a shame," Stephen agreed. "Like five years ago."

"And here we all are. How's the love life, by the way? You seeing anybody these days? Been meaning to ask."

Stephen shot him a sideways look. He kept in fairly regular touch with Perry and Will, and they always asked, so they knew perfectly well who he mostly wasn't seeing these days: all the available women of Chicagoland. Life was pretty simple. He'd gotten used to it that way.

Besides: it was hardly fair to compare every first date for the rest of his life to what he'd had with Emma, once upon a time. After all, it had taken six semesters, two summers, and countless excursions as pals before some hidden mechanism in the cabinet drawer flipped, and friendship with Emma Grant had opened up into something else entirely.

Looking back, it seemed so simple to imagine what should have been. If he'd gone with her to Boston for her third-year law internship, for example, instead of staying home at their apartment in Chicago to save money. If they hadn't cut so many corners rebuilding after Hurricane Ryan passed through. If either one of them had done any number of things that neither one of them—for whatever bunch of insufficient reasons that made no sense now—had been equipped to do at the time.

But what had anybody ever gained from wringing out their should-have-beens?

"You can be a stubborn fellow when you want to be," Perry said. "Anybody ever tell you that?"

"Yeah. You. Just now."

Perry sighed wistfully. "Still, we *were* kind of hoping to see a little bedroom farce action this weekend. Mistaken identities, doors opening and closing, people sneaking up and down hallways...the cute thwarted heteronormative couple getting together in the end...you know. A classic."

Okay, fine: deep down, Stephen supposed he'd probably been hoping for about the same dumb thing. Maybe without the doors and the sneaking. He wasn't about to admit that to Perry, the overstretched gossip. "You mean this isn't farcical enough for you?"

Indeed, in the past few minutes, the air seemed to have swollen with that pleasant, damp-earth aroma that meant only one thing. Stephen held out his palm for Perry to see. Sure enough, a raindrop fell on it.

"Yep," Perry said. "I felt one too."

They both looked up. The dark sky above the road almost seemed to be boiling, lowering itself toward the treetops. The treetops themselves had begun swaying in earnest. All at once, the wind seemed to barrel across the Rock like a train.

"Shit," Stephen said. "We'd better book it."

So they did, taking off at a run, giggling like idiots as the sky opened up and the rain came down. Instant deluge: as hangover cures went, it made for a hell of a cold shower. They headed off the track and into the cover of the trees, but even still, they were soaked to the skin in no time flat. And the ground was uneven in the timber. There were rocks and dips and fallen branches, all manner of pitfalls about, and quickly their shoes were caked with slick wet fir needles. Nobody needed to turn an ankle or bust a leg out here, and they were as wet as they were going to get anyway, so they abandoned the woods and retook the path again.

Soon the trees thinned into another clearing. Even from fifty yards, they could barely see the darkened cottage through the wind-whipped sheets of rain. *Here's your tempest*, Stephen thought, once again thinking of Ryan on the roof.

Something told him he'd be thinking back to that moment for a very long time to come. The light tower pulsed at the end of the nearby spit, its bright white beacon strobing the rain into strands of beaded glass. The cottage came into relief for a moment—a small Cape Cod with wood shake siding and a covered porch—then slowly faded back into the murk.

This place had a far different character than the big house at the opposite end. Stephen had assumed that Ryan had built everything out here, but now he wondered if Mags and Luna's place was perhaps the island's original dwelling—perhaps from a time when the automated, skeleton-framed tower on the spit had been an old-fashioned lighthouse. The tour hadn't included such historical details, and none of them had thought to ask, but it was easy to imagine. It was as if they'd stumbled out of the trees and found themselves in Nantucket.

They made a break for it, splashing through puddles, clambering up onto the porch like it was a wooden raft.

"Holy shit," Perry laughed, swiping water from his hands, shaking his hair like a wet dog. "This is bonkers."

Stephen reflexively tried the door, expecting it to be locked like every other door on this island. He was astounded to feel the knob turn freely in his hand. "I don't believe it."

Perry pumped his fist. "Open sesame." He followed Stephen inside, crowding him forward, both of them dripping all over everything.

"So waaarm," Perry said. "So not raining."

Stephen fumbled for a light switch, found one, flicked it on...

...and nearly jumped out of his skin when the woman in her underwear let out a startled cry.

She stood in the middle of the small living room in nothing but a sports bra, matching briefs, and what looked like some kind of virtual reality headset over her eyes and ears. Her fingertips bristled with haptic sensors, wires taped up and down her bare limbs. Other sensors were taped here, there, everywhere.

Perry matched her with a yelp of his own. Stephen's heart pounded. Good grief. How was there anyone here? She tore off the headset, eyes wide. When she saw the two of them dripping in the doorway, she shouted, "What the shit!"

Stephen and Perry stared at each other, then at the half-naked woman. Without the headgear, Stephen recognized her immediately, even though she'd been wearing an entire skirt and blouse the last time he'd seen her, back at Link Village. A thought flashed in the back of his mind: Perry had gotten his farce after all. They blurted her name together:

"*Kai?*"

CHAPTER 12

EMMA FELT CERTAIN she was dreaming. According to the window monitors, a storm had blown up outside. The world had gone dark, obscured by curtains of rain. The windows facing the water showed pictures of whitecaps; the windows facing inland showed pictures of swaying trees. In a house made of reinforced concrete, with soundproof panels blocking all the glass, they could barely hear any of it happening. It was like watching Weather Channel footage from someplace else.

Meanwhile, on the boat, Ryan had taken cover below deck. He'd carried them into a small aft cabin off the lower lounge, where he'd remounted the tablet and closed the door behind him. Now he sat on the edge of a narrow daybed, swaying with the movement of the boat, arms planted beside him like buttresses.

"I don't get it," Beau was saying. "You built Link Labs with your own two hands. I know you've hit some rough spots, taken a few shots in the press, whatever. Who cares? Our guy says your share price is set to shoot through the roof again. Nothing but runway. It doesn't make any *sense* to throw in the towel now!"

Lainie couldn't agree more. "Of course it doesn't. To hell with the haters. How many people use Link?"

"Three billion and change," Beau filled in. "*Including* the haters."

"Three billion people! Ryan, you've literally helped change the world, why on earth would you—"

"Guys, I understand," Ryan told them. "It's a big download, you're getting it all at once, and it all sounds pretty crazy."

"*Pretty* crazy? Buddy, no offense, but you sound batshit insane right now." Beau leaned back, crossing his arms defiantly. He looked to Emma and Will for support. "Guys, back me up."

Emma had nothing for him. In the midst of everything else, they all seemed to have forgotten that they themselves were locked inside Ryan's house against their will. On a private island. With no way to get off without him, no way to contact another soul. Their entire environment was literally at his fingertips; Ryan had only to pick up his tablet to put them all in the palm of his hand. For all they knew, it was still sunny outside. He could be playing them a video of a storm right now, and they'd never know the difference.

"Ultimately, it's a matter of contingencies," Ryan explained. "At least that's what we call it in the company governance plan: Contingencies and Emergency Succession." He pointed toward the closed cabin door. "And it's where they've got me by the balls."

Will said, "Contingencies?"

"Terminal illness, for example."

A light bulb came on for Emma. "Your board found out you were sick."

Ryan sighed. "I lied to Stephen when I told him only my doctors knew. That was true for a long time, but it's not true anymore, and believe me: as far as that pack of jackals in there is concerned, Christmas came early. So now, as if dying painfully weren't enough, I've got a coup to put down before I go."

"Ryan, listen to yourself! Coup? Put down? You literally *kidnapped* these people?"

"I invited them all to an emergency retreat to discuss the most sensible transfer of power." Ryan shrugged. "They arrived yesterday morning."

Emma thought back to their tour of Link Village. Of course some part of her had wondered why Ryan hadn't been there to conduct it himself, but then, that was Ryan. He was a very intelligent, very busy guy. And he'd always had his own reasons for things.

"Wait a minute," Will said. "They've been here? With us? This whole time?"

"There at the Rock? Yes. Chained up in the basement while we got drunk and watched MTV, no." Ryan waved away the thought. "Resting comfortably at the cottage. Mags and Luna both have medical degrees and half a dozen Peace Corps tours between them. I simply asked them to be a little more liberal with the lunch menu than they were with dinner, that's all. No Stanford MBAs were harmed, you can rest assured."

Emma heard what he was saying...but it took a few seconds before what he was saying sank in. She thought back to this morning. When was the last time she'd slept in past sunrise, hangover or no hangover? Then she thought all the way back to last night. What was the last thing that happened before she'd fallen asleep? She honestly couldn't remember.

"Are you saying...," she started, marveling at how absurd it sounded. "Ryan, did you *drug* us?"

On-screen, Ryan's eyes didn't change. But he also didn't answer the question right away.

It was all the answer any of them needed. Lainie looked like she'd been sucker punched. "Ryan!"

"Only a little," he finally said. "Just enough to ensure an early bedtime. I had lots to get done."

Beau said, "Whoa."

"I did say Luna's risotto would put you in a coma."

Emma couldn't begin to gather her thoughts. Nobody seemed able to respond.

Will finally sat forward, rubbing his face with his palms. When he took his hands away, he looked ten years older. "What did you mean when you said Perry and Stephen are being collected? Why can't you just unlock the house so they can come back in?"

"That's what I've been trying to explain."

"Breathe on Perry wrong and he gets pneumonia. You know that. We almost lost him to the virus last year. Now he's stuck out there in this?"

"Okay," Ryan said. "You're right, I'm sorry. This wasn't part of the plan. Operation Perry and Stephen is delayed momentarily due to the weather, but radar says it'll pass soon. For now they're just cold and wet. Which does not cause illness, as we know."

Speaking of storms, Emma had never seen Will's face go so dark so quickly. She thought he might get up and kick a hole in the TV screen.

"But now's not the time to split hairs," Ryan hastened to add. "Where are they right now?"

"Who knows?" Will snapped. "They stopped trying to get in half an hour ago. We haven't seen them since before the storm started."

"Got it," Ryan said. "I can see you all need a little time to absorb things. Let's pause here. I'll come back to you with a status report."

Emma said, "Ryan, don't you dare..."

But he was already gone.

Kai returned to the seaside-chic living room dressed in a long cable-knit sweater over leggings. She'd stripped herself of spare wiring. Her feet were still bare.

"Nope, no problem," she was saying into the phone against her ear. "They're already here. No. Drying out—I told them to help themselves to the firewood."

"Some device free weekend this is turning out to be," Stephen said. "I'm starting to think there's more of a signal out here than Ryan lets on."

Perry glanced at Kai and chuckled. "I'd say there's a lot more going on out here than Ryan lets on."

They'd immediately taken Kai up on lighting the small stone fireplace. Stephen raided the basket of kindling on the hearth while Perry hit the rack of split cordwood on the wall. The logs were just now starting to crackle and pop. The rain still pounded against the shingles overhead. Stephen's teeth were still chattering.

"Got it," Kai was saying. "Yep. Nope. Absolutely. We'll be fine." She hung up and said, "Your clothes will dry faster if you get out of them. Drag those chairs over, you can hang stuff. I'll get you some towels."

"Please, don't go to any trouble," Stephen said.

"What's the matter, shy?" She winked. "You've already seen me."

"Um...yeah. Really sorry about that."

"I'm kidding. No worries."

"None at all," Perry said. "Neither one of us is interested in naked women, it seems."

Stephen sighed heavily, rolling his eyes. Perry cackled at him and stood. Kai watched them with the attentiveness of a zookeeper.

"Permission to disrobe accepted," Perry said, stripping out of his sodden shirt and trousers, down to his boxer briefs, where his modesty kicked in.

"Don't go anywhere." She disappeared again.

"Guess I am sort of chafing," Stephen said, joining him.

Perry turned his backside toward the fire. "This kind of reminds me of that night we got caught out at White Bear."

"With fewer tornadoes."

"But more cottages."

Kai returned with a stack of fluffy white towels. Stephen thanked her, wrapped one of the towels around his waist, and said, "Kai, not to be nosy, but…what are you doing here, anyway?"

She waved her hand. "I was just playtesting some new interface hardware we're developing. Perfect spot. The less ambient light the better."

Perry raised a finger. "And clothing."

"That too." She laughed. "I swear, I didn't even hear you guys until the lights came on. Anyway: that was kind of a top secret prototype you just saw. *Nobody's* supposed to see it yet. So…mum's the word?"

Perry pantomimed zipping his lips, tossing the imaginary key into the fireplace.

Kai wiped imaginary sweat from her brow. "Whew."

"I mean…here, at the cottage," Stephen said. "I thought this was Mags and Luna's place."

"Oh, it is," Kai said. "They had their own plans this weekend."

Perry slipped him a glance. Stephen pretended not to notice. "Well, sorry again. We'd never have just walked in on you like that if we'd known anybody was in here."

"Totally not a problem. You must have been drowning out there."

"I guess we had the impression the house would be empty all weekend."

"Exactly," Kai said. "That thing you saw me wearing really is top secret. Your friend Ryan can be pretty cagey when he's got something big in the works."

"Yes," Perry deadpanned. "We were reminded of that just recently."

Stephen knew he was enjoying himself. Perry liked awkward. *I'd say there's a lot more going on out here than Ryan lets on.* But Stephen was getting a tingle in his bullshit meter. Yes, of course he knew what Perry was thinking, and yes, he'd had the same first thought himself: Emma may have been right that Jud Bernal only had eyes for Kai…but maybe it was, in fact, *Ryan* and Kai who had a little something extracurricular going. Maybe this wasn't exclusively an old-friends weekend for him after all.

But the more he thought about it, the less it tracked.

Meanwhile, Kai hadn't blinked.

In fact, that's precisely what he'd noticed: after her initial surprise, she hadn't batted an eye over any of this. He held the towel with one hand as he stooped to move his shoes closer to the fire. "That was Ryan just now, huh?"

"He called to let me know you might show up. I guess you were faster."

"You should have given us the phone," Perry said. "We have a few comments for his suggestion box."

"I bet you do." She laughed. "I think he was embarrassed. Sounds like his big escape room extravaganza backfired a little. You poor guys."

"I owe you five bucks," Perry told Stephen. "You totally said escape room."

"You can pay up later."

"Good. My wallet's in my pants, and my pants are over there."

"Everybody's waiting for you back at the big house," Kai said. "But please, hang out, dry out, wait 'til the weather clears. These midday squalls usually pass pretty quickly. I was going to make tea—either of you guys want a cup?"

"Tea would be lovely," Perry said.

Stephen offered his friendliest smile. "If you're already putting a kettle on…"

"Back in a flash."

While she was rattling around in the kitchen, Perry said, "You're evil. I love it."

"Don't get fancy," Stephen told him. "I'll handle this investigation."

Pretty soon, Kai came back with two steaming mugs, tea tags draped over the rims. She handed one to Perry, one to Stephen. "Forest Berries. Hope that's okay."

"They're all okay." Perry breathed in the steam and sighed. "All the berries of the forest. You've saved our lives."

"It was nothing."

Stephen sipped his tea. It did taste nice. "How'd you get here, anyway?"

"Ryan brought me out," she said. "Early this morning."

"Some boss *you've* got. Isn't it Saturday?"

Kai laughed. "We don't call it 'work-life balance' at Link. We call it 'work-life synergy.'"

"How twenty-first-century," Perry said.

"Good thing I love what I do, right?"

Stephen said, "If you don't mind my asking, what do you do? Like, title-wise. I imagine it's not 'Weekend Playtester,' right?"

"Director of Communications, technically," Kai said. "But we don't stand on titles much. Everyone sort of fills in where we're needed."

"As long as the cottage is empty anyway," Perry said.

She touched a finger to the tip of her nose. "You could be Link material."

Director, Stephen thought. Kai couldn't have been much older than her early thirties, and she was already not standing on titles for one of the most prominent tech companies in the world. He knew what Perry would have said: *Perks of sleeping with the boss, no?* But Stephen didn't get that vibe.

"I like Perry's idea," he said. "We should call Ryan back. I've got some work-life synergy concepts I'd like to share with him."

"Oh. Sure. Well. He...sort of told me not to do that."

"Coward. He's ducking us, isn't he?"

"Of course not!" she said. "But I do get the impression he's hoping to salvage the itinerary he's got planned."

"Give us a hint. What's next? Weed out the weaker members? Form our own system of government?"

Perry said, "He's not going to hunt us, is he?"

She laughed, making a warding gesture with her palms. "I wouldn't know, guys. And even if I did, you won't catch me leaking. I love what I do, remember?"

Stephen sipped his tea. "What did you say you do again?"

Kai looked back and forth between them, standing there in their towels and teacups in the dancing light of the fire. "Are...you two okay?"

Perry grinned. "Don't mind him. He's suspicious by nature."

"I think I'm getting that."

"Sorry," Stephen said. "Occupational hazard."

"Oh? What line of work are you in?"

"Polygraph examiner."

She finally blinked.

"Job screenings, mostly," Stephen said. "Pretty boring stuff."

"He's being modest. He owns a whole company." Perry leaned over, did a stage whisper behind the back of his hand. *He even works with the police.*

"That's overstating. The company's only me." Stephen smiled. "Really I'm just a technician with a psych degree."

"Wow," Kai said. "That must be interesting work."

"Pretty controversial in the clinical community, if you want the truth. If we were in court right now, my results wouldn't be admissible."

"Well, I think it sounds...," she started, trailing off before she'd finished telling them what she thought it sounded like.

Perry raised his mug, still grinning.

Kai glanced between them again, but she knew she was busted.

"Shit," she said.

CHAPTER 13

AFTER TOUCHING BASE with Kai, Ryan took a moment to check in again with Jud Bernal, temporarily reassigned from his primary duties overseeing the prep work at Link Village.

Immediately, Jud texted a succinct reply: *5x5*. In Bernalese this meant either "Everything's okay" or "Don't bother me, Boss, I'm flying a helicopter." Either translation sufficed for the moment.

Meanwhile, the storm had died down over the water, easing the motion of the ocean considerably. Nevertheless, Ryan opened the aft cabin door to find his six captives looking decidedly green around the gills.

"I don't feel well," a trembling voice said. "I need...I don't feel well."

The voice belonged to Amanda Driesen-Briar. Forty-one years old, their youngest sitting member. CEO of a promising cloud analytics start-up. Mother of two charming, whip-smart little blond mini-Amandas, ages three and five. Strands of hair sticking to the sweat on her forehead.

As soon as she spoke, the others joined in, voices rising and mingling in a generalized chorus of upset.

Ryan couldn't exactly blame them. The truth was, he didn't feel so hot himself. Over the past thirty minutes, a hot coal had developed in the pit of his stomach. While he'd brought along a number of options for dousing it, he needed to stay as clearheaded as he could until things were back on track. He'd popped a few ibuprofen, but that was sort of a laugh. Nothing to do but ride it out for now.

"At least none of you barfed," he said, passing out waters from the mini-fridge and Dramamine from the med kit. "In tight quarters like this I'd say that's one for the yay column."

The members of his governing board were crammed shoulder to shoulder on the white leather sofa section of the VanDutch's lounging saloon. Except for being mostly over-the-hill millionnaires tied together in a line, the scene almost reminded him of the challenge photo he'd added to the tablet UI—the whole gang from Stillwater back in the day, goofing around with Will's camera in 205 Anders.

"Just what are you trying to accomplish?" Tom Carver demanded to know. Square-jawed, thick-bodied, fifty-five years old; Ryan's chief operating officer. Also chief organizer of this underhanded little revolt-that-wasn't. "Who were you talking to in there?"

"If you must know, Tom, I'm entertaining old friends this weekend." When Tom refused to accept his designated water bottle, Ryan dropped it in his lap. Tom huffed and sat up straight. "Who knows, maybe they'll be your replacements? There happen to be six of 'em, one for each seat. I guess we'll see!"

"You're insane."

"That's a distinct medical possibility," Ryan said. "But no matter what happens, at the very least, I won't be your chairman after this. That ought to make you happy."

Without warning, the hot coal in his stomach suddenly became a hot knife. Instantly he buckled, grinding his teeth. Ryan stepped back into the counter of the small kitchenette behind him; at the same moment, the boat hit a swell, nearly sending him to the floor. He grabbed the doorway into the forward master cabin and steadied his balance, tried to control his breathing. He saw Carver smiling.

"I'll tell you what's going to make me happy," Carver said. "I'm going to sit here and wait until that happens to you again. When it does?" He raised his bound hands. "I'm going to get up and strangle you to death. That's going to make me *very* happy."

"Tom, shut *up*." Bhavna Patel. Exec VP at Werner-Wagman. Also president of the largest women's nonprofit in Washington State. Divorced. Daughter in med school. "Ryan. Please. You're clearly not well."

Ryan took a deep breath, exhaled it slowly. "I've been better, it's true."

"Then stop this now. I don't know what you want from us. But I've known you for many years. And I know this is *not* who you are."

"Who I am." He straightened himself carefully. "That's exactly the question, Bhav. Who I am, who you are, who we are as a company."

Carver expressed an astounding amount of confidence for a man tied up in a passenger hold on open water: "From now on, that's for us to decide."

"Let me see if I can illustrate the question in a way that clarifies things for everybody." Ryan opened a bottle of water for himself and took a small sip. He had to work to keep it down. "Who remembers the Ship of Theseus?"

Blank faces.

"Oh, come on."

"Please just say what you mean to say." Elijah Stanhope, Outside Director. Former CEO of three different Fortune 500 organizations; former executive secretary for the US Department of State. Sixty-seven years old. Five grandkids.

"See, this is why we've never completely gotten along." Ryan pointed back and forth between himself, leaning against the kitchenette counter, and the lot of them, tied up on the lounging couch. "You're all impressive, you're all intelligent, you're all accomplished. But you've got no time for *philosophy*."

"No, Ryan." Oliver Chen. Fifty-eight. CEO of Caishen Capital. "It may make things easier for you to think of us as greedy philistines, but no. We've never completely gotten along because you're the chairman of your own board, your ownership stake makes you the deciding vote for every decision this company has ever made, you are historically quite averse to accepting an opposing viewpoint, and..."

"And in the past three years," Tom Carver jumped in, "your decisions, quote-unquote, have cut our active user base by fifteen percent and our average trade price by—"

"But enough about what we can do for our shareholders," Ryan said. "As the ghost of my old professor Mendota might explain, the Ship of Theseus is a way of discussing the problem of *identity*. Our sense of what makes a thing what it is. How that sense of a thing persists over time. For example: Imagine the Ship of Theseus returns from battle, goes into dry dock, and starts to rot. So you replace a rotten plank. Is the Ship of Theseus still the Ship of Theseus?"

"Uh-huh. Now I get it." Carver snorted. "Without you, the whole ship goes down, is that it? Here's a news flash—"

"Let's say you replace two more planks. How about now? Is the Ship of Theseus still the Ship of Theseus?"

"I would say," Bhavna offered calmly, "that the spirit of the battle is still in the ship. Therefore, the ship that returned from the battle is still the Ship of Theseus."

Ryan smiled. "Not bad, Bhav. You're a born metaphysicist."

"But..."

"But how many planks would it take before the Ship of Theseus *stops* being the Ship of Theseus? Exactly." Ryan noticed the water bottle trembling in his own hand. He took a sip to cover the tremor. "Let's imagine you take apart the entire ship, store the wood in your garage for a year, then use the original plans to rebuild the whole thing in your driveway. Is *that* still the Ship of Theseus?"

"Nobody wants to take Link apart." Valeria Cordero. Outside Director. General counsel to the largest industrial engineering firm in North America, fifty-two years old. Two boys and a girl, all between the ages of twelve and seventeen. Husband in a wheelchair. "Quite the contrary, in fact."

Ryan nodded. "I believe you, but that's longer-range, bigger-picture stuff. Here's how the Ship of Theseus question applies to us right now."

He made his way carefully to the narrow closet that housed the boat's electrical system, opening the door so the group could see inside.

"Who can tell me what these packages contain?"

Everyone craned for a look. Amanda's eyes grew wide as she surveyed the rectangular white bricks stacked in among the wiring harnesses, breaker panels, and backup batteries.

"Oh my God," she said. "Is that...*cocaine?*"

Ryan choked on his water. Amanda. Goddamn, it hurt to laugh right now.

"Composition C-4," he said. "About twice this much in the engine compartment as well. I'd show you, but we'd have to go up top, so you'll just have to take my word for it."

He had everyone's full attention now. Even Tom's.

"But as you feel yourselves tempted, over the course of this adventure, to reconsider the idea of mutiny," Ryan advised, "I'd factor in the explosives. And what you do or don't know about my ability to set them off. Otherwise, we'll all know in a hurry how fast our own little Ship of Theseus loses its identity."

He gave them a moment to absorb this new information.

Almost to himself, Tom Carver murmured: "You actually *are* insane."

"Well, Tom, in this situation, I suppose it's like the kids say: fuck around and find out."

Stripped of bravado, Carver now looked to the others for help. He found none forthcoming. He shook his head slowly. "Shithouse crazy."

Ryan shrugged, checked his wristwatch. "Speaking of, does anyone need to use the facilities before I hand out sandwiches?"

CHAPTER 14

Okay, look," kai told them. Confession time at last. "There's going to be a corporate announcement in a couple days."

"What kind of announcement?" Stephen asked.

"A big secret one," Kai said. "Ryan wanted it managed from here, away from the jackals—that's his word, not mine. Come Monday morning, we'll also have attorneys, others from the executive level, a couple of extra hands from my group. I'm just the advance team."

"It sounds like quite an announcement," Stephen said.

"And that's all you're going to get me to say about it," Kai said. "If you two want more, you'll have to beat it out of me, and even then you won't get much. Because I don't know much myself, yet. There's an internal briefing scheduled for Monday morning."

Stephen and Perry exchanged glances.

Kai picked up on that, leaned forward. "What do *you* guys know?"

"Very little," Stephen said.

Perry added, "And you'll have to beat it out of us."

They'd all taken seats in the living room, where the small fire crackled along. Everything felt perfectly cordial. Everyone had their own fresh mug of Forest Berries tea. Judging by the feel of their laundry, Stephen and Perry would soon be wearing pants again. Outside, the rain had stopped; amazingly, sunlight was already beginning to filter back in through the cottage windows. Kai had been right. These squalls passed quickly.

"Just out of curiosity," Stephen said, "why are you here so early?"

"Early?"

"You said this wasn't happening until Monday."

"I need to set up. A few workstations, network switch, VPN connections to our press portal, test the satlink, a few other odds and ends."

"You can do all that?"

"And my makeup too."

"Sorry, that's not what I meant," Stephen said. "I just thought you said you were PR."

"I said director of communications, but I understand what you're asking. Most people with a job like mine have a background in journalism or similar, yes. Mine happens to be in IT and informatics."

"Inforwhatics?"

"Computer stuff," she said.

Perry said, "They all fill in, remember?"

Stephen still had questions. Quite a long list of them. For example: If Ryan wanted her bunkered out here all weekend, why hadn't she simply flown out yesterday with the rest of them? Was he announcing this double-top-secret new virtual reality product she'd claimed to be testing? Or was he preparing to disclose his illness to the world? Both? Why do it on a holiday? What was this so-called Stillwater Seven reunion really all about? Was there no proper clothes dryer in this place? Where *was* Ryan?

And how, exactly, had he known to call Kai just now?

"Sounds like you've got a lot to accomplish," he said. "Guess we'd better let you get back to it. Thanks for the tea."

"And the towels," Perry said.

She rose with them, collecting their empty mugs while they put themselves back into their clothes. Still damp, but much better. Warm and damp, at least. As he was lacing up his musty shoes, Stephen said, "Can I ask you one last question?"

"Fire away."

"Are you completely, totally, one-hundred-percent-absolutely sure," he said, "that you have nothing to do with that lockdown back at the other house?"

She laughed. "Completely, totally, one hundred percent."

Her eyes shifted up and to the right when she said it. Quick as it was, Stephen couldn't fail to notice the tic.

However, contrary to a popular myth still promoted faithfully by cop shows on television, this was not, in fact, a reliable indicator that she was lying again. In this case, it was simply an indicator that Kai was twenty years younger than they were.

She had much better hearing.

He heard it himself a moment later: the faint but unmistakable *whop-whop-whop* of an incoming helicopter.

"Wonder who that could be," he said.

Kai expressed confusion. But as the sound of the chopper entered Ryan's airspace overhead, she finally acknowledged it with a grin. "Oh. Ha, sorry. I hear it now."

That was how he knew she was lying again.

Nearly half an hour passed before Ryan reappeared on the big TV. The sun had returned to their window monitors. Ryan's setting had transformed from a seesaw back into a boat.

When he finally came back on-screen—same station, same lower cabin—he looked noticeably different to Emma.

It was the first time all weekend he'd looked so obviously unwell. His color had blanched, making the dark rings under his eyes stand out. In ultra-high-definition, the beads of sweat on his pallid skin gave his complexion the look of room-temperature cheese.

"Ryan," she said, "I think you need help."

"Just a flare-up. It'll pass." He tried a smile. "Stress isn't great for this."

That wasn't entirely what she'd meant. "How could we make this situation less stressful?" She looked to the others. "Anybody have any ideas?"

"Emma," Lainie said. "Just stop. Look at him."

A dozen sharp replies leapt to mind, but Emma bit them all down. She found that she didn't much *want* to look at the stranger on-screen with them right now. He resembled Ryan, and he spoke with Ryan's voice, but whoever this was, it couldn't be Ryan Cloverhill.

"All right," she said. "Fine. Ryan, tell us what we need to do to get you, and those people on board with you, back here safely."

"Okay, here's the deal," Ryan said. "As I was saying before the previous inter-mission, I've reached that point where it's time to think about legacy. I've already made my own decision on that topic, but it's a big one. Really big. And even though I can guarantee I won't be changing my mind... let's put it this way: even *I'm* not a big enough egomaniac to bypass the checks and balances."

"Whatever it is you're thinking about doing, don't do it," Beau said. "There. Easy. You're welcome."

Ryan chuckled, then pressed his fist into his right side. Then he squeezed his eyes shut and pressed harder.

"Oh, God," Lainie said. She reached her hand toward the television. "I just hate this."

As the moment passed, Ryan gave a wan smile. "Sorry, what was I saying?"

Emma said, "Checks and balances."

"Right." He cleared his throat, seemed to center himself. "Not too long ago, somebody told me that I had trouble accepting opposing viewpoints. I admit it: he was right."

"Any one of us could have told you that," Will said.

"So I'm not sure if you'll believe me when I say this, but here's the truth: In all my years on earth, the six of you are the only people I've ever genuinely trusted. Definitely the only people I've ever trusted more than myself."

Emma said, "Ryan."

"That's why I'm counting on you to make a decision of your own. Because you're the only people in the world who can."

"No problemo," Beau said, cracking his knuckles. "You came to the right place. Lay it on us, buddy: What do you need us to decide?"

"I need you to decide whether to stop me or not."

Lainie said, "From inexplicably blowing up your own life? Your own com-pany? You need *us* for that?"

"Bingo," Ryan said. "I mean, you should know, I've taken steps to mini-mize collateral damage. Link Labs is closed worldwide for US Labor Day—a little thank-you to employees for a hell of a tough year. The Village is off-limits all weekend. I'm deactivating all gates and badge readers as a precaution. I've got a crack team in charge of keeping the blasts professionally contained, but we're still talking about a populated urban area. And if there's one thing product development has taught me, it's that nothing ever goes completely according to plan. As if we haven't proved that today already."

Everybody looked at each other.

Beau said, "Wait. What?"

"Your decision," Ryan repeated, "is whether or not to stop me from blowing up my own company. I thought we were on the same page."

Lainie's eyes widened slowly. She sat up straighter. "I thought you were being figurative!"

"Oh, no," Ryan said. "There's actual detonation involved."

Stephen and Perry stood just off the porch, watching the Sikorsky circle, bank, then lower itself toward the helipad on the far side of the island.

"I have to say," Perry mused aloud, "this place smells amazing after a rain."

"I have to say I'm not loving the sight of that helicopter."

"I think you're being paranoid."

"Can't imagine why that would be."

"Come on," Perry said. "Let's get back. Maybe Jud's got the spare house key."

But Stephen wasn't so sure that was the right idea. He couldn't explain why, really. Just that his bullshit meter had kicked into overdrive. "I think I'd rather speak directly to management."

"No go, remember?"

"We'll see about that."

Stephen turned toward the porch, intending to go back inside the cottage and insist on using Kai's phone. But he pulled up short, the sole of one damp shoe glued to the tread of the first step.

Kai stood in the open doorway. She looked apologetic.

As if she would rather not be pointing a small handgun at them.

"I'm sorry, guys," she said. "Unlucky timing. Maybe it's best at this point if we all sit tight for a few."

Perry's face had gone slack. When he looked at Stephen, his eyes spoke volumes: *Are you seeing the same thing I'm seeing?* His mouth said nothing, and that was saying something. It was a rare moment indeed that found Perry Therkle lost for words.

So Stephen said, "Your job description really does cover a lot of ground, doesn't it?"

"This is new territory, I admit. And I really am sorry." She beckoned them toward her with her free hand, holding the gun close to her body, as if it might jump away and escape.

Stephen didn't move a muscle. "If you're sorry, how about putting that thing away? I don't like it pointed at me."

"I don't like it pointed at him either," Perry said. When she turned the gun toward him instead, he put up his hands. "Okay, that's worse."

"Then let's just go back inside for now, okay?"

"Come on," Stephen said. "You're not really going to shoot us, are you?"

Her eyes flashed, and she raised the gun a few inches. All at once she looked a lot more comfortable with it. "I don't know, Mr. Technician with a Psych Degree, why don't you tell me?"

CHAPTER 15

THE ONLY WAY to effectively govern a diverse society, Ryan Cloverhill once scrawled on a public restroom wall, *is through benevolent dictatorship.*

This had been the spring break they'd all driven from Stillwater up to Grand Marais, hoping to catch the forecasted appearance of the aurora borealis over Lake Superior. Ryan and Perry, as Emma recalled, had been tripping balls on psychedelic mushrooms at the time; they were the only two among the group who saw any Northern Lights that weekend. When Ryan finally came down, and the others had shown him the Polaroid account of his unprovoked outburst of drug-induced graffiti, Ryan claimed no recollection of the restroom, the wall, or ever having subscribed, even temporarily, to the proclamation itself.

It's counterintuitive, he'd joked on the long drive home. *Nobody achieves power through benevolence.*

Yet somehow, as enduring chief of the global Linkverse he'd created, "benevolent dictator" became the term most commonly applied to Ryan Cloverhill's management style.

"Savvy investors have long understood two things about Link Labs," a reporter for *Forbes* once wrote. "First: the corporate governance charter is printed on toilet paper, which is housed under lock and key in Ryan Cloverhill's personal executive crapper. Second: it's hard to argue with a 30% average annual return."

But making money hand over fist, it turned out, didn't do much to stop the rise of politically motivated conspiracy theories around the Grayson Point school shooting, to name an example. It didn't stop hate groups from using the Linkverse to organize larger parades. And it definitely didn't improve the ability of average humans to play well together in large, unrestricted groups.

Which was why he'd famously spent the past few years pouring untold resources into cleaning up his own worldwide town. In the last half-decade,

Ryan's company had developed revolutionary algorithms for filtering hate speech, misinformation, disinformation, propaganda, and other "digital toxins," as he called them. These days, Link Labs invested as much in its fact-checking division as it did in developing code. Link's various integrated platforms now banned all forms of paid political advertising. They handed out lifetime restrictions to individual users who violated their policies like Premier League football officials handed out penalty cards. Even the mission statement of Ryan's behavioral research group had changed fundamentally. The division's prime directive was now to *mitigate*—rather than intentionally amplify—the naturally addictive qualities of the Linked experience.

But was any of it working?

"Do you know who I find myself thinking a lot about these past few years?" Ryan asked them. "Since before the diagnosis, I mean."

Emma said, "I give up."

"People like Oppenheimer. Kalashnikov. Ethan Zuckerman. Dr. Frankenstein. Do you know what they all have in common?"

The atomic bomb, the AK-47 assault rifle, a patchwork monster animated by lightning bolts...Emma felt herself playing right into his hand. This was classic Ryan. He'd always had an uncanny ability to make you feel like an active participant in his way of thinking.

Beau said, "Who's Ethan Zuckerman?"

"The guy who invented the pop-up ad."

"Oh," Beau said. "That guy."

"But what makes them all alike?"

"They all developed something revolutionary," Will said.

"Exactly right." Ryan touched his finger to the tip of his own nose. "And they all had regrets."

Emma said, "*This* is how you've chosen to handle your regrets?"

"I know. It seems a little disproportionate at first." Ryan winked at the camera. "Who knows? Deep down, maybe I really am a Bond villain."

Beau cocked his head. "Heeeyyy..."

Emma closed her eyes. He'd heard them all talking on the trip out yesterday. Which meant he'd even bugged his own helicopter.

Of course he had. It physically pained her to think that her oldest friend had somehow gone this far over the edge. Ryan: the kid up the street, whom she'd walked with to Morningside Middle every day for three grades. Who'd eventually come to spend more of his free time at the Grant house than he had at his own. Like a hot poker jabbing her in the side, that's what it felt like. Was there such a thing as phantom cancer?

"Just kidding," Ryan said. "But do you see why I need your help?"

"No," Emma said.

"Think back to those trips we used to take. Hell, everything we used to do together, pretty much. Everybody always wanted something different. We'd make a production out of the simplest thing."

"You mean we'd fight like a bunch of cats and damn dogs," Beau said.

"Yet we always managed to find a compromise. We've always been seven very different people, but whatever we ended up choosing, it always turned out right, even if it was a disaster. Because we always did it together."

"But, Ryan," Will said, "you're not talking about whether to order pizza or Chinese. You're talking about...Jesus, man. You're talking about blowing up *buildings*."

"And yet, the same principle applies," Ryan said. "And that's what I need from you now. One last time—for old time's sake, if nothing else—I need you guys to fight like cats and dogs. Argue, get mad at each other, then compromise. Because this decision needs to be unanimous."

"I still don't get it," Beau said.

"Your tablet contains a library of material you can use to inform your deliberations over the next"—Ryan checked his wristwatch—"thirty-four hours and change."

Emma said, "What material?"

"A few studies. Effects of social media on productivity, sleep, depression, anxiety, relationships, self-esteem. None of it's conclusive, but it's a start. There's some trendline data from Pew on fertility and reproductive rates over the past thirty years. There's also some analysis on the hole I'm preparing to blow in the US economy. Projected job losses, secondary impacts on advertising and retail, along those lines."

"Ryan..."

"I've also included some of our own internal analytics. For example: Would it surprise you to know that the average Link user between the ages of nineteen and thirty-two interacts with our user interface, in one way or another, just over seventeen times an hour? That's a screen tap every three and a half minutes. On *average*." He pointed. "There's a good one in there from the *American Journal of Preventive Medicine*. It finds that the heaviest social media users in that same age-group are roughly twice as likely to report feelings of social isolation. Social *isolation*! Any fans of irony in the audience?"

"And when we were all locked down for months on end during that awful pandemic," Lainie said quietly, "what kept us together? What kept kids in school? What kept businesses doing business? What kept..."

Ryan nodded his encouragement. "Now you're talking. That's exactly the kind of conversation I'm asking you guys to have. You said it yourself, Lainie: Link helped change the world. Now I'm asking you to decide for all of us whether that's a version of the world worth keeping."

"Buddy, I gotta say, I'm with the ladies on this one," Beau said. "You're not making a hell of a lot of sense. I mean, come on. What about..."

Ryan showed them his palms. "I already told you: I've made *my* decision. Is it correct? That's your debate. After the guys get back, you can choose to stop me, or not stop me, or do nothing at all, which is effectively the same as not stopping me...Although, from your perspective, not quite."

Emma said, "How?"

"Glad you asked. It's time we went over the terms and conditions. They're kind of important."

"I mean, how do we stop you?"

"Ah." Ryan smiled. "Who's up for a good old-fashioned game of Trolley Problem?"

CHAPTER 16

WITHIN FIFTEEN MINUTES of returning to their seats in the newly sun-dappled living room, Stephen heard heavy footfalls on the porch. He glanced at Perry, who sat with a scowl, watching the dying fire.

"Thank God," Kai said, rising from her perch on a barstool halfway across the room. She hustled to open the front door.

Jud stepped inside. "You good?"

"I wasn't sure what to do," Kai said.

"No worries." He kissed her on the lips. "I'll get 'em back where they go."

So Emma had these two pegged right from the beginning, Stephen noted. He really needed to start paying more attention. For example: Jud's weekend attire. Today he wore a tight-fitting sleeveless holster shirt tucked into tactical pants, with a bulky diver's watch on one wrist. His exposed shoulders were bulbous, striated with muscle. One shoulder displayed a tattoo of a skeletal frog with a long-handled trident in its mouth. The firearm concealment pocket under his other shoulder was visibly not empty.

As for guns, Kai handed him hers, grip first. "Maybe you'd better put this on a high shelf somewhere."

"Nah. You keep it." Jud deftly checked the chamber, engaged the safety, and placed the gun on the driftwood entryway table, patting it affectionately. "It makes me feel better."

"Aw," Perry said. "They make a cute couple, no?"

Stephen had been focused on Jud's tattoo. Though it didn't make him feel much better about their current situation, Emma wasn't the only one who'd had him pegged. Right off the bat, Stephen had guessed ex-military. "I guess you're on the work-life synergy plan, too, huh?"

Jud grinned. "Twenty-four-seven, three-sixty-five."

"Well, it was nice seeing you guys," Kai said. "It started weird, and it ended weird, but I guess we all survived."

"It sort of feels like the weekend might still be young."

"Ha. Don't worry, you're safe with Jud. Sorry I went all Calamity Jane on you."

With that, Jud gave Perry and Stephen a friendly nod. He stepped to one side, gesturing toward the open front door. "All set, then?"

A good old-fashioned game of Trolley Problem.

Straight out of Honors Philosophy 101.

Oh, how Professor Mendota had enjoyed blowing the minds of his introductory students with the Trolley Problem. How old had the man been back then? Sixty? Seventy? The hair in his ears had been like tufts of steel wool. Emma wondered when he'd finally retired. Or maybe he was still there, doddering around like Methuselah, croaking on about ethics and what it was like to be a bat.

The Trolley Problem was a classic thought experiment. It went more or less like this:

You're aboard a runaway trolley heading for five people tied up on the tracks. Do nothing, five people get splattered. Pull a lever, and the trolley diverts to a second track. This other track has only one person on it. So: if you decide to pull the lever, the trolley kills only one instead of killing five... but it would be your deliberate action that caused the person's bloody death. What do you do?

How much bonding had the Stillwater Seven done over the Trolley Problem that first semester on campus? With enough fuzzy navel premixed in a two-liter Sunkist bottle, you could go on for hours, or at least until Letterman came on, arguing and laughing and coming up with variations:

What if the people tied to the tracks were strangers?

What if you knew them personally?

What if the single person was a pregnant woman? What if the single person was a murderer?

What if the five people on Track A were innocent children, but the single person on Track B was president of the United States? Or a scientist who would go on to cure some horrible disease—cancer, for example—if only you didn't hit them with a trolley?

Wait: What if pulling the lever *released* the five people in the nick of time... but they were a small tribe of starving cannibals now free to dine on the poor tied-up soul one track over? What if it wasn't a trolley but a machine gun? No, wait; just listen: What if the machine gun was a chain saw, and the chain saw was duct-taped to your hands, and...

"So, these are your levers," Ryan said. The tablet screen now showed them two large, color-coded emblems: a red clover on the left, a green clover on the right. "Red for Stop; Green for Go. That should be simple enough to remember."

Back in the sunlight above deck, remotely controlling their device from his anchored location in parts unknown, he walked them through a tutorial of the tablet's specialized interface.

"Now, here's the kicker," Ryan explained. "Once you choose, you're locked into that path."

Beau said, "What if we change our minds?"

"As your customer service representative, I can back you out of the next step, but only in a qualifying emergency, as determined by me. So choose wisely. For example."

The red clover pulsed, simulating a finger tap. The screen faded out, and a new screen faded in. This one, labeled with a smaller version of the same red clover, contained six empty ovals lined up in a row.

"As you've already figured out, these are where your thumbprints go," Ryan said. "One from each of you. As I mentioned, this decision needs to be unanimous, and we need all six thumbs to execute the agreement. Which is, of course, why we can't proceed without Perry and Stephen, but don't worry. According to my intel, they'll be along directly."

"I've been wondering about that," Will said. "How does this thing know our thumbprints in the first place?"

Ryan waited for him to arrive at the answer on his own.

Will closed his eyes. "We loaded them in ourselves."

"Sorry. Dirty trick, I know." Ryan nodded seriously. "Six thumbprints, one from each of you, authorize your decision. And again, this step is final."

Lainie said, "What does red do?"

"Sends a relay signal to enough explosive material to turn this boat into floating matchsticks."

He gave them all a moment to absorb the preposterous statement he'd just made.

"You'll find our charter in the document library. Review the requirements under the Catastrophic Events clause for more of my logic on that. But in a nutshell, it's like I said: Red means Stop."

Emma believed he could have given them a year to absorb it, and it still wouldn't have made a difference. She heard herself say, "Green..."

"Simply notifies me we're a go," Ryan finished. "I'll take care of the rest myself."

───────────────

They walked back the way they'd come, Stephen and Perry strolling side by side, just as before. This time with an armed escort.

The ground to either side of the path was spongy, sucking and popping as it soaked up the rain. The return of sunlight brightened the fragrant timber all around them; the trees sparkled and dripped, emerald green beneath a ceramic-blue sky.

Jud trailed just a few steps behind, cutting a line dead center on the path. He moved with a kind of athletic saunter, bare arms loose at his sides. He didn't seem opposed to friendly chatter. For example, when Perry said, "Jud, can I ask you a personal question?"

Jud said, "Sure."

"Are my friend Stephen and I your prisoners right now?"

"You're definitely my responsibility." Jud's tone was matter-of-fact, but not threatening. "But I wouldn't classify you as prisoners, no."

"Oh. Okay, just checking."

"No restraints, and my hands are empty. That's a couple ways you can tell."

Stephen felt his tension rising with each step they took along the path. Each step farther away from the cottage. The nape of his neck physically itched. He kept his hands in his jacket pockets, told himself to breathe in and out like a normal person. To distract his brain, he said, "Can *I* ask a personal question?"

"Don't see why not. It's nice out, we're all pals."

"Coronado, or Virginia Beach?"

Perry gave him a funny look, but Jud only smiled. "I heard you were the observant type."

"The bone frog gave you away."

"You serve?"

"More of an indoors kid, myself."

"Got it."

"Friend of mine in Chicago has one." Stephen patted his own shoulder, then put his hand right back in his pocket where it belonged. "But he's been out since the first Gulf War. He's a police detective now." Stephen almost added, *Homicide*, then thought, *Don't push your luck.*

"Well," Jud said. "It's good to have friends. Coronado, by the way."

"I love how you guys include me in your conversations," Perry said. "It makes me feel like I have friends too. What the hell are we talking about?"

Stephen said, "Ever met a Navy SEAL before?"

"Only while daydreaming."

"You've met one now."

Perry glanced back over his shoulder. "No shit?"

"Negative shit," Jud said. "Retired."

"Wow." Perry faced front again. "This isn't like I imagined it at all."

Jud chuckled behind them. "Kai said you guys were pretty funny."

Just then, Stephen heard a muffled ringtone from one of Jud's pockets. His heart leapt into his throat and sat there, pounding away. He felt light-headed all at once. His fingers tingled. Under his breath, he muttered, "Shit."

Perry looked over. "Now what's the matter?"

Without turning his head, Stephen muttered, "Get ready to run."

Green for Go.

As simple as a few taps on a screen.

In addition to the Village, fewer than fifty miles to the east of Sham Rock, Link Labs employed a dozen hyperscale server farms in the United States, the

Netherlands, Norway, Sweden, and Finland. Marvels of modern computing power. Those near the Arctic Circle had received numerous citations from international green technology groups for leveraging year-round cold air temperatures and ample natural water supplies, enabling them to operate at peak energy efficiency. Millions of square feet. Ever-growing exabytes of data housed across multitudinous storage arrays. All built to withstand everything from suburban hackers to foreign governments to geomagnetic superstorms.

All of it—the entire vast NeuraLink network—prepped to go boom.

"I call it the Pineapple Drive," Ryan told them. "Will, you'll like this, it's very *Mission Impossible*. High-density charge cell baked right into a solid-state drive—I designed it on contract for the NSA ten years ago, before they scrapped the program. Stable as a table, indefinite shelf life, the blast stays contained. No surviving data, no debris. Every server in every rack in our entire fleet now has them installed. Once the central AI is down, I can brick the whole net with a batch command."

Beau said, "Pineapple what, now?"

"Explain it, Will. You always knew your World Wars."

Everyone looked to Will, who sat shaking his head in disbelief. "I think he means like an Mk 2."

"Ding! Got it in one."

Beau looked confused. "The Volkswagen?"

"The hand grenade," Will sighed. "The GIs called them pineapples."

"Why?"

"Because it looked like a pineapple."

"Huh," Beau said. "But why would you do that?"

"Call it a nuclear option," Ryan said.

"In case of *what*?"

Emma thought back to a Ryan-related news item she'd seen last year. A report from some technology summit or other, Link Labs announcing an end-to-end refresh of its server hardware. Disaggregated this to leverage that and optimize whatever. In the tech world, apparently, this was quite a big deal. She said, "You've been planning this a long time."

"There's a lot of gray in words like *long* and *planning*, but yes, I try to look ahead."

"How many people are involved?"

"Not nearly as many as stormed the Capitol because of some shit they read on the internet, I can tell you that," Ryan snapped. Then he sighed. "Sorry. Let's just say we're a nimble project group and leave it at that. The job prerequisites were skill, effectiveness, discretion, and an appropriate degree of ethical scalability vis-à-vis compensation."

Will stared hard at the television. "Once the central AI is down," he repeated. "What does that mean?"

"Right. That part's a little more lo-fi."

"But what does it mean?"

"Basically a fuckload of water gel and Semtex," Ryan said. "Jud's team is handling that now."

Green for Go. The boat and its passengers would be spared, but Link Labs headquarters—aka "One"—would be leveled to the ground, along with the rest of Link Village. After that, Pineapple Drives would begin popping off at Link data centers across the United States, northwestern Europe, and Scandinavia. After that, the Linkverse would be no more.

"It's an extreme statement, I admit," he said. "But I've learned the importance of showmanship. These days, you need a little extra flash and bang if you really want to get your point across."

Emma said, "What *is* the point?"

"Don't worry, I've prepared a more conventional statement on that. For right now, the point is, my communications team will alert the relevant authorities in advance. There will be a small preliminary detonation to establish credibility before I drop the plunger for real. We've got estimated response times for full evacuation of the surrounding area, as well as capability assessments for the local emergency medical infrastructure. All that said, the target count for human casualties is zero. It's important that you know that."

"So, you're not *planning* to kill anybody, then."

Ryan winked. "I may be a genius, but I'm not an evil genius."

Emma found herself studying his face on-screen, suddenly wishing very much that Stephen were here. If anybody could give them a qualified second read on this, it was him. NSA? High-density "charge cells"? It all sounded... Well. Hadn't Ryan said it himself? Very *Mission Impossible*.

Emphasis on *Impossible*.

Beau said, "Couldn't you just unplug everything?"

Ryan laughed. "I swear, I love you guys."

"What?" Beau looked around innocently. "I was being serious."

"The great thing about rubble," Ryan said, "is that you can't plug it back in again. Do you know what makes me different from Oppenheimer, Kalashnikov, and Ethan Zuckerman?"

"Jesus Christ," Emma said. "Not this again."

"None of them could put the toothpaste back in the tube," Ryan said. "Any asshole can look back at the end of their life and say, 'Gosh, if only I knew then what I know now. If only I could take it back.' Well, guess what? I'm at the end of my life. And I *can* take it back."

"You're talking about a bunch of web apps," Will said, "like they're the atomic bomb."

"In Nagasaki and Hiroshima, Fat Man and Little Boy killed a quarter million people by some estimates," Ryan said. "Check the library after I hang up—we've got a decade's worth of analytics on traffic deaths that occurred while the driver at fault was interacting with our interface. At the current rate, I feel like I can say with some confidence that we'll be outperforming the A-bomb within your lifetimes."

He looked at each of them wistfully.

"Believe me, guys: upon reflection, I see plenty of other things about my own time on this planet I'd change if I could. But I *can* change this. Can you imagine having that kind of opportunity?" He smiled. "Or I'm a dangerous crackpot who needs to be neutralized. Frankly, I'm starting to have moments when I'm not sure I know the answer myself anymore."

"Ryan..."

"Like I said before, that's why I need you guys here. Besides: if you really think about it, you all bear some responsibility."

Beau said, "How do you figure that?"

"If I'd never met Emma, I'd never have made it to Bardsley. Without all of you, I'd never have made it *through* Bardsley. If Rollie and Em hadn't gotten together, I probably never would have gone off to California, and if I'd never gone to California, none of us would be here now. So in a sense," he said, lacing his fingers together, "from a chain-of-influence perspective, this is just as rightly your decision as it is mine."

Will leaned back. "That's bullshit."

"Maybe," Ryan said. "The good news is, there's a win-win option for all of us."

"Ryan, please," Emma said. "Climb down out of the clouds, stand here on solid ground with the rest of us, try to think like a regular person for just half a minute, and tell me: How could anybody possibly win from *this*?"

"Once again, Em, you bring me straight back to the point," Ryan said. "Last thing, before I leave you to it: What, ultimately, does red clover/green clover mean for you? Stay with me, here's where it gets interesting."

CHAPTER 17

Pᴇᴏᴘʟᴇ ᴄᴏᴍᴍᴏɴʟʏ ᴀssᴏᴄɪᴀᴛᴇᴅ surges of adrenaline with heightened performance: increased mental acuity, feats of supernormal strength.

Stephen had always experienced the opposite effect. For him, a sudden bath in fight-or-flight hormones more often seemed overwhelming, like gasoline flooding a carburetor. If anything, it made him feel weaker, not stronger. Literally sapped of physical effectiveness, mind blank as a dead motel key card.

As an educated professional, he understood the scientific findings related to the periaqueductal gray region of the midbrain—the link in the limbic chain that governed one's emotional and behavioral response to threatening stimuli.

As a guy under armed guard, he still nearly shit himself when Jud's phone rang.

"Yep," Jud answered. His face clouded. "Hang on, slow down."

"*Go*," Stephen whispered to Perry. He could barely feel his extremities. "*Right now*."

But it was already too late. Jud's eyes snapped up, locking first on Perry, then fixing hard on Stephen. Stephen heard Perry gasp beside him.

"Found it," Jud said, slowly lowering the phone. "Really bad idea, Mr. Rollins."

Stephen nodded. "It feels like it." He'd nearly dropped Kai's gun on the ground, fumbling it out of his pocket. Small as it was, it still seemed too heavy to hold steadily. His hand was trembling. He steadied his feet and cupped his free hand under the base of the grip. He could barely hear himself over the rush of blood in his ears. "Believe me, I wish it weren't happening."

"Obviously, I'm slipping," Jud said.

"Don't beat yourself up. I wouldn't have expected me to do this either."

Approximately ten minutes prior to this moment, as Stephen and Perry had trudged out of the cottage, Kai had stepped in to give their custodian one last, lingering kiss. It was in that briefest of moments, while Jud's attention was divided, that Stephen had done it. Almost without thinking—like grabbing his car keys on the way out the door.

The thing had been just sitting right there on the little driftwood table. He barely even had to reach. He just palmed the small gun casually into his jacket pocket, as if he'd done it a thousand times. He'd been waiting for someone to notice ever since.

"Well, you seem to know how to hold that thing. Sort of."

Stephen wasn't a gun owner, or even a gun liker, but he'd been target shooting with his cop pal back home a few times. Enough to know the basics. "I know where the trigger is, anyway."

"For your sake, let's hope you can aim." Jud did not appear the least bit tense. On the other hand, he did not seem incapable of tearing Stephen's arms out of their sockets and beating him to death with them either. "That's a Sig Sauer P238 you have there. Subcompact frame, chambered for .380 ACP. Great little gun. Not my first choice for stopping power."

"I'll take your word for it."

"So, what now?"

Stephen hadn't thought that far ahead yet. "First, I think we should switch places. You walk up front, we'll tag along. Oh: Your gun. Hand that to Perry."

Perry said, "What do you want *me* to do with it?"

"And your phone, also," Stephen said. "Unlock it first. We'll call Mr. Cloverhill on the way."

"Yeah, none of those things are going to happen," Jud said. "Let me tell you what *is* going to happen. You doing okay, Mr. Rollins?"

"Hanging in there so far."

"That's good. Now. As long as you don't discharge that firearm, I'm not authorized to hurt you. But I *am* going to relieve you of that firearm. If you really want to keep it, you'll need to shoot me, and if you shoot me, you're definitely going to need to kill me, and if you kill me, then you'll have a dead helicopter pilot on your hands. You don't seem like you actually want that, and I've got a really long list of shit I still need to get done today. So why don't we make this easy on ourselves and let me hang on to that weapon for you?"

"Or you could tell us what the hell is going on."

"I'm not authorized to do that."

Stephen was beginning to wonder how they were going to resolve this. Jud was right: he wasn't prepared to shoot anybody. What had he been thinking? "What *are* you authorized to do, exactly?"

"Get you back with your friends, safe and sound."

"Then why are you armed?"

"Washington is a shall-issue state, and I passed the background check."

"You're not playing this game right."

"I think that makes two of us," Jud said. "But it really doesn't have to be so complicated."

Stephen spared Perry a quick glance. Perry stared back at him as if waiting for a reasonable, clearly stated plan.

Jud said, "It's Steve, right? Okay if I call you Steve, Steve?"

"It's Stephen," Stephen answered. "But I don't see why not."

"Stephen, I'd feel a lot better if you at least indexed your finger while we talk."

Stephen knew what he meant: *Please take your finger off the trigger until you're absolutely positive you're ready to shoot me.* He left his finger right where it was. "Let me see if I understand. Mr. Cloverhill wants us back in that house, and you're here to make that happen."

"That's correct."

"But if you were to hurt one of us, or presumably both of us, Mr. Cloverhill would not be happy with you?"

"Also correct," Jud said. "But there's an order of priority here. My advice to you is, don't make me prioritize."

"I think you might be reading my mind."

"Am I?"

"Priorities. It's two against one."

"Technically, that's true. But your math won't work out, Stephen. Please trust me on that."

"I trust him," Perry said.

"No, obviously. That's not what I'm saying. What I'm saying is, Perry and I are two individual people." Stephen glanced at Perry again, thinking, *Please listen carefully.* "You're only one individual person. I know you have your own gun and everything, and I presume it's filled with a number of individual bullets, but if you're really not authorized to actually shoot us, then... if all of a sudden one of us were to run off that way, and the other ran off the oth—"

But he never got to finish the thought.

Jud made his move while Stephen was talking, quick as a striking rattler. Stephen saw the flinch, and his own reflex mirrored it.

He jerked the trigger. Mostly by accident. The firecracker pop split the whispering stillness, clattering through the trees.

At the same moment, something hit him square in the face, hard as a rock. Everything flashed white, and his eyes filled with water. Had the gun malfunctioned? Blown up in his face? He couldn't see anything. Did he have a face left? He should have indexed his finger.

But no, somewhere in the confusion, his brain had captured an image: Jud's phone spinning toward him through the air like a small rectangular Frisbee.

Then his wrist popped, pain flared, and the gun wasn't in his hand anymore. A bone-crunching impact drove him off his feet. Or maybe the impact was him hitting the ground. Either way, he couldn't breathe anymore.

When he regained his faculties, Stephen coughed and tried to push himself up, felt new pain in his wrist, collapsed back onto his face. The bone above his right eye throbbed painfully. His wrist throbbed painfully. When he rolled onto his back, gasping for breath, the bright blue sky above the treetops hurt his eyes. Crushed oyster shells clung to his cheek.

Jud stood over him, Kai's gun turned backward in his palm, knuckles planted on his hips.

But he wasn't looking down at Stephen.

He was looking off into the trees.

Shaking his head slowly.

Bright red blood ran down his bare arm.

Amid all the throbbing, Stephen felt a swell of triumph. He looked at the sky and listened carefully to the faint, muffled sound of feet pounding wet fir needles, crunching on twigs, receding little by little into the woods. He thought, *Haul ass, Perrier. Go, my son!*

Above him, Jud sighed heavily.

"For fuck's sake," he said.

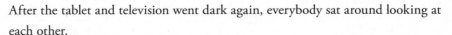

After the tablet and television went dark again, everybody sat around looking at each other.

Beau shook it off first. "Did he really just say all that?"

Will sighed, rubbed his face, spoke from behind his hands. "I think so."

"He's pulling our leg," Lainie said. "Surely."

Beau said, "You don't think he's really gone crazy, do you?"

"Even if this is all a big put-on, he can't be entirely sane," Will said.

"And he was clearly in pain," Lainie said. "You all saw his face. I don't think he was faking that."

"I don't either," Emma said.

"Okay, let's go over this again," Beau said. "I just want to make sure we all heard what I think I heard."

"We heard it," everyone else said together.

Trolley Problem:

Your oldest friend has planted a thirty-acre bomb in a populated urban area. Only you can stop him from setting off the explosion.

Push the red button, and the crisis is averted. But it means deliberately murdering your friend, along with six strangers.

Push the green button instead, and your friend will destroy several large buildings near downtown Seattle in broad daylight, disrupting a national economy and instantly unemploying thousands. But you'll personally become wealthy for life.

Stand idly by, and your friend carries out his plan anyway. But you get nothing. You'll know you did nothing.

And so will the rest of the world.

What do you do?

Red meant Stop. According to Ryan, they'd be kicking off the signal that caused his boat to detonate, sending him and his entire board of directors full fathom five. Ryan would claim responsibility for the explosion in a detailed manifesto to law enforcement and the media, to be released and authenticated posthumously. Their involvement would be protected by the power of the Pineapple Drive (along with self-purging event logs aboard Hermes Junior 1, the satellite responsible for relaying said signal—the first of three experimental geosynchronous "smallsats" the company had launched to great fanfare last year). Controlling interest in Link Labs would pass to the six of them.

Green for Go. Ryan claimed he would carry out his stated plan, living long enough to accept responsibility in person. His board members would be released unharmed. All active, nonexecutive employees would receive severance payouts according to time of service. After his death, which would most likely occur in prison while awaiting trial, what remained of his personal fortune—setting aside noncash holdings and a constellation of decoy accounts earmarked specifically for the feds—would transfer to the six of them. After expenses, and a permanent endowment to the Cloverhill Foundation, their individual cash windfalls would land at a neat $100 million each. Attorneys would be in touch.

"Emma," Beau said, "is any of that true?"

"Why are you asking me?"

"Who else? You're the only one of us who'd know."

"Guys, I don't think I know him as well as I thought I did," she said. "Not anymore."

"I mean the legal stuff," Beau said. "You're the only lawyer here."

She should have known. This was Beau Hemford she was talking to.

To answer his question, none of it *sounded* credible...but Beau gave her too much credit. Her expertise was in intellectual property law, not whatever you'd call this. Aggravated probate? If anybody died, their families would surely file claims against the Cloverhill estate. If he really did blow up an entire office complex on domestic soil, surely the Patriot Act would come into play somehow. Surely investigators would be able, eventually, to find their way through whatever financial maze Ryan had constructed for them. *Surely* they'd be tied up in civil forfeiture proceedings for years to come.

But Ryan Cloverhill had defied all reasonable odds before. If any of this were true, and it somehow played out exactly as he planned...who knew? It wasn't as if there was precedent for such a thing, as far as Emma knew.

"Sorry," she said. "I could text somebody or do some research, but without a connection, I have no clue."

Will said, "I think that might be part of the point."

Doing nothing—no clover—also meant Go. Ryan would carry out his plan. His board would be released unharmed, but the Link Labs workforce would not be compensated. After all: it wouldn't be a Trolley Problem if doing nothing came free of charge. The lockdown would end Monday at noon. The Stillwater Six would be free to recount their experience to authorities. For choosing nothing, they would receive nothing.

"Thirty-four hours, hell," Beau said. "Do we need thirty-four seconds? Green button! Let's do this."

Will snorted. He seemed to need the laugh.

Beau said, "What? I wouldn't know the first thing about running his company. Would you?"

"That's hardly the…"

"A hundred mil each, nobody gets hurt, no strings attached? How much sweeter does the pot need to be? This Trolley Problem literally solves itself."

"Nobody gets hurt?" Emma gave him a look. "That seems highly arguable, Beau."

"Okay, fine. Nobody dies, then. And everybody gets paid."

Will said, "Blowing up an office park in the middle of a major American city on a holiday weekend. What could go wrong?"

"He said zero casualties, remember?"

"He also said nothing ever goes according to plan." Will took an exaggerated look around the locked-down house, taking a quick head count of their group with a finger. "I'd say that seems about right so far."

"Fair point." Beau shook his head. "But according to him, he's going through with it anyway, right? Even if any of us *did* know how to run a global tech company, we obviously can't blow up seven people."

"What if it's thirty people by mistake? What if toxic dust gives a bunch of first responders cancer? How's that green button looking now?"

"Yeah, but…I mean, if you *knew* there was a chance all that could happen… shouldn't you stop it?"

Will sighed. "But we obviously can't blow up seven people."

"That's what I said."

"Emma, call him back," Lainie said. "Honey? Which part did he say to tap?"

Beau said, "Lower left corner."

"Tap it," Lainie said. "I have questions."

"What questions?" Emma said. "Obviously, we do nothing. Either he's telling us the truth, or he's so far gone that this is his idea of a joke, but what's the difference?"

"What's the *difference*?"

"Lainie, I'm not participating in this," Emma said. "Come on."

"Just call him back."

"Are you really going to indulge..."

"Oh, Jesus Christ, Em, who fucking died and made you Queen of the Inside?" Lainie pushed herself up from the sofa and stalked toward Emma, arm outstretched, fingers grasping. "Give me the damn thing, I'll call him back myself."

"Wow." Emma handed her the tablet. "Call him back then."

"Thanks, I will. Honey?"

"Lower left," Beau said.

Lainie tapped the screen and looked expectantly toward the television.

There was a long pause.

Then the screens winked to life with an ascending chime. Ryan was there, grinning. "Already?" he said.

But Lainie had grown so impatient during the ten seconds it had taken to rub him back out of his lamp that she'd tapped the lower left corner again, just at the exact right moment to immediately hang up on him.

Descending chime. Dead screen.

"Shit!" Lainie said.

Beau sighed from their couch. "Just tap it again. Then don't touch anything."

CHAPTER 18

Oɴ ʏᴏᴜʀ ғᴇᴇᴛ, dipshit," Jud said. "You've got work to do."

Stephen cautiously picked himself up off the ground, making no sudden movements, watching Jud closely.

Jud paid him little mind. He'd removed his watch and rolled his blood-slick right arm forward, craning to look at his own shoulder. Stephen's wild bullet had gouged a deep furrow across the bone frog's back. Blood dripped from Jud's fingertips, spattering the oyster shells at his feet in bright crimson droplets.

"You cut him in half," Jud said.

Stephen didn't know what to say. "Sorry about that."

"Thanks, that really helps." He probed gingerly near the wound with his index finger, looked at the finger, sucked off the blood. "Whatever. Ain't my first scar. Find my phone."

"Where did it go?"

Jud gestured off to the side of the path. "It bounced off your face and flew over there somewhere."

Stephen's eye felt hot and swollen. He could see the outline of his own eyelid. When he touched the spot, his finger came away bloody. He cradled his wrist close to his body: also hot and swollen, with an invisible nail through the middle.

"It's only sprained," Jud said. "You'll be fine. Start looking."

Stephen had questions, but he decided to save them for later. The crunch of oyster shells under his feet sounded the way all his joints felt when he moved. He stepped off the path, did a half-hearted scan of the forest floor around him. He scuffed through the needles a little with the toe of his shoe.

"Look faster. By the way: if you try running, I'll paralyze you from the waist down."

Stephen stooped, elbows on his knees; the movement made his eye throb harder, blurring his vision. The nail in his wrist started wiggling around. He groaned and straightened again.

Jud sighed. "Up."

"What?"

"Hold it up. Above your heart."

Stephen raised his right hand to shoulder level, glancing toward Jud's bleeding shoulder. "Doesn't that hurt?"

"About a three."

"On a scale of four?"

"Just find my goddamn phone."

Stephen walked around, back and forth and in widening circles, scuffing through the tree litter. Occasionally he looked up, tried to find landmarks to estimate their location along the path. All the trees looked the same. The path had curved gently, so he couldn't see the cottage behind them. They weren't far enough along yet to see the big house ahead. He wondered which way Perry had gone. He hoped he'd found a good hiding spot. He wondered what he'd do next, if he were Perry. Had any of this accomplished anything?

After a few fruitless minutes, Jud sighed again and said, "Forget it. Let's go."

"What about Perry?"

"What about him?"

"We can't just leave him."

"You should have thought of that before you pointed a gun at me."

"Aren't you supposed to bring us both?"

"Don't worry, I'll find his ass. Now. For the last time, nicely: move."

Stephen didn't see many options. Hand still raised, he got back on the path and started trudging.

"Not that way," Jud said. He pointed back the way they'd come, in the direction of the cottage.

Stephen shrugged and reversed course, tensing internally as he passed the retired Navy SEAL he'd just winged. Jud watched him with a dour expression, shaking his head slowly, like a disappointed coach. Then he shook blood from his own fingertips and fell in behind.

Five minutes later, the cottage reappeared. Kai was waiting on the porch.

When she saw them, she hustled down the steps and across the clearing, calling, "Jesus, I heard the...Where's the tall one?" Her eyes widened as they neared each other. "Why are you bleeding?"

She brushed past Stephen and went straight to Jud, who held her at arm's length to keep the blood off of her. He leaned across the gap between them to peck her on the cheek. "I'm fine. Little mishap."

Kai wheeled around, made a fist, and nailed Stephen hard in the shoulder. "You *shot* him?"

The impact of the punch traveled straight down his arm to his injured wrist. He squeezed his eyes shut. When he opened them, they were watering. "Ow."

Kai dismissed him with a scowl. Back to Jud. "Come inside. Let's get you fixed up."

"It's fine," Jud said. "Little scratch."

"Uh-huh. I'm stitching it."

"Later." Jud hooked his clean arm around her and continued on toward the house, shoving Stephen along with his bloody hand. "Right now I gotta quit playing grab-ass with these two and get this mission back online. You got a spare handheld?"

"In the house with the gear. Who'd you leave in charge?"

"Einhorn."

"You're kidding."

"He'll be fine."

Stephen didn't know who Einhorn might be, or what he'd been left in charge of doing, but Kai certainly looked skeptical about it. "If you say so."

Inside, she tossed Jud one of the damp towels Stephen and Perry had used to dry themselves off. Jud now used it to keep blood from dripping on the floor on his way to the kitchen. He parked Stephen at the farmhouse-style table and washed his arm at the sink, using his bare fingers to rub soap suds directly into the wound. He did it like washing an elbow or rinsing off his diver's watch; no wincing, no flinching, simply a task to complete. Stephen could barely watch him do it without feeling queasy.

Kai came in with fresh towels, a basket of first-aid supplies, and a new phone just like the one Jud had used to disarm Stephen fifteen minutes ago. "Let me cover it, at least."

"Just patch it over," Jud said, patting his arm dry with a clean towel. The towel came away red. He winked. "It'll clot pretty soon. I'll come back later for the full treatment."

"Damn right." She tore open a large self-adhesive gauze pad, squirted a line of antibiotic ointment down the middle. She squinted, aligned, then pressed the pad directly over the slashed bone frog.

Jud helped her press down the edges. "Do me a favor and get him some ice, will you?"

Kai rolled her eyes, found a plastic baggie in a drawer. She filled the baggie with ice cubes from the freezer, zipped the top closed. "I'm still pissed at you, but here."

Stephen thanked her, took the baggie, and tried to decide where to put it: eye socket or wrist? He chose wrist. The cold felt glorious for a moment. Then it turned the invisible nail into an invisible ice dagger.

Jud tore open a second, larger pad with his teeth. Kai took it from him. He thanked her again. While she worked on applying the second layer, he took the new phone and placed a call.

In a moment, somebody answered.

"Checking in," Jud said. "Affirmative. Long story." He paused. "Negative. One down, one to go. Full report from the air. About that, hate to ask, Boss, but I'll get there faster if…Affirmative. Affirmative." He paused again, listening carefully. "Copy. How long will it take you to…No shit? That was fast. Affirmative. Out."

Stephen said, "Can I talk to him?"

Jud ended the call, shoved the new phone into a trouser pocket, and looked over at him. "Okay, hero. Time to go."

Stephen thought about it, reconsidered the wisdom of saying it, then said it anyway: "What if I still don't want to go anywhere with you?"

"Then at that point my priority waiver kicks in." Jud looked at him squarely. "Do you understand what I mean by that, Mr. Rollins?"

Stephen sighed, lifting his aching body off the wooden chair. "You might as well keep calling me Stephen."

"Now you're making better choices." Jud pointed toward a back pantry. "Door in the corner, then down the stairs."

Stephen looked to where Jud was pointing. Back at Jud.

"Go," Jud said. "If I were planning to bury you in the cellar, you'd be getting stiff already."

So Stephen followed instructions, feeling his heart begin to pound again. It didn't help the throb in his forehead or wrist. Jud said a few words to Kai in a tone too low to overhear; then Stephen heard footfalls behind him.

He found the door tucked back in the corner between wooden shelves lined with dry goods. He took a deep breath, twisted the knob with a squeak of tarnished old brass, and pulled the door open.

"Down three steps, then reach to the left. The light's on a string."

Stephen ventured three creaky steps down into the cool, musty darkness. He gritted his teeth, holding the ice pack against his hip with his sprained wrist so that he could feel along the rough wall with his good hand. When the wall suddenly stopped being there, he reached out into the empty space, found the string. Gave it a pull. A single bare bulb cast the remainder of the staircase, and a bit of cracked cellar floor, in low yellow light.

"Down to the bottom, turn right, then stand aside," Jud said.

Stephen continued to follow instructions, wondering about Perry, thinking, *This was a mistake. I should not have done this.* At the bottom of the stairs, he turned right and stood aside, crunching over a few dead insect husks scattered on the floor. Jud came down the stairs behind him.

Stephen found himself at another door in the middle of a poured concrete wall. This one looked different: newer, heavier, smooth steel. He saw a small black glass window mounted in the wall near the pull handle. Jud walked past him to the door and pressed his thumb up against window.

Servos whirred as the window slid open, the cavity behind it illuminated, and a keypad emerged.

Blocking Stephen's view with this body, Jud punched in a long string of numbers. There came a hiss and a series of heavy clunks—the sound of pneumatic locks releasing. Jud pointed to the door and said, "Open that and go through."

Stephen didn't move.

"I'll be right behind you," Jud said. "Or dragging you behind me. You can choose."

So once again Stephen took a breath, reached out with his good hand, and pulled the door handle toward him. The door opened with a hermetic sucking sound, like Kai opening the freezer upstairs. Stephen stood before deep, echoing darkness.

Then another light snapped on. Then more, a long repeating sequence of them, tripping awake one after another down a seemingly endless concrete corridor.

"Left foot right foot," Jud said. "You're doing fine."

CHAPTER 19

Accecording to the tracker, Jud's phone hadn't moved in nearly twenty minutes when the call from com unit 7 finally came in. It had just been sitting there, a pulsing dot, somewhere between the house and the cottage. For all practical purposes, and a few impractical ones, Sham Rock's mesh video network covered the main traffic areas of the island. But there were blind spots, and Jud's phone, naturally, had parked itself in one of them.

Now that he finally understood why, Ryan didn't know if he felt more or less bothered.

Jesus. What a couple of lunatics.

So where the hell was Perry Therkle now?

Back above deck, tablet in hand, he scrolled through the exterior security feeds. No answers to be found there.

Meanwhile, from below deck, Tom Carver's bellyaching started to sound like it might actually be serious. He'd been shouting for Ryan's attention for the past ten minutes; the longer Ryan let him squawk, the louder he shouted. But his tone had changed from angry to pained, and now sounded legitimately despondent. Ryan cursed aloud to nobody but the gulls overhead. He mounted the tablet in the helm console and went below to see how to make the racket stop.

"I can't feel my hands," Carver said, raising his flex cuffs. Were there actual tears in his eyes? "I think you cut off the damn nerves or something."

"I'm told that's what happens when you try to get out of them," Ryan said. "They just get tighter."

"Well, it hurts. Bad."

"I thought you couldn't feel them?"

"It's both!" Carver cried. "It hurts *and* they're numb."

If this was a ploy, it made up in credibility what it lacked in flair. Tom did look pretty damned uncomfortable.

Ryan scanned the others. Oliver and Amanda sat with their heads back, eyes closed, bobbing along with the movement of the boat. Val Cordero sat in a more rigid posture, leaning forward, elbows on knees. Elijah Stanhope stared straight ahead at nothing.

Only Bhavna met Ryan's eye.

"Please," she said. "Couldn't you at least loosen them? He's learned his lesson."

Ryan struggled to find sympathy. His gut hurt all the way through to the middle of his back, and he couldn't loosen that. Nor had he brought it on himself.

Still: on a personal level, there never had been any love lost between Tom Carver and Bhavna Patel. He supposed there was something to be admired in her appeal on Tom's behalf. If the gang back at the Rock surprised him, and she were to die in a red clover, he supposed it could be considered a tragedy.

Up top, the tablet chimed.

"All right," he told them. "Tom, I have other priorities, but I promise I'll change out your cuffs within the next hour. I suggest you use that time to reflect on your predicament. It'll help you avoid similar mistakes going forward. Later, we'll discuss supervised mobility privileges for everybody."

Over Tom's angry appeal, he went back above, took a deep breath, put on a smile, and answered. "Already?"

Lainie Hemford's worried face filled up the screen.

Then the call abruptly went dead.

Then the tablet sounded a security alert, which meant that Jud had used his temporary new credentials to access the tunnel back at Sham Rock.

Jesus! Being a Bond villain was hard. Ryan ignored Lainie's return call and checked the feeds again. He'd call them back after Rollins was home safe. It wasn't like they were going anywhere.

Which was, even he could acknowledge, the final irony. As the head and public face of Link, a person had to get comfortable with the idea of being admired and hated by total strangers. But until the last election cycle, he'd never received what law enforcement, or any reasonable person, might consider a credible death threat.

These days, they were a regular part of life. So he'd spent an absurd amount of money building a veritable fortress, where he could be at least reasonably assured of not dying. And now here he was, barely a year after construction, dying anyway. Instead of locking his enemies out, he'd locked his friends in.

Or at least he'd damn well tried.

In one frame, he saw Jud entering the tunnel from the cottage end, none other than Stephen Adelaide Rollins in tow. Jud had what appeared to be a bloody bandage slapped over one shoulder. Rollie held his arm close to his body like a big dumb bird with a busted wing. Full report from the air, Jud had said. This had better be a good story.

In the meantime: Perry.

According to the Doppler, they had at least an hour, maybe two, before a new storm system rolled over them. But for now, the skies were clear. Prevailing wind was 26 knots north-northeast at 400 feet.

So he launched the camera drone from his secluded cove at the south edge of the San Juans.

The UAV unit was based on a commercially available model designed primarily for broadcast work and 4K filmmaking. He'd refitted it with his own signal-encryption firmware, a high-range Comsat transceiver, and a supercharged battery system, then rebalanced weight ratio, netting himself an effective range of fifteen miles. He'd have an eye in the sky over the Rock inside thirty minutes.

Logically, there was no question that Jud Bernal was more than capable of rounding up two middle-aged liberal arts graduates on his own. But Ryan was forced to acknowledge that he'd piled an awful lot on the man's plate for one day. And he needed him back at the Village ASAP.

Teamwork time.

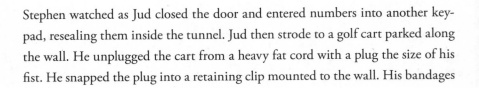

Stephen watched as Jud closed the door and entered numbers into another keypad, resealing them inside the tunnel. Jud then strode to a golf cart parked along the wall. He unplugged the cart from a heavy fat cord with a plug the size of his fist. He snapped the plug into a retaining clip mounted to the wall. His bandages had already soaked through, but he seemed to have perfectly good use of the arm. He nodded toward the cart and said, "Hop in. You're driving."

"Where does this go?"

"For a stupid guy, you seem like a pretty smart guy," Jud said. "I bet you'll have that figured out by the time we get there."

Stephen cast his gaze as far as he could down the crisp rectangular profile of the tunnel stretching out before them, which disappeared around a gradual curve in the far distance. The obvious answer popped into his mind. Where else would they be going, if not the big house? "You must be shitting me."

"Congratulations, you're officially a VIP," Jud said. "Now shag ass, I'm getting short on time."

So dumbfounded by this new discovery was Stephen that he'd almost forgotten how much his wrist hurt until he'd settled into his side of the cart. He gripped the wheel, then pulled his right hand away, sucking air through his teeth.

Jud reached down for him and punched a power button in the dash. The button glowed to life, and the cart produced a faint hum. Next, he twisted the transmission knob to F for Forward. "Okay. Let's go."

Holding his right wrist in his lap atop the ice baggie, steering with his left hand, Stephen pressed the accelerator experimentally, and forward they went. He banged the rear tires steering away from the wall, jostling their shoulders together, causing the ice bag to slide off his knee and drop between his feet. Then they were off, tooling along down the smooth corridor under whisper-quiet power.

"I don't remember reading anything in any of the magazine articles about a half-mile-long secret tunnel," Stephen said.

"Wouldn't know. I don't read those magazines. Let's pick up the pace a little, Grandma."

Stephen gradually pressed the accelerator pedal to the floor. The cart wasn't built for speed, but they zipped along at a brisk enough clip to put a breeze in their hair.

The tunnel was about double the width of the cart, with perhaps seven vertical feet between ceiling and floor. Stephen marveled at the construction of it. He marveled at the existence of it. Why would Ryan build such a thing? He probably could have built himself a guest island with all the dirt he must have excavated from this one. Stephen began to wonder more seriously if his old friend really did have a screw loose somewhere. Maybe even a retaining bolt.

"Can I ask you a question?"

Jud said, "Sure."

"How long have you been with Link again?"

"Didn't we go over this?"

"Remind me."

"Coming up on ten years," Jud said. "Mr. Cloverhill hired me a couple years after I got out. I wasn't in a very good spot back then, but he gave me a shot. Started out checking badges at the front desk."

"I thought you said you started out driving?"

"Yeah, well. Sounded better than receptionist."

"Why did you leave the military?"

"Shattered my knees." His tone remained perfectly conversational. "But don't get any new ideas."

Stephen glanced over. Jud rode casually, one foot on the dash, like they'd just made the turn at the clubhouse and were heading for the back nine. "You still move pretty well."

"I get by."

"And how *did* you come to work for Ryan, anyway?"

"You mean Mr. Cloverhill?"

"I thought Kai said he mostly goes by Ryan."

"He probably mostly does," Jud said. "I still call him Mr. Cloverhill. And none of this matters. I'm a motivated employee with passion for my work, and that's really all you need to know."

"I guess the money must be good."

"Very. Start letting up, we're almost there."

Stephen saw the end of the tunnel approaching. He slowed down, braked, and brought the cart to a stop near a door that looked identical to the one they'd left behind.

"Stand over there," Jud said. "Don't forget your ice."

At the door, Jud repeated the process: thumbprint, keypad, *hiss-clunk*. This time he opened the door himself and gestured Stephen through. "Ibuprofen for pain and inflammation," he said. "Hit the ice again in three hours. Enjoy the rest of your weekend."

Stephen walked through the door, passing from the industrial chill of the tunnel into a perceptibly more residential warmth. He turned and said, "Look, can you at least tell me..."

But Jud was already closing the door in his face with a clang. There was a pause; then the locks reengaged.

Silence.

Stephen turned to find himself in a basement room of the big house, where he'd started his day: large, open plan; flat wool carpet; track lighting. He saw modern art and vintage arcade machines evenly spaced along the walls: *Galaga*, Rothko, *Ms. Pac-Man*, Pollock, *Donkey Kong*, O'Keeffe. There were billiard, air hockey, and foosball tables scattered about the central space. The glassed-in corner looked out on giant video screens depicting a vacant patio rimmed in seagrass.

He couldn't begin to know what to make of it. Stephen followed the hallway leading out of the room until he spotted the floating stairs going up. He could hear voices now, somewhere above him. Arguing.

He took the stairs up to the main floor. The others were gathered in the sitting area, bickering heatedly. Will noticed him first: a glance, then a double take, eyes widening.

Emma noticed Will, then followed his eyes all the way to Stephen, confusion on her face.

"Hey, guys," Stephen said. "I'm home."

CHAPTER 20

EMMA SAID, "*STEPHEN?*"

She vaulted herself out of the sofa, heading straight for him. Stephen hadn't had the first clue how good it would feel to see her until she was there. He accepted her hug with a gratitude that bordered on craving. It hurt all over.

"Where did you come from? How'd you get in?" She looked at his face. "What *happened* to you?" Then she saw his wrist. "Where'd you get ice?"

"I've got a lot to tell you guys," Stephen said. "I don't know if you'll believe any of it. I'm not even sure I do."

"Just try us," Beau said. "We've got some crazy shit to tell you too."

The others trailed after Emma, milling around him. Everybody looked shell-shocked. Stephen still couldn't get over what he was seeing: window views replaced by giant video screens, just like in the basement, everywhere he looked. *They really could see us in here*, he thought.

But he must have thought it aloud, because Emma said, "They who?"

"Can we go sit down?" Stephen said. "I feel like I fell off a bridge."

"Get over there," Beau said. "What do you need?"

"I could use a glass of water."

Beau peeled off in search of water while Emma and Lainie stood aside, opening a path to the furniture.

"We've been trying to call Ryan back," Lainie said. "He's not answering."

"Call him back? You talked to him? Call him back how?"

"Buckle up, mister," said Beau, returning to hand Stephen a glass. "You're in for a ride."

As Stephen took the water, he caught Will's eyes. They hadn't yet returned to normal size. If anything, they'd only grown wider.

"Where's Perry?" he said.

OUTSIDERS

CHAPTER 21

THOUGH HE'D LEARNED much over the years from his hardy, corn-fed Midwestern husband, Perry Therkle, generally speaking, had not been built offroad-tough.

He'd grown up in Westchester, for Christ's sake. Despite ready access to the vast natural splendor of New York's Hudson Valley, his childhood outdoor activities had consisted primarily of the members-club variety: golf, tennis, sailing, crew.

But he'd sucked at, and therefore hated, all of them. When it came to sports, he'd been a disappointment to everybody: six feet four by the eighth grade, but only 162 gangly, uncoordinated pounds. As for camping and related pursuits, he did not pursue them. Young Perry Therkle did not adventure: he hit his head a lot and knocked things over accidentally. Yes, he'd grown into himself eventually. Yes, he'd learned where to purchase extra-long bass guitar straps and how to enjoy himself within many of his various discomfort zones. But a glass of good wine on a high veranda *overlooking* trees: that was still middle-aged Perry Therkle's idea of a good time in the great outdoors.

Tempted as he was to blame Stephen for his current predicament, Perry couldn't deny his own participation in it, having bounded off into the forest at the sound of that gunshot like a fifty-year-old spotted fawn. The first time he'd glanced over his shoulder and couldn't see the path anymore, he'd hidden behind a tree, tried listening for the sounds of pursuit over his own jackhammering heart. Additional gunshots, for example. Footsteps. A sneeze. Any kind of life-threatening sound at all.

When he heard nothing, it finally occurred to him that he'd just abandoned one of his oldest friends in the clutches of a trained killer, so he began creeping back, skulking from tree to tree like a cartoon villain, as quietly as he could manage.

Perry didn't know what good any of this would do. In fact, he was pretty sure any gesture of heroism on his part would do nobody anywhere any good of any kind at all. The Therkles ran away from gunshots. They did not move toward them.

But what was he, an asshole? Rollie might have been an impulsive idiot, but he was *their* impulsive idiot, and—impulsively idiotic though he may have been—he'd stuck his neck out for all of them. Whatever happened, Perry couldn't just leave him there on the chopping block alone.

So the moment the path came back into view, he ducked behind another tree, a big old fir roughly three Perry Therkles wide. Peering around it carefully, he could see Jud in the distance, overseeing Stephen, who seemed to be wandering around aimlessly with his hand in the air. It was all very confusing until he heard Jud's barking voice, which carried well in the timber: *Forget it. Let's go.*

That was when he understood that Stephen hadn't been wandering—he'd been looking for something on the ground.

And he knew right away what that something was.

A few moments later, as Jud marched Rollie back down the path toward the cottage, Perry ducked behind his tree and pumped his fist silently. He waited there until they were out of sight.

Then he waited until he couldn't hear the sound of their footsteps crunching along the path anymore.

Then he waited another fifteen minutes until he was damned sure they were good and gone.

Then he popped out from his hiding spot and hustled over to finish finding that phone.

They sat together around Ryan's fossilized dinner table, watching Stephen Rollins get angrier.

"If not for those people, I'd push the red clover right now," he said, tossing the tablet onto the table with a rubberized thud. "He's a fucking psychopath! Why wait for the canc—"

"Stephen, don't," Emma said. "Enough for now."

Angry as she was herself—as close as she'd come to thinking the same thing herself—Emma didn't want to hear Stephen give it a voice. Nobody needed that energy now.

Plus, after Ryan's quip about Bond villains, she wouldn't be surprised if he could monitor every word they were saying. In fact, the more she thought about it, the more she'd be surprised if he weren't. For all they knew, he could see them right now.

Stephen saw all their faces, sighed, and lowered his eyes. He sat and placed his palms down on the table. Immediately he winced, lifting his injured hand again.

"Sorry," he said. "I'm just..."

"We get it," Will said. "Believe me."

Emma reached out, took Stephen's good hand. He met her eyes briefly, then looked away. But he gave her fingers a squeeze.

Will was the first of them to arrive at the simple observation that they were all attempting to run on stress alone. "It's midafternoon," he sighed. "Maybe we should eat something."

"He's right," Emma agreed. "I can't think anymore."

"I'm sorry, Em," Lainie said, her voice nasal, eyes still red from crying. "I didn't mean to be such a bitch before. I..."

"Me too," Emma said. She went around to Lainie's side of the table, where Lainie was already standing in wait.

Big hug. Friends again.

They found the Sub-Zero stocked with all manner of lunch options. Nobody felt like taking another run at the leftover lamb chops, and the risotto was definitely out. So they voted in simple ham sandwiches and made an assembly line: Beau stacking, Lainie buttering, Will at the stovetop with a grilling pan.

While those three did that, Emma went upstairs and found a bunch of first-aid stuff in a closet. She brought the whole basket down and told Stephen to quit fidgeting while she doctored the abrasions on his cheek, the cut over his eye.

"Ow," he said.

"I said hold still."

"I forgot I was bleeding up there."

"You're not anymore. For a minute I thought I saw bone, but it's not so bad. What are all these flecks of..."

"Probably oyster shells."

"Ah. Yep."

There was an elastic compression bandage in the supply basket. She got it started around his wrist, then let him take over.

"So," she said, going for a distraction while she watched him wrap. "Jud and Kai, huh? I told you."

"It's a modern fairy tale, all right. With his-and-hers sidearms."

"At least you got to see her naked."

"Only mostly naked, but that's a good point," Stephen said. "I wish I'd told him that."

Emma laughed. It felt good. Good to laugh, good to have him back. And he did seem to be back, finally. It was in his eyes.

Now they just needed Perry.

Perry and a plan.

"Soup's on," Will called. Plates clattered in the kitchen.

Emma said, "I didn't know I was this hungry until I smelled ham."

"Me either," Stephen said. But he seemed distracted. Lost in a sudden thought.

"What is it?"

He blinked. "Nothing."

She decided not to press for now...but Stephen Rollins wasn't the only person here who could tell when somebody was lying. She used her lightest touch to pat his newly wrapped wrist. "Sit tight, Clubber. I'll bring you a plate."

"I'm okay. Thanks, Em." He rose from the table. "For a lawyer you make a good combat medic."

"Combat," Emma said, rising with him. "You got hit in the face with a cell phone."

As soon as he found it, nestled screen-down against the base of a tree amongst the needles and cones, Perry knew he had decisions to make.

First on the list: *Now what?*

The phone itself, like the tablet they'd found earlier, was not a model Perry recognized. It was small but heavier than average, with a shockproof case and a short, fat stub of antenna on top. There was no visible product badging or external buttons. Just a glowing white clover insignia that faded in when he turned the device over in his hand.

He touched the screen, did some experimental swiping: up, down, left, right. The clover pulsed with each new movement, but that was all. So he touched the clover itself. The phone vibrated briefly, and the clover turned red. Wrong answer.

The longer Perry stood there fiddling, the more exposed he felt. He tried to think like a Navy SEAL. Or a fugitive. Anything other than an out-of-work corporate management consultant with a scuttled early retirement plan, which was what he was.

Judging by the relatively small amount of blood spattered about the path—and by the relatively normal way Jud had seemed to be moving—the man was far from mortally wounded. This left Perry to presume that Jud and Stephen would be heading back this way eventually—probably as soon as Jud had tended to his injuries.

He further presumed that Jud probably had some kind of supercommando people-tracking skills. Unless that helicopter had the ability to land in dense trees, he would likely begin that tracking on foot, here, where things had gone haywire.

Or maybe he'd call in backup instead?

Or maybe he already *had* backup? Possibly Navy SEALing its way toward Perry from the helipad right now?

Perry tried to think. He wasn't good at this. He wished Will were here; he'd have some ideas. Will was a mechanical engineer; he knew how to solve problems. He'd grown up on a farm, dammit—he knew about outdoor things. Will owned every season of that TV show with the good-looking survivalist who taught you which plant or bug or frog you could eat if you needed life-sustaining nutrition. Perry preferred the one where celebrity experts judged high school show choirs, but how was that going to help him here?

Shut up.

Think.

He tried to decide if he should make his way back toward the big house, away from the cottage, or stay put and find a new place to hide somewhere in the trees. He didn't know how much time he had before Jud returned. He didn't know what would happen if Jud found him. He knew he didn't want to get caught in the open.

But he didn't know what would happen if he could somehow stay hidden until nightfall either. He only had his yellow windbreaker, and it would get plenty cold out here after dark. What if it stormed again? What if it got dark and cold and *then* stormed again? What if there really were wolves?

He started with something he could accomplish easily: he untied the highly visible yellow windbreaker from around his waist, rolled it up in a long tube, then retied it like a belt, pulling his shirt down over it.

There.

This gave him his next idea. Using the edge of his shoe as a rake, Perry tilled up all the oyster shells that had blood on them, covering them over with oyster shells that did not have blood on them. He smoothed over the area he'd disturbed as best he could with the flat of his sole. He ended up with a wide discolored spot in the middle of the path, the rain-dampened shells from underneath now churned up to the top.

But the sun was out again. The wet patch would dry. It would probably look fine in no time, indistinguishable from the rest of the path. Jud would have no clue how to get his bearings now.

Right?

Sure.

Covering this obvious landmark gave Perry a third idea. He gave the same shoe-raking treatment to the marks Rollie had made in the shells while getting body-slammed. Next, he jogged up the path for a hundred yards or so, toward the big house.

Then he ducked off into the timber—this time opposite the direction he'd escaped the first time—and doubled back. When he could see the wet patch again from the trees, he headed farther into them. He lucked into a nice big deadfall—a pair of old cedars that had toppled onto their own branches, partially onto each other. Somehow, they reminded Perry of himself and Stephen. He made this his spot.

His idea was pretty basic: he'd watch the path from a camouflaged position until Jud and Stephen reappeared. It was, after all, the only direct route back to the big house. With a small amount of luck, he'd have enough time between now and then to come up with a plan for what he would actually do when he saw them. With a gigantic amount of luck, he'd figure out how to make an emergency call on this stupid cloverphone before it did.

At the moment, it didn't look promising. Perry felt like one of those apes jumping around the mystery monolith at the beginning of Kubrick's *2001: A Space Odyssey*.

Seriously: How was this thing supposed to work? He sat on the ground and leaned back against a cedar trunk. He tried tapping, double-tapping, triple-tapping, tapping different locations around the screen. He tried swiping with one finger, two fingers, three fingers. He tried pinch-zooming with his thumb and index. Basically everything short of shaking the whole thing like a maraca. He even tried voice activation, holding the device close to his lips and whispering, *Unlock, you fucker.*

No dice. No matter what he tried, invariably, one of three things happened: (1) The clover pulsed white; (2) the clover pulsed red; or (3) not a damned thing. Meanwhile, the dampness from the ground had soaked through to his ass. So much for dry pants today.

The sudden vibration of the phone in his hand startled him so much that he spasmed and dropped the whole thing. The phone bounced off his shoe and into the ground litter.

Perry scrambled to his knees, soaking them for a change, pawing around through the wet needles and rough twigs, trying to zero in on the exact spot from which the chirping tone still emanated.

At last he found it. He scooped the phone up mid-ring. The caller ID screen said...

RC

…above a small, pulsing green clover emblem.

It took Perry a moment to register what was happening.

Then he smiled. *Gotcha.* He touched the green clover with his thumb, raised the phone to his ear, and said, "SEAL Team 6 Outdoor Adventures, how may I direct your call?"

CHAPTER 22

OVER SANDWICHES, STEPHEN elaborated on the tale of his cottage adventure with Perry. In the best of moods, he was not a natural-born dinner table raconteur. His UpLink feed consisted primarily of random re-Links from two or three years ago. His prevailing social media philosophy was, *Who gives a shit what happened to me today?*

But Emma had to hand it to him: he seemed to sense how eagerly Will soaked up every detail and leaned into the role of storyteller, really painting them a picture—of the forest, the storm, of building a fire. Of the look on Kai's face when they'd walked in on her. Of the look on Perry's face when Stephen had pulled an actual gun out his jacket pocket. The whole performance was a welcome distraction—and not the first time she'd wondered what he might have been like as a father, had things gone differently.

But then lunch was over.

With food in their bellies, the five of them left their dirty plates in the sink and followed him down to the strange door in the game room on the lower level.

"It leads all the way to the cottage," he said.

Will said, "Why would he have this?"

"I'm starting to think *why* is a dead end."

"Guys, none of us know what his life is really like," Lainie said. "If we were Ryan, maybe we'd want an escape tunnel too."

It took some doing, but Emma held her tongue. To her credit, Lainie still wanted to give Ryan the benefit of the doubt—which was, in some ways, what had always made Lainie Hemford such a good friend. She deserved as much time and space to come to terms with all this as any of them.

At the same time, it was getting harder to look past the simple, awkward truth: with *(I)n (R)eal (L)ife*, Blainey had a livelihood stake in this Trolley Problem of Ryan's the others did not.

Maybe none of that mattered now. She could see her friend hugging that tablet like a protection charm. Trying to square the world she was experiencing with the artfully filtered, selectively curated world she preferred.

And why not? It occurred to Emma that maybe all lifelong friendships required a certain amount of artful filtering.

It also occurred to her that she was the only one here equipped to fully understand what Lainie was going through at this moment. Yes, of course: whether or not he'd admit it out loud, Beau would be missing their twins. He could be a lunkhead, but nobody could accuse him of being a checked-out father.

Still, Emma knew it went deeper for Lainie. She'd already confessed that this—far more than their precious UpLink feed—was her true qualm with the weekend's "no devices" rule. She wouldn't be able to check in on the boys, who were living away from home for the first time, just starting their second weekend at college.

Lainie had always been a tad superficial. Always a little too status-obsessed. But she had levels, and on this level, Emma knew just what she was feeling, because she'd felt it herself. She'd felt it almost the moment the house locked down around them: an immediate, nearly overpowering urge to connect with Kyle.

It had been only two weeks since they'd moved him into his own first-year dorm at Vassar—Emma, her ex, and Kyle's latest step-bot, his second in five years. Will and Perry even showed up for the occasion, living within an easy drive as they did; it had helped so much to have them there. *See you in Seattle!*

Now it was Labor Day weekend. No classes Monday. What was her own kiddo doing right this minute? Studying? Getting to know the people he'd reunite with three decades from now? The people who might help him move his own kid into a dorm one day?

It was entirely possible. She supposed it was just as possible that he was alone, hanging out with his old high school buddies on GamerLink instead.

What was the weather like in Poughkeepsie right now? Emma wished she'd given in to temptation and called him one last time before giving up her phone, instead of convincing herself to refrain from helicopter-momming him to death from afar. They'd spoken only the morning before, on her way to the boarding gate in Denver; she already knew he was doing fine. Such an easygoing personality, such a good head on his shoulders. Kyle always seemed to roll with the punches, even when he'd been small.

But something about standing there in Ryan's basement, pondering a steel security door that led to an underground tunnel, which led only deeper into Ryan's troubled psyche, made Emma want nothing more than the sound of her son's voice in her ear.

"I don't suppose you happened to catch the combination," Beau said.

Stephen shook his head. "It was a lot of numbers."

"How many?"

"He blocked my view." Stephen gestured toward the window concealing the keypad. "Besides, even if I knew the code, we'd need Jud's thumb to get to the keypad anyway."

Beau's face fell. But he quickly brightened again, waving off all obstacles, real and imagined. "Well, that's no problem. We just smash the glass."

Emma noticed that Lainie's facial expression also had fallen. To Beau, she said, "Hon, can we talk a minute?"

"But we still don't know the code," Will said. "We also don't know if it's the same code on both sides. Even if we could get in, what if we can't get out? We could end up trapped in a tunnel instead of trapped in a house."

"So we smash the keypads too," Beau said. "You're good with this stuff; you can just hot-wire the damn things. Right? Just like you did with Ryan's old Honda after we lost the keys in the lake that time."

Will looked doubtful. "That was an '86 Prelude. This is . . ."

"Hon," Lainie said.

"I know, I know," Beau said. "But wires are wires, right?"

"I bet he'd know if we tampered with them," Will mused aloud. "Some kind of alert system."

Beau looked around. "Where's the fuse box in this joint?"

Emma noticed that Stephen's attention had wandered again. She lowered her voice and said, "You had that same look at lunch. What are you thinking about?"

He glanced above them, nowhere specific. He used his nonbandaged hand to pantomime a common action: writing something down on paper.

Emma nodded. So she wasn't the only one who'd considered the possibility that Ryan might be tuning in. "Guys, we need to keep thinking this through," she said in a normal tone. "Let's do it upstairs where we can watch for Perry."

Lainie said, "Beau!"

At last, Beau blinked. He looked at his wife and said, "Yeah, sure, honey. Of course. You guys go ahead, we'll catch up."

Emma wondered what that was all about.

Whatever it was, it would keep. They left Beau and Lainie in the game room and went back upstairs. They found a pad and pen in a kitchen utility drawer.

Stephen awkwardly scribbled a line using his uninjured, nondominant hand. He showed Will and Emma the sloppy scrawl:

You did those plays in college. Ever miss acting?

Will looked at him curiously. Stephen scribbled another line:

Think you could play a guy in a diabetic coma?

Will leaned back. He glanced toward Emma.

She snapped her fingers, pointed at Stephen: *not bad*.

Will reached for the pen and added his own line to the pad:

Insulin shock first, then coma. More believable.

CHAPTER 23

KEEPING HIS VOICE low, scanning the timber warily, watching the path from his crouch behind the deadfall, Perry spent half a minute explaining to a frustrated, unwell-sounding Ryan Cloverhill how he'd come to answer Jud's company phone.

Sick or not sick, whenever Ryan attempted to get a word in, Perry defended the floor long enough to apply some preliminary scolding: for stranding them in a rainstorm, for sending a man with a gun to unstrand them, for keeping his diagnosis a secret for so long. These things just for starters.

"But I'll forgive you for all of it," he murmured in closing, fading his own volume again, "if you stop what you're doing and come back here. Whatever this is, it's not fun anymore. Let us help you."

Ryan sighed in his ear. His breath sounded ragged. "Pear, don't say you want to help me if you don't really want to help me."

"Oh. Are we pouting? Sweetheart, please."

"Then you'll do me a favor? Remember, you're sad I have cancer."

"I also have pine needles in the crack of my ass." *Fir needles*, Stephen's voice whispered helpfully in the back of his head. *Different trees.* "What favor?"

"Next time you see Jud, will you please just follow his instructions? Stephen's back at the house, everybody's waiting. Will's worried about you."

"I'm sure he is." Perry felt a flash of real anger. Who did Ryan think he was trying to manipulate? And why? "But Stephen's at the cottage. With Jud. Right now."

"He isn't. I can patch you through to the house if you don't believe me."

"There's only one way back to the house, and I've been watching it the whole time. Nice try, though."

"Look," Ryan said. "We're wasting time, and my goddamn stomach is killing me, so if you won't let me prove it to you, can't we just agree to help each other out? You're on your own out there, which is completely pointless, and I need all six of you together, or none of this works."

"I thought you said pancreas."

"What?"

"You just said your stomach was killing you. You told Stephen it was your pancreas."

"Jesus, Perry. Who ever said 'My pancreas is killing me'?"

Perry conceded the point. "None of what works?"

Now came a long pause, followed by another sigh.

"Okay, fine," Ryan said. "This isn't how I planned things, but you've missed the feature presentation, so you'll have to settle for the recap. Let me switch us to video mode; it'll help make things more clear."

Why did Perry feel so certain that Ryan just wanted to get a look at his current location? He crouched lower, still scanning the trees. "I think I'm good. Make things more clear now."

For good measure, Ryan had thrown in a tablet function he called the Decompression Chamber: a repository of Bardsley-era music, movies, and television episodes they could send to various endpoints throughout the house entertainment system. Somebody got the idea to play music to cover their deliberations, just in case Ryan really was listening.

Lainie handed Emma the tablet across the dining table. She didn't seem to want to be the one holding it anymore.

So Emma took a spin through the Chamber and found something perfect near the top of the list: Alanis Morissette, *Jagged Little Pill*. She smiled and said, "Here we go, Lainie. This will solve everything."

She called up the first track, sent it to Main Floor 1, and pushed up the volume slider on-screen with her fingertip. God, the instant memories that flooded back the moment the music kicked in—how long had it been since she'd listened to this?

Even Will found a momentary smile. "Maybe it's good that Perry's not back yet. He still hates this album."

For Emma, it was the bittersweet soundtrack to the end of an era. She'd just gotten her acceptance to Pritzker the week this record came out. How many times had they played it? She wouldn't know how to count. That whole last summer at the duplex it was like they simply couldn't tire of these songs. She and Lainie eventually made it a game, wailing the lyrics into whatever nearby objects passed for microphones until Perry, already bound for grad school himself, fled the room, or covered his head in pillows, or offered to smash the disc into jagged little pieces.

Across the table, Lainie smiled too. But there didn't seem to be much feeling in it. "Can we please listen to something else?" she said.

Emma looked at her, but Lainie wouldn't look back. So she complied without comment, pulling up something mellower, bringing the volume down a notch or two.

Meanwhile, Beau turned to Stephen and said, "I saw this thing about people on chemo going nuts. Could that be it?"

Lainie said, "Honey, I don't think that's really true."

"I've read a few case studies," Stephen said. "There have been psychiatric complications with certain people and certain chemotherapy drugs. Cognitive changes, anxiety, manias, yeah. But it's not really my area."

"He said he'd been pursuing experimental treatments," Emma said. "Who knows what he's been taking?"

Will said, "The whole thing does seem a little..."

"Grandiose?" Stephen offered.

"That's the word."

"He always has been."

Lainie scowled. "That's not true."

Emma wasn't so sure about that. "He does keep comparing himself to Oppenheimer."

"Well, I guess you know him best," Lainie said. A little petulantly? Emma thought so. "I just don't think we're being very fair."

Will threw up his hands. "Lainie. Seriously. Fair?"

"Fair, unfair, whatever," Stephen said. "I still don't believe he'd risk letting one of us die over this."

He dropped his voice to lay out his plan. It really was smart and simple, in Emma's view. Possibly even simple enough to actually work: they'd call Ryan on the tablet, show him a credible medical emergency inside the house, tell him Will's insulin wasn't helping, and force his hand.

"I don't know," Beau said. "He might be crazy, but he's not stupid. You don't think he'd sniff that out in about two seconds?"

"Probably," Stephen said. "But he'd never be able to know for sure. Any more than we can know how much of what he's telling us is real. He's forcing us to call his bluff. Why not put him in the same position?"

"Ready for my close-up," Will said.

Emma nodded. "I still like it. I'm in."

Beau looked at Lainie.

Lainie looked at the table.

To both of them, Emma finally said, "What?"

Beau leaned back slowly. "Well, look. Let's just suppose—I mean just for argument's sake—that he's not bluffing. Everything's just what he says it is. It's up to us to choose our own adventure."

"Come on," Stephen said. "I mean, you know what this is, right? You do remember?"

"Yeah, yeah, pull the lever, don't pull the lever, Trolley Problem, he told us. I know," Beau said. "I'm just saying: What if these levers really do work?"

"Suppose they do," Stephen said. "You're ready to red-clover seven people?"

"Jesus, no!" Beau said. "Who said red clover?"

"Just let him finish," Emma told Stephen. "He listened to you."

Stephen nodded. "You're right. Sorry, Beau. The levers really work. So?"

"So, theoretically, those tied-up people *aren't* people he paid to act like hostages, and they're not all laughing their heads off over afternoon drinks on the boat right now. That being the case, we'd all agree, red clover's out." He looked around the table. "Am I right so far?"

"I won't speak for anybody else," Emma said, "but you'd have to take my thumbprint off my cold, dead hand."

Beau looked at Will, then Stephen. "Well?"

Will rolled his eyes.

Stephen said, "No, Beau. In theory, I would not pull the lever that blows up the boat."

"So, that leaves green clover or nothing. Either way—theoretically—Ryan's gonna do what he's gonna do. Right?"

Emma didn't like the way he kept coming back to this. Lainie hadn't looked up from the table since Beau took over the conversation. She could sit here with them, but she couldn't meet anybody's eye.

What had they been discussing down there in the game room? Emma would truly love to hear that conversation now. But she couldn't, so she took a breath and said, "Beau, what are you trying to say, exactly?"

He looked around the table as if waiting for somebody to fill in the rest. When nobody did, he sighed and leaned forward.

"Okay, I'll be the asshole who says it out loud." He glanced briefly toward Will, then spread his hands to the rest of them. "Are we really pretending that nobody at this table feels the need to at least *discuss* the matter of six hundred million dollars?"

Perry laughed.

Too loudly.

He clammed up immediately, knowing he'd potentially just given away his position. But come on.

"My," he said. "That all sounds very elaborate."

"If you hang on a sec while I put us on video, I'll introduce you to the board. It's only fair for you to get a look at the people whose lives you'll be considering."

"Pineapple Drives." Perry had to hand it to him—as a put-on, it had pizzazz. "I'm glad you've had fun, amigo. But can you please explain the point of this exercise when we all came here just to see you in person for a few days? The weekend's half over already. Will and Emma have their hearts set on orcas before this is over."

"Trust me, it's not an exercise."

"Trust you." Perry ducked down farther behind the deadfall, keeping his eyes peeled. Were there cameras hidden in the trees somewhere? No, of course not: that's why he needed them back in the house so damned badly. Perry couldn't believe he hadn't thought of it before now. "You're secretly filming all this for Blainey's Netflix thing, aren't you?"

"It's not a reality show either. It's just reality."

"Uh-huh. Cool."

"Perry, listen to me carefu—"

"Please tell me," Perry said, "that you didn't bring us all here just to prank us into the world's most elaborate game of Trolley Problem. That's obsessively weird even for you."

"Perry, ask yourself one question," Ryan said. "If this were a prank, do you really think Kai's gun would have been loaded?"

It seemed like an excellent point. Perry felt prickles on the back of his neck, and his hands went clammy. Could Ryan possibly be serious?

How could he be?

"Maybe a demonstration will wrap this up," Ryan said. "I see my dots have joined."

"Your what?"

"Do me a favor. Observe this, then report to the others. Hand the phone to Jud, will you?"

Perry snapped his eyes to the path. Still empty in both directions. He scanned the trees.

Then he heard someone clear their throat behind him.

Still half-crouched, he spun around, heart flopping in his chest. And there was Jud, not five feet away. Patiently sitting on his heels, arms resting on his knees. His right arm was covered in blood-soaked bandages.

"Fuck me," Perry blurted, nearly toppling over sideways. His heart pounded so hard that spots floated in his vision like gnats. Or maybe they were actual gnats. Either way, he felt close to passing out.

"Howdy, Stretch," Jud said.

Perry couldn't think. "How did you do that?"

Jud waggled another phone identical to the one in Perry's hand. "GPS locator.

Borrowed Kai's. Plus air support." He pointed straight up to the sky. "Wave hello to the boss."

Perry looked up into the blue above the treetops. A black object hovered directly over them. Suddenly a sound registered; the faintest insectile hum. Perry realized he'd been hearing it for some time without fully realizing it, blending as it did with the rustling of the treetops. Absently, he raised the phone back to his ear and said, "Ry?"

"Haloo," Ryan said. The drone bobbed up and down in the air, its hum shifting pitch as if in greeting.

Meanwhile, Jud rose to full height and stepped forward, reaching down toward Perry with his free hand. "Is that for me?"

Numbly, Perry handed him the phone.

Jud put it to his ear and stepped away. "Here. Negative. Site one reports on schedule. Copy. Affirmative. Back in the air in…" He checked his watch. "Twenty? Copy. Out."

While Perry leaned against the dead cedar trunk, trying to pull himself together, Jud pocketed Kai's phone. He stooped and placed the one he'd just been using on the ground at his own feet.

Then he took two steps back. After a few quiet seconds passed, he looked at Perry and explained: "Satellite delay."

Perry had no idea what he meant until a split second later, when he jumped at the sound of a muffled *bang*. As if mimicking him, the phone hopped in the ground litter, seemingly under its own power.

Jud stooped again, picked the phone up in two fingers. He blew off the schmutz, front and back, then tossed the phone to Perry.

Perry caught it, fumbled it, held on mostly by accident. The phone felt hot. The screen was shattered, case pulped outward. He could smell burnt electronics.

"Pineapple Drive," Jud said. "Pretty cool, right?"

Perry stared at the phone. Stared at Jud.

Jud casually reached under his arm, finally removing his own gun from the pocket built into his tight-fitting shirt. "Questions?"

This gun looked much bigger than the one he'd taken away from Stephen. Jud flicked something with his thumb, then held the gun down by his leg, muzzle pointing toward the ground. His trigger finger pointed the same direction, laid safely along the outside of the frame. Something odd Jud had said to Stephen bobbed randomly to the surface of recent memory: *I'd feel better if you indexed your finger.* So this was what that meant.

Perry did have questions. Plenty of questions. But he couldn't seem to think what any of them were.

CHAPTER 24

I'M JUST SAYING," Beau kept saying, "people demolish buildings all the time. You heard all the precautions he said he's taking. He can afford the best people in the world, right?"

Stephen said, "Listen to yourself."

Beau said, "What? I bet he'd do a better job than Joe Dynamite and Sons. Have you ever known anybody as detail-obsessed as Ryan? In theory..."

"In theory, you're just saying you'd sponsor an act of domestic terrorism," Emma said, "if the guy was a friend of yours, and there was enough money in it?"

"Jesus, no!" Beau said. "Not when you put it like that."

"That's how I'd put it."

But Beau wasn't finished. "I'd sign off on a construction demo, though. If I knew I was working with professionals. Look, just hear me out."

Emma, Will, and Stephen sat by impatiently while Beau laid out his logic, which really was not so complex: if—in theory!—red clover was out, and if removing that option removed their ability to change the fate of Link Labs or, ultimately, Ryan Cloverhill...and if they had some reasonable assurance that no innocent people would be harmed, including themselves...then should they really be so quick to pass up enough wealth to make Solomon blush? Especially if Ryan covered them with the lawyers and, you know, whatever.

"Hell, forget about us; what about all those employees?" he said. "Go green, and a bunch of programmers get to play hacky sack for a few weeks. Paid! Do any of 'em get that the no-clover way?"

"That's rationalizing."

"He set the terms, not us," Beau said. "And what *about* us?"

"What about us?"

"Any one of us could give the whole wad away if we felt that guilty about it. Imagine all the good *that* would do in the world."

"In theory," Stephen said dryly.

Beau pointed at him. "I'm just saying."

"I still don't think we'd ever lay a finger on a dime of that money," Emma said. "In theory."

"Yeah, but you can have all kinds of theories," Beau said. "That's what makes it theoretical."

Emma looked at her old friends from across the table. Her longtime roommate, and the guy who'd made her so happy for so many years: Beauregard Jamison Hemford III. The bright-smiling fellow who had so effortlessly wiped away the lifetime of self-esteem debt young Lainie Calissa Goss had carried with her to campus like luggage, all the way from Marin County to Stillwater.

This was coming from both of them...but thinking back to that odd exchange in the basement, it also seemed clear enough to Emma which one of them had brought it up first.

Was it surprising? Not surprising? Both?

She knew that Lainie, deep down, felt jealous of Emma and Ryan's childhood bond: that it had survived, that it had sustained no permanent damage, that it existed at all. To UpLink Lainie, Emma suspected, it just didn't seem quite fair.

But that was just one of the differences between UpLink Lainie and Bardsley Lainie: Bardsley Lainie hadn't felt left out in the least. *Don't get me wrong, we all love the guy,* she'd said back then, after everything went nuts. *But he's one strange little twig. Who wouldn't pick Stephen?*

It was only since Ryan Cloverhill had become Ryan Cloverhill that Lainie's viewpoint seemed to have changed. And now?

Well. In some ways, their UpLink personas really were authentic. Amplified for clicks and likes, maybe...but they were peas in a pod, Beau and Lainie, and they always had been. And Lainie had always been the mayor of that relationship.

"I'm not saying it's worth thinking about," Beau concluded. "I'm just saying...maybe it's worth thinking about?"

Stephen said, "Why do you keep looking at Will?"

"What do you mean?" Beau said. "I'm looking at everybody."

Stephen turned to Will.

Will shook his head slowly. "He's looking at me because I recently confided in him—confided; Beau, you understand what *confided* means, right?—that we've been a little tight."

"What?" Stephen said. "Since when?"

Emma sat up and leaned forward. She knew Will and Perry had had a tough couple of years, but she'd never heard either one of them mention money trouble. "What happened? I just saw you two in August. What's going on?"

Will sighed. "You guys know Perry got so sick. Then he couldn't travel for a while, lost his job in June. We'd already sunk a bunch into the house, and the recession shelled our investments, and..."

"Perry hasn't been working?" Emma couldn't believe this news. She'd probably asked a version of that basic question every time they talked. It was standard checking-in chitchat: *How's work?* Lately, now that she thought about it, Perry usually said *Can't complain* and changed the subject. Suddenly she felt like a dolt. "You guys!"

"We didn't want to say anything," Will said. "Perry made me promise. I don't know what I was thinking when I told you, Beau."

Beau looked sincerely chastened. "I'm sorry, buddy. I swear, I didn't tell anybody except Lainie." He gestured toward Stephen. "I can't help it if I forgot we were sitting with Carnac the goddamn Great over here."

Carnac the Magnificent, Emma thought. Beau always got everything just slightly wrong.

Stephen ignored him altogether, focusing instead on Will: "How tight is tight?"

"Stephen," Emma said. "Come on."

"I just mean, can't we help?" He looked almost professionally offended by this revelation. "I can't believe I didn't pick up on any of this. I've been practically damn naked with your poker-faced husband today."

"Well, that makes one of us." Will chuckled a little. "Guys, don't worry. We're not losing anything important. This is exactly why we didn't want anybody to know. One way or another we'd have been right here, even if Ryan hadn't paid our way."

Emma reached over, took Will's hand. He kissed her knuckles.

"We'll be fine," he said. "And I don't care if we each get a hundred billion, I don't want anything to do with that money. In theory or for real. Perry won't either. I promise you that."

"Perry," Stephen said. "I'm giving that guy a piece of my mind when he gets back here."

"You'd better not, Rollie. I'll never forgive you."

"Yes, you will."

"Okay, fine. But still: please don't."

Stephen shook his head and looked grumpy. Beau shook his head and looked embarrassed. Lainie hadn't looked up from the table a single time through all of this.

Emma called bullshit. "Lainie, you've been awfully quiet," she said. "I'd like to hear what you have to say."

Lainie sensed them all looking at her. "I feel bad for Will and Perry too."

Nope, Emma thought. *Don't think you can cop out on this and let Hubby take all the flak.* "I mean about this green-clover idea of Beau's," she said. Knowing full well that what she was about to say next was flat-out mean. Knowing she should stop herself from saying it, unable to stop herself from saying it anyway: "Are you sure a hundred million is enough to make up for losing all those followers?"

This brought Lainie's eyes up at last, flashing like distant thunderclouds. Emma knew that look. Had been doing her best to provoke it, if she was honest with herself. She readied for battle.

Bring it on.

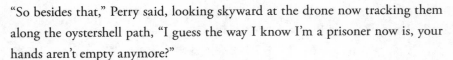

"So besides that," Perry said, looking skyward at the drone now tracking them along the oystershell path, "I guess the way I know I'm a prisoner now is, your hands aren't empty anymore?"

Behind him, Jud said, "You're catching on."

Perry wondered what time it was by now. The sun was definitely well into the western sky. He was starving. And parched. His fluid intake for the day had amounted to two cups of coffee and two mugs of Forest Berries tea, and all that running around in an actual forest made a fellow thirsty. Had he seen any berries in his travels today? Maybe they were an urban legend. Or a different forest. Or he just hadn't noticed.

At any rate, he hadn't peed since the six of them had returned from the boathouse this morning. This morning didn't even feel like today anymore. He had a headache. His fingers were scraped and sticky from pawing around in the needles and twigs, and he'd bent back a nail. Even his shoe had come untied.

Fuck it. Perry let the strings flap. Civil disobedience.

What were Will and the others doing right now? Was Stephen really there with them, as Ryan had claimed? Why was Jud walking him toward the cottage instead of the big house?

He supposed there was a way to research at least some of these things. So he asked Jud: "What time is it? Do you have any water? Why are we going to the cottage? Is Stephen still there?"

"Around fifteen-thirty," Jud said. "No, but you can have some soon. Because I said so. And, no."

"Thanks, Alexa."

"She works for somebody else."

Perry glanced over his shoulder, realizing he had no idea what time "fifteen-thirty" was without doing math. He supposed it didn't really matter. He glanced up at the drone again—the goddamned all-seeing Ryan-bot and its faint, ever-present hum. It was starting to creep him out.

So he stopped walking and turned around.

Jud stopped with him.

The drone stopped and hovered overhead.

Perry said, "Jud, you strike me as the type who's been around. Done a lot of things, met a lot of people. No?"

"You win that bet."

"Here at home and in faraway places?"

"Around the world twice and talked to everyone once. Just like the song says."

Perry didn't know what song he was talking about. He didn't much care. "In your opinion," he said, tossing another glance up toward the hovering drone, "based on your personal experiences, has my very good friend Mr. Cloverhill become a madman?"

Jud actually seemed to consider the question. Finally, he shrugged. "If he is, he seems like a high-functioning one. And he offers a hell of a benefits package."

Fair enough.

"Let's move."

Perry turned and walked on. Jud fell in behind. The drone tagged along.

As they rounded the last bend in the path, the cottage came into view once again—an entirely different view when not obscured by gloom and sideways rain. He imagined himself and Will out here, whiling away their retirement years in a spot near a spit like Mags and Luna had found for themselves.

Impossible, of course. For Mags and Luna, too, he felt pretty certain, without a benefactor like Ryan Cloverhill. Still, Perry could imagine it clearly. It made a nice picture.

Red means Stop. That was what Ryan had said on the phone, the raving wacko. *Green for Go. Your doting husband can show you everything as soon as you're finished dorking around out there.*

But what was he really saying? Admit your price, and something like this could be yours? Perry couldn't imagine what need in Ryan this deranged production of his fulfilled.

With clear skies, he could see the edge of the bluff beyond the cottage. The vast, denim-blue water beyond the bluff. He almost remarked on it over his shoulder, something along the lines of *Nice backyard.* But he stopped himself. Because there was something else:

There, in the water. Maybe a thousand yards out, just off to his left. Moving slowly toward his right:

A boat.

A big boat. Hundred-footer at least. Big enough to cut an aggressive-looking profile even at this distance. It was a profile that said: *I am not a recreational craft.*

Perry knew immediately what kind of craft it was. White, with a pilothouse. A mast and crow's nest on top. A big yellow boom crane on the aft deck. He could see the unmistakable markings on its forward hull: a fat red diagonal band with a narrow blue stripe behind it. At least they were unmistakable if you'd grown up near a coast.

Because that was a Coast Guard cutter.

Perry felt his heart skip a beat. Were they out on maneuvers? Regular patrol? He pretended he hadn't noticed a thing, casually sweeping his eyes as if taking in the full breadth of the glorious view. But his mind was suddenly spinning. He felt tingly all over.

What could he do?

Surely he couldn't do nothing. Not with a big gleaming law enforcement vessel within sight. Was there any kind of play to be made here at all?

Perry couldn't think of anything. He didn't have a flare gun handy. He saw no way to quickly build a signal fire without Jud noticing. He could make a break for the bluff and wave his arms like hell, but what would that accomplish? He'd seen this end of the island from the water for himself; there would be no way anybody on that boat could see him from way out there, unless somebody happened to be scanning the island through a lens. Right?

"I wouldn't bother," Jud said, as if reading his mind. "They won't see you."

Perry felt all his skin tighten. How did he *do* that? What did they teach these pricks in Navy SEAL school?

He said, "Who won't see me?"

"Good answer."

Jud's smug alpha effectiveness pissed him off. People pointing guns at him and following him around with drones pissed him off. It wasn't fair, Mags and Luna out here in this quaint little Cape Cod with the wraparound porch, drugging houseguests and playing Sea Hags of the Sound. Also, Perry had been lying out of politeness before: He'd hated that Forest Berries tea. It tasted like mulberry bird shit.

And Ryan.

What in the name of all holy Christ had become of Ryan Cloverhill? Who did that guy think he was? Ryan Cloverhill?

Perry watched the cutter crawl behind the cottage, disappearing from view as if it had never been there at all.

But based on its trajectory, it would reappear shortly.

And that was when the idea came to him. Instantly, Perry made a decision. Just like that. It was surprisingly easy.

He stopped walking. Bent to one knee. Finally tied his flapping shoelace.

Jud sighed. "You really can't wait to do that?"

"Guys with long legs have to be careful," Perry said. "We go down easy. Like baby giraffes."

"Seems like you could have thought of that half a click ago."

"Tell me about it." What the hell: Perry went for a double knot. "Hey, out of curiosity, what's Mr. Cloverhill paying you for all this extra duty, anyway?"

"I swear you and your shrink buddy share a brain."

"That's what my husband says. I was just wondering how much it would cost you if you really did shoot me." He glanced upward toward the drone again. "Right in front of him."

"I don't think either one of us wants to find that out. Or your husband."

"That's what I thought." His other shoe wasn't untied, but he retied it anyway. "Know what else I just thought of?"

"Nope."

Scuffling his feet to cover the sound, Perry closed his hand around some oyster shells as he stood up again. As many as he could grab without making a production out of it. He felt surprisingly calm just then. It was as if the whole world suddenly slowed down, became easier to understand. He said: "How much longer my legs are than yours."

With that he spun, sidearming his oyster shells straight at Jud's smug alpha face.

Naturally, Jud saw all this coming a mile away. He wasn't fooled in the least. He simply moved his head to the side; the entire fistful of shells sailed harmlessly past him, scattering in the air, pattering ineffectually back to the ground wherever they happened to land.

But Perry had already bolted: Away from the cottage, away from Jud, in roughly the same direction the cutter was cuttering. Out toward the spit.

He'd wanted a much bigger jump, and he'd only bought himself a couple of steps; this was going to be over before it started. Despite his aversion to sports, Perry had taken up running with Will for exercise and rehabilitation. He'd actually grown to enjoy it; they'd even entered next year's New York City Half Marathon together. It was good to have goals.

But he'd been off awhile, and long legs or not, he couldn't imagine being any match for Jud in a sprint.

But a quick glance over his shoulder showed that Jud wasn't even chasing. He was just standing there, one foot slightly forward, knees slightly flexed, both arms extended.

Shit.

Wrong bet.

Jud's voice rang out: "Stop there, Mr. Therkle, or I *will* fire."

But Perry had already made his decision. This was no time for baby giraffes. He pumped his arms and stretched his legs, thinking, *He's not going to shoot. This is without question the dumbest thing you've ever done. He's not going to shoot. Will would shit himself if he could see how heroic you were being right now. He's not going to shoot. You're going to die.*

"Last warning!"

Perry glanced to his left and saw the cutter crawling back into view. He saw the front door to the cottage banging open, Kai emerging to see what was going on this time. He saw the drone pacing him.

He thought: *Stuff this in your Trolley Problem and smoke it, Mr. Cloverhill.*

Perry ran in a probably ridiculous serpentine pattern as he aimed for the navigation tower due ahead, a hundred exhilarating yards in the distance. It rose before him like a red-and-white candy-striped ladder to the sky, a skeletal beacon against the blue. Perry could feel imaginary bullets burrowing into his back like murderized bees. He pumped his arms harder, stretched his legs farther. *He's not going to shoot. He's not going to shoot.*

And, sweet baby giraffes, it was actually true.

CHAPTER 25

THE TOWER WAS a triangular lattice of tubular steel surrounding a central nerve pipe. Its frame was widest at the base, narrowing as it climbed forty feet straight up into the sky. As he reached the structure, Perry realized there were at least two immediate problems with his plan.

First: He was going to have to climb that goddamned thing.

Second: Jud, it turned out, was willing to shoot after all.

Perry heard the crack of the first gunshot and felt the impact of the bullet almost simultaneously. The round chewed up a spot in the ground just inches ahead of him, kicking up dirt and pebbles. Close enough that he could actually feel the percussion of it through the soles of his deck shoes.

His first reaction was complete, mind-blanking panic. He had never been shot at before. It was terrifying. It made a person want to stop what they were doing immediately.

But it also confirmed that he was on the right track. He'd officially come around to Rollie's way of thinking: they were all in real trouble out here. In this strange new state of clarity, Perry's mind put two and two together: *He's going for my legs.*

Didn't they always say that cops, in shoot-outs with robbers, sometimes fired dozens of rounds without actually hitting anything? If that was true, then it was probably really hard to hit moving legs, even for a trained professional.

Or maybe it had been only a warning shot. There was no way to know for sure without stopping to ask. The important thing was, no bullets had hit him so far.

The tower's lowest crossbar started well above his waist, where he'd tied the windbreaker he now planned to use as a signal flag. Upper body strength was not high on his résumé.

But he spotted a service ladder on the far side, facing the water. Perry glanced back, saw Jud coming. To his surprise, the exceedingly fit young man, who normally moved like a chilled-out panther, did not seem to run very well. Less like he imagined a Navy SEAL and more like an actual seal.

Clearly, Jud had sustained some kind of serious injury in his past. Jesus, what a break. Perry wondered which kind of animal was better on a narrow service ladder: seal or baby giraffe? *Let's make it a contest,* he thought, and broke around to the far side of the tower.

He was only a few rungs up when Jud's next shot clattered through the latticework, ringing through the painted steel piping. On the ladder, with the water at his back, Perry could see Jud elevating his aim.

He climbed faster, hand over hand, size 14 after size 14, intuiting that elevation was more his ally than Jud's. For visibility, yes. But also to confound his pursuer. The higher Perry went, the farther he'd fall when Jud finally hit him, a scenario Jud was duty bound—not to mention financially beholden—to avoid.

His third shot clipped the edge of the ladder directly in front of Perry's right knee; the vibrations thrummed in his hands and feet. In the absence of sudden agonizing pain, he kept on climbing. Rung. Rung. Rung. Steady. As. She. Goes.

Little by little, one rung at a time, Jud was getting smaller, the ground farther away. Thank goodness it wasn't Will on this ladder, with his deathly fear of heights. Perry couldn't quite understand why he wasn't more afraid himself right now. More confirmation that he was doing the right thing.

Right?

Best to not overthink it.

He kept climbing. Sure enough, the shooting stopped. Perry looked up, estimating that he was perhaps halfway up the tower now. He also learned that looking up was a huge mistake; the lamphouse at the top, outlined against the vast blue sky and the moving clouds, gave him a powerful sense of vertigo. Suddenly Ryan's drone dropped into Perry's field of view, startling him with its angry-wasp buzz. He gripped the ladder tightly and anchored himself again, eyes back to the ground. He waited for the momentary disorientation to pass.

Now a much smaller Jud had given up shooting and was heading for the ladder himself. Perry checked the water off to his right (which way was starboard, again? Jud had explained all this in the helicopter). He tried to judge how much time he had before the cutter passed the light tower.

He could still get higher.

He showed the drone his middle finger, then grabbed the next rung.

The tower began to narrow slightly on either side of him as he neared the top. It felt much windier up here. Looking down was no longer a comforting thing, especially looking down past the edge of the bluff. He must have been sixty or seventy feet above the waterline at this point. And look—there was a smaller dock on this side of the island. He hadn't even noticed it on yesterday's tour. The spitside dock looked like a weathered gray tongue depressor from up here. If only there had been a boat attached to it.

Now the ladder started to wiggle under new weight as Jud started climbing up after him.

And Perry Therkle was officially as high as he dared to climb. He hooked an elbow tightly around the vertical rail and kept his eyes glued to the rung in front of him. He used his free hand to lift his shirt and untie the yellow windbreaker. Why had he knotted it so damn tight? Why wouldn't his hand stop shaking? *Easy*, he thought. *Do not drop your signal flag.*

He checked the cutter's progress. Shoulders open now, he could extrapolate an invisible line from the patrol boat's bow. As he did so, he spotted something even farther out in the water:

A series of tiny, glossy black crescents gleamed in the long afternoon sunlight, surrounded by sparkling wavelets. Just a momentary glimpse. And then again—there! In a slightly different position this time. Perry felt a flash of delight as he realized what he was seeing:

Ryan's pod of orcas.

How he wished in that moment that Will was on this ladder with him after all.

The cutter was getting closer.

Jud was getting closer. Perry could see the frustration in his upturned eyes.

Somewhere above him, Ryan's drone buzzed.

He looked out toward the far water again, hoping for one last glimpse, wishing the animals were closer. He felt unreasonably disappointed. Where had they gone? Out on the horizon, as far out as he could see, dark clouds appeared to be massing again.

The knot came loose in his fingers. His pulse kicked up. *Pay attention.*

Jud was only ten rungs away now, close enough that Perry could hear him easily when he spoke: "Come on, man. Let's get off this tower before we kill ourselves. Come down with me now."

He could see Kai far below, closer to the tower than the cottage; she stared up at them, shielding her eyes with one arm as she watched the world's slowest chase scene unfolding. Perry raised his eyes again to the approaching boat. He wished it were closer too.

But the orcas were gone, and help was as close as it was going to get. So he steadied his breathing, adjusted his armlock on the ladder, and carefully removed the rolled-up jacket from around his waist.

"Mr. Therkle," Jud said. Too calmly. So calmly that his tone, by itself, struck Perry as a comment; an experienced evaluation of the dangerous lunacy of their current position. "Perry. It's Perry, right?"

You're goddamned right it is, Perry thought.

He unfurled his flag and let it fly.

CHAPTER 26

THINGS INSIDE THE house devolved in a hurry.

Stephen stayed with Will and Beau at the table as Emma and Lainie parried and thrusted all the way into the living room. They dueled there awhile, until Lainie retreated, and Emma pressed the attack down the nearest hall. It started as an argument about choosing the green clover, then became an argument about who had the right to judge whom, then became an argument about who'd *always* thought they were better than the other, and how wrong they were.

And it felt to Stephen like they were just getting limbered up. As their voices receded somewhere into the other leg of the L-shaped house, he believed he had a pretty good picture of the group's collective mental state at this point. Emma had always been the best of them, or at least the most even-keeled. But there was no question that she'd been the one to draw first blood with Lainie just now. If Emma Grant was on the attack instead of making peace, you knew things were hosed.

Beau looked sincerely pained. "Sorry, fellas."

"Not your fault," Stephen said. "Although you probably could have given the green-clover thing a rest."

"Why?" Beau said, immediately stiffening. "There's no room for discussion in this group anymore? We all just follow Emma and Stephen because they know best?"

"Guys," Will said. "Come on."

Stephen sighed. It was so easy to forget about Will sometimes. He was naturally soft-spoken and made so few waves. Now that he thought about it, maybe Will Shrader was the most even-keeled of them all.

"You're right," Stephen said. "Beau, I apologize. I'm not fit for human company right now."

Beau waved it off. "Forget it. We're all on edge."

But his face had gone glum. And Will seemed to be putting out an odd vibe all of a sudden too. Stephen began to sense some unspoken understanding between the two of them. Nobody seemed to want to look at anybody else.

"Okay," he finally said. "What am I missing?"

Beau gestured vaguely toward Will. "Go ahead and tell him. I did it to you."

Will shook his head. "You didn't mean to."

"Tell me what?"

"Aw, hell," Beau said. "Will and Perry aren't the only ones up to their tits."

"What?"

"We're bankrupt," he said.

"Not yet," Will added quickly.

Beau waved that off too. "All but the paperwork. In the meantime, we're in default on the mortgage. We've got creditors living in our colons. The boys just started college, and we can't even pay for the first semester. And then what's next for them? I mean, God knows I love 'em, but let's face it: they ain't exactly scholarship material." He tried a grin. It wasn't remotely convincing. "The truth is, we came here planning to beg Ryan for a bailout."

Stephen couldn't have been more surprised if Beau had told him they'd given away their worldy possessions and joined a commune. "Beau," he said. "Jesus, I don't know what to say. I thought you guys were going gangbusters."

"Smoke and mirrors," Beau said.

"Hey," Will said. "That's not true." He looked at Stephen. "He's not telling you the whole story."

"What happened?"

"Lots of terrible decisions," Beau said. "It doesn't matter."

Stephen wanted to press, but Beau was clearly humiliated enough. Stephen glanced at Will. Will's eyes said it all: *Let it go for now.*

So he said, "I'm so sorry."

"It's our own damned fault."

They sat and looked at the table together for a while. They couldn't hear Emma and Lainie anymore. The house had gone quiet.

In the uncomfortable silence, Stephen had an unpleasant thought. "Did Ryan know about any of this?" He looked at Will. "Either of you?"

Will shook his head. "Only if he's psychic."

Beau shrugged. "We wanted it to be a surprise."

"But even if he did," Will said, "I still can't figure out why he'd put us through this. It doesn't make any sense."

"He did say he wanted us to fight like cats and dogs," Beau said.

"Well, mission accomplished," Will said. "But *why*? He knows we'd never choose red. He obviously wants us to choose green, but he gets what he wants even if we don't. If what he *really* wants is to blow up his company and leave us all his money, why not just...do that? Why do we need a Trolley Problem?"

"Because he wants us to choose it," Stephen said.

"But *why*? Why does he need us to be his accomplices? Does he feel guilty about how rich he is? Does he want to prove we're all capitalists at heart? What does he care? He's Ryan Cloverhill."

"Maybe it's a loyalty test," Beau said. "To prove we're worthy."

"Of what? To be knights of the realm? I'm a mechanical engineer." Will shook his head. "Stephen, come on. Help us out. You're the one with the psych degree."

Stephen didn't know the answer either, but he didn't need a psych degree to speculate. Will said it best: he was Ryan Cloverhill.

"I think he means to do exactly what he means to do," he said. "He always has. He just wants the illusion."

Beau said, "What illusion?"

"That he's not alone."

Everybody sat with that.

"That might be the saddest thing I've ever heard," Beau finally said. "Thanks."

Stephen nodded in Will's direction. "He asked."

Will sighed. "I just want Perry back."

Of course he did. With everything going on it was almost easy to forget that Perry was still locked outside.

"For what it's worth, Jud's under strict orders," Stephen said, trying to be encouraging for a change. "He'll get him back here safe and sound. Probably any minute. He's ten feet tall and wearing a bright yellow jacket; he can't be that hard to find."

Will laughed a little. "And not much of a woodsman."

Beau said, "Actually, maybe that's an idea."

"What is?"

"Hear me out. Rollie's bum wing aside, we're all reasonably healthy individuals. We'd get our asses kicked in any bar fight, but there's kitchen knives and cast-iron pans and shit like that around here. Maybe we should be camping out downstairs by that door. The second it opens, we pile out and gang up on him, all three of us. On Jud, I mean. Not Perry."

Will looked around. "I don't know where the cameras are, but I'm sure Ryan's watching. He'd warn Jud what we're up to."

"Good point. We should try to find those. Put tape over 'em or something."

"We'd probably stay alive longer if we focused on trying to find a way out of here," Stephen said. When he saw the look on Beau's face, he added, "Maybe having Will go to work on those keypads wasn't such a bad idea."

Just then, Lainie returned.

Silently, she crossed the living room and walked straight to the table. Her eyes were red, still overcast. Her facial expression seemed actively neutral to Stephen—like she was working hard to look like she wasn't working hard to hold something in. She leaned past Beau and picked up the tablet from the middle of the table. "I'm going to go study," she said.

She looked at none of them. Beau reached out to touch her, but he touched only air. Lainie had already slipped away. She headed toward the floating stairs leading up to the bedroom level.

Emma followed twenty feet behind Lainie. She paused in the living area, waited respectfully for Lainie to clear out, then approached the table herself. Stephen caught her glance, tried to read her eyes. They seemed to say: *Don't ask.*

Will said, "Friends again?"

Emma waited for Lainie to disappear upstairs. Then she took a deep breath and exhaled. She hadn't looked at Beau yet.

"Not quite," she said. "We'll get there."

They all heard the bedroom door close firmly. Not quite a slam.

Beau sighed, starting to rise. "I should go. To be continued."

Then they heard the distant click of the door locking.

Beau sat down again.

Emma said, "Continued with what?"

CHAPTER 27

Lᴇᴜᴛᴇɴᴀɴᴛ ᴊᴜɴɪᴏʀ ɢʀᴀᴅᴇ Junipero "Jud" Bernal, retired, couldn't believe the dumb luck these two idiots kept having. Or how many dumb green bubblegummer mistakes he'd allowed himself to make—probably starting with too easily taking the boss at his word: *These are soft, fearful men, Jud. They're like me. Just get them home without scratching them up, okay?*

It was his own damned fault for treating this like what it should have been: a milk run. For getting distracted by everything he still had on his plate back at the Village. He'd been too busy worrying about getting Therkle back to the house and getting himself back to South Lake Union so that he could finish overseeing his small crew there—keeping things on schedule, inspecting every charge himself, generally crossing the i's and dotting the t's for the fireworks on Monday. Cloverhill might have been stretching him a little damn thin here, but that's what he was paying change-your-life money for. End of the day, who else was there to blame?

Damn sure not Kai. This was his end of the mission, not hers. And somehow, inexplicably, here he was: thirty feet up a goddamn pole and running out of options.

On the bright side, that was a 210-foot cutter out there, not a VTS patrol tub. Most likely out on a maintenance run from Port Angeles, possibly even a full deployment. Those guys handled drug traffic. Commercial fishing operations. Oil spills. Heavy rescue. They weren't concerned with Sham Rock.

On the other hand, in the highly unlikely event they happened to notice a guy on a light tower half a mile away, waving a canary-yellow jacket around in the sun glare, they'd almost certainly radio home. If that happened, Jud could handle it...but as complications went, it would be a thousand times better to avoid.

So now he had to somehow make Therkle stop waving that jacket without knocking him off this ladder.

I persevere and thrive on adversity, he thought as he climbed around to the inside of the ladder, hustling up to Therkle's rung from the opposite side.

The fool was hanging by an elbow as he waved the jacket back and forth in broad, flapping swaths. Jud stepped onto the tops of his three-eyed boat shoes and stood on them with all his body weight, pinning Therkle's feet to the narrow rung.

Therkle cried out in very sudden, very sharp pain. Jud couldn't blame him; there wasn't much to those shoes, and it had to really fucking hurt.

He simultaneously reached around the outside of the ladder and grabbed Therkle's shirt, yanking his free shoulder back toward the ladder. But the guy was so tall, and flailing so much, it was like trying to wrestle a berserk circus clown on stilts. Using only one hand.

Under the ever-present watch of Cloverhill's buzzing drone overhead, Jud repositioned his grip. He wrapped his wounded arm around the ladder and around Therkle's back, grabbing more shirt for purchase and squeezing with all his strength. He sent a short punch through the rungs into Therkle's midsection to soften him up, then whipped that arm back around the other side of the ladder. He pulled the taller man toward him and pinned him against the rungs, locking his own grip hand-over-wrist in the middle of Therkle's back.

Jud gripped him tightly, a bear hug with a steel ladder sandwiched between them, his eyes more or less even with Therkle's quivering Adam's apple. Therkle was still shrieking in pain, every so often words like *get-off-get-off-get-off* surfacing from the gibberish.

"Be still!" Jud shouted, letting off the guy's feet, planting one of his own in the narrow space of rung between Therkle's, letting his other hang free. There was nowhere else to put it and still keep the armlock intact.

He was pouring sweat now, which only made things harder. His only secure point of positive contact was two inches of rung and the narrowest part of his own slick wrist, in between his watchband and his hand. He rolled that hand toward Therkle's spine, hooking his fingers around the heel of his palm. If he lost his grip at this precise moment, they'd both be screwed. Firmly and clearly, he said, "Grab the ladder with both hands, right by my ears. Do it right now."

Therkle coughed, panted, wheezed. But he grabbed the ladder. The bright yellow jacket floated down and away like a shred of torn sail. Now Jud's own arthritic knee was the only thing screaming at him.

"You piece of shit," Therkle blurted, his voice trembling.

And that was where everything started to go very, very wrong.

Later, Jud wouldn't be able to reassemble the next sequence of events in exact order. He only knew it started with Therkle making a grab for his sidearm.

Jud was fully extended, hugging Therkle against the ladder, when he felt Therkle's right hand come off and begin rooting around under his own left arm.

He couldn't defend his weapon without relinquishing his grip. Couldn't maintain stability with one leg planted and one hanging free in space.

All he could do was shift his grip to the small of Therkle's back and climb down a rung, moving his whole body ten inches lower, taking the gun physically out of reach.

But at the same time, Therkle got the idea to push *his* body away from the ladder. He had too much leverage, and his arms were too long, and Jud couldn't hang on. His greasy grip slid apart.

He felt the yawning, dizzying sensation of falling suddenly backward into emptiness. The next few beats were a flurry of disjointed moments, like watching video on fast-forward—recognizable flashes here and there but everything blended, indistinguishable. Somehow, in his memory, the video leapt ahead and resumed normal speed here:

Jud's knees locked around the rung he'd been standing on.

His left hand gripping steel two rungs above.

And Cloverhill's friend clinging for his life to Jud's slick right arm.

His terrified eyes locked on Jud's. His long legs bicycled in space, thirty feet off the deck below.

"Stop moving!" Jud shouted, every muscle straining, tendons like high-tension wires. "Stop! Be still!"

"I'm slipping!" Therkle cried out, panic spiking his voice.

"Just hang on," Jud said, his left hand already trembling with fatigue. He guessed Therkle stood six-six; he wasn't broad, but tall guys were often larger-framed than they looked. This one might have been narrow to the eye, but he went two hundred pounds, easy. Jud's awkward grip on the rung above them would fail before much longer.

"I'm going to swing you back to the ladder," he said. "Eyes forward. Find a rung with your feet first. Then grab on. One hand at a time. Copy?"

Therkle nodded rapidly, eyes wide, swimming with fear. The guy was going to hyperventilate and pass out if he didn't start breathing right. He'd clawed off Jud's bandages and raked open the gash on his shoulder; new blood streamed down Jud's arm, mixing with the sweat, making everything slipperier.

Jud's left hand slowly began loosening involuntarily. Roaring with effort, he drew Therkle back toward the ladder.

But the motion caused Therkle to slide farther down his arm, screaming and digging in with his nails. The fingers of his left hand snagged the fat body of Jud's Luminox wristwatch, his right arm now wheeling free.

"Reach!" Jud shouted, tapping the last of his strength, digging deeper in that moment than he had since his last sleep-deprived week of BUD/S training school. The pain around his Navy-issue cobalt-chrome knee joints was blinding. *"Reach!"*

Therkle's outstretched fingers were six inches from the ladder when Jud's watch band snapped free.

And then the man was falling. Swimming in the air with his long arms and legs, gaining nothing, only losing altitude. Jud watched his eyes all the way down. He could see them change the moment Therkle understood exactly what was happening.

Then he hugged onto the ladder with both arms, roaring again as he rammed his own forehead against the rung in front of him. *Fuck!* He felt his skin split, felt blood trickling, stopped before he knocked his own compass off-kilter.

Twenty feet above him, Cloverhill's drone buzzed, pinned dead still against the moving clouds. Still watching.

Out in the strait, the SS *Puddle Pirate* crawled along on its merry way.

Jud squeezed his eyes closed.

He felt like shrieking at the goddamned sky. What was it about hanging out inside an impregnable luxury home for a couple of days that seemed so categorically *unappealing* to these assholes?

He'd seen guys miraculously survive higher falls than this. But one more look at the pile of wrong angles at the base of the tower told him there was no point even hoping that Therkle might be one of them.

Jesus. And for what? Jud had actually liked the annoying pain in the balls.

What was the *point* of this? Nobody on this island was in actual danger! They already shoveled their entire privileged lives onto Link without a second thought; if Cloverhill really, truly wanted to play God, he could probably ruin any one of them with a laptop while taking his morning dump. Habits, proclivities, daily routines, personal finances, personal contacts, reputations in their respective communities—you name it, he had one-stop access. Even offline conversations, if you owned a voice-activated LinkBase 365 and ran it in monitor mode to make turning on the lights in your house three percent easier. But take away a couple doorknobs for five minutes, and suddenly they're deprived of all liberty?

Don't want to play along? Fine. You're too *moral*? Got too much *integrity*? Great! It's your loss; you still go home Monday; your buddy Cloverhill still gets his in the end. It was almost the definition of no harm, no foul. In the meantime, chill out, have a cracker, put some wine in your face. Was it really so hard?

This was bad. This was worst-possible-scenario, Mayan-calendar bad. What a goddamned waste of everything. *Think.*

The pain in his knees finally centered him.

That, and the ever-present buzz above his head.

And the thunderheads in the west. Jud could see the dark bank rising up from the horizon like a hazy, distant mountain range. Another storm on the way.

So he took one more minute of rest.

Then, without another glance toward his hovering sentry, he chinned himself up on the high rung and pulled his legs out and under him again. He thought: *The ability to control my emotions and my actions sets me apart from other men.* He climbed back around to the correct side of the ladder. *I persevere and thrive on adversity.*

He started back down.

CHAPTER 28

KAI WAS WAITING for him, crouched over Therkle's broken body. She hadn't lost her cool. But she was far from okay.

"Tell me he's breathing," Jud said.

Her face broke his heart. "Jay. Look at him."

Jud nodded. "That's what I thought."

"Why did he *do* that! Oh my God. The poor stupid jerk!"

Jud looked up. Cloverhill's drone hadn't moved. It hovered there, a hundred feet directly above them, a black spot on the sky. For a moment, he had an urge to pull out his sidearm and shoot the thing down. But why waste a bullet? It would solve nothing. Not now.

Kai stood and joined him. "Which one of us calls him?"

As they stood there watching, the drone abruptly climbed another fifty feet straight up and zipped away.

"We don't," Jud said, watching the black dot grow smaller, retreating over the water, back in the direction it had come. It finally disappeared into the black horizon. They were alone again. "This changes everything."

"He saw what happened," Kai said. "You did everything anybody could possibly do. He saw it."

"I had one job."

"He'll have to understand."

"You sure about that?"

Kai said nothing. She just stared at the man on the ground.

"Come on," Jud said. "We need to move."

Eyes still on the body, she said, "What about him?"

"He's on his own now. Just like us."

She blinked at that.

"Okay," she finally said. "You pack up here. Wash, rest your knees. I'll go get Brutus from the other side. We can load everything in the back. I'll stitch you up in the air." She stood on tiptoe, inspecting the gash on his forehead, where he'd banged his own head against the ladder. "The arm, anyway. Need to take care of this new one before we leave. Can't fly with blood in your eyes." She shook her head at him. "Dummy."

Brutus was her nickname for the heavy-duty utility vehicle Cloverhill kept in one of the storage buildings. It had a cargo bed. Enough to get all their gear to the bird in one trip. It was exactly what Jud had been thinking himself when he'd started down the ladder.

But now he had other plans in mind.

"No time," he said. "We've got an hour before that weather hits, tops."

"What are you thinking?"

The money transfer would hit their accounts the moment Cloverhill received a clover signal from the house, that's what he was thinking. Ten million each: that was the deal. There were substantial bonuses to be paid automatically once Monday went off successfully, no pun intended. But they were past worrying about extras now.

And red was good as green, as far as Jud and Kai were concerned. Red clover hit their accounts before the last of the VanDutch's fuel slick burned away. In the same move, eliminating the man who could make it all vanish.

Frankly, Jud felt worse about the poor mangled son of a bitch ten feet away from him now than he'd feel about the six faceless jerkoffs on the boat with Cloverhill. At least Therkle had balls. Would any of them climb a light tower for anybody else? Jud, as Cloverhill's head of security, couldn't remember a single one of them ever so much as asking how his day was going. As for Cloverhill himself?

Good guy. Jud owed him a lot. All in all, he probably didn't deserve what was about to happen to him.

But it *was* his system.

And he was already a goner anyway.

"All we need is that tablet and six thumbprints." He nodded toward Therkle's corpse. "There's one of them now."

She looked in his eyes for a long moment. Then she shook her head. "Forget it. Too risky."

"No risk, no reward."

"I didn't sign up for this." Kai shook her head again. "It's plan B time. I say we get out while we can. We'll end up with enough."

He kissed her. "Twenty million. That's what *I* signed up for."

"I thought you signed up for *us*." She leaned back. "No? Not the case? I misinterpreted?"

"That's what twenty million bucks is," he told her. "You, me, and no more worries. Smooth sailing all the way to the end. With a pile left over for the kids."

"Who you having kids with?"

"Just thinking out loud." He shrugged. "Besides, without you, it's only ten million."

That got him a knuckle punch right in the bone frog. It hurt.

"I don't need his twenty million," she said, wiping her bloody fist on his shirt. "We can sell Gully to the highest bidder. Three phone calls. Give me seed money and five years, I'll make us our own twenty million."

"I believe it," he said. "Still."

She buried her face in his sweaty neck and hugged him the way she always did: with everything. Blood or no blood, it didn't matter to Kai. She felt taut and electrified against him. Like the future.

"We can pull this off," he said. "If you patch me up fast."

Kai stepped back from him. She looked once more at the man on the ground. Poor stupid jerk indeed. She cursed under her breath. When she looked back at Jud, her eyes were wet. "He liked my tea."

Jud pulled her close again.

Kai hooked his arm over her shoulders and crutched his busted ass back to the cottage.

⸺✕⸺

There was new weather coming.

Ryan Cloverhill didn't like what he saw on the horizon. He didn't like what he saw on the radar map. Most of all, he didn't like what he saw, at altitude, when Perry finally emerged from the timber, into the clearing at the cottage end of the island, marched along by Jud Bernal:

The USCG *Active*, the medium-endurance cutter out of Port Angeles, powering out toward open water on an unpublicized run.

The question of what they were doing out there, and when they would be coming back, was for another time. Because just then another wave of nausea hit him, this one so hard and sudden it was all he could do to mount the tablet and make it back to the swim platform in time.

God. He felt bone weary, weak as a cat. Gut full of red-hot razor blades. He'd finally given in and hit the Roxanol, which left him dizzy, with a pounding headache. He hadn't been able to hold down any food since morning, and his bowels had fallen into anarchy; he'd taken to hanging one bare end or the other off the platform out of convenience, with incidental consideration for his captive guests below deck. When this was over, somebody should create a humanitarian award in his name. The Ryan Cloverhill "Who Died in There" Medal of Dignity.

Meanwhile, schools of herring had been feeding on his ever-expanding bio-slick. It was disgusting.

How many of them would end up in nets? How many would end up in salmon that ended up in nets? How many supermarkets would one day sell a tin or a can containing a fish that had foraged, directly or indirectly, on the great Ryan Cloverhill's cancer waste? Even as he prepared to destroy his life's work, he couldn't help connecting the world. Wasn't that visionary of him?

On the other hand, the feeding fish reminded him that it was long past time for snacks and wellness checks down below. It had been ages since he'd heard a peep out of Amanda, Oliver, Valeria, Elijah, Bhavna, or Tom. They'd been on the tether now for hours. Ryan didn't know how he was faring as a captor on the Geneva Convention scorecard at this point, but he knew he was getting sloppy. Fighting dehydration and fatigue. He needed rest himself. Badly.

Soon.

For now, he hiked up his pants and made his way back to the helm. He sagged into the pilot chair.

Then he sat up straight, staring at the first thing he spotted on-screen:

A flash of yellow.

Perry's windbreaker. The same one he'd been wearing right here aboard the VanDutch yesterday. The same jacket that had been so helpful, earlier, in spotting him from the air in heavy timber.

Only he wasn't wearing it now. He was waving it.

Clinging to the top of the navigation tower like a gangly, underfed King Kong, waving the jacket for all he was worth. With Jud Bernal clambering up the service ladder behind him.

Ryan couldn't understand what he was seeing. He'd looked away for less than five minutes! How had this *happened*?

How, in a million years, had Jud Bernal *allowed* such a thing to happen? He was a goddamned mercenary guarding perhaps the least athletically inclined human being Ryan had ever known. What in the name of Tim Berners-Lee was this overtrained limo driver *doing* down there?

He ripped the tablet from its mount and shouted at the screen: "Perry, goddammit! You're going to..."

...fall.

Horror-struck, Ryan watched it happen as if in slow motion:

He watched as Jud grappled with Perry on the ladder.

He watched as the yellow jacket floated away, down and away. Down and away, gently fluttering to rest on the water against the pilings of the spitside dock.

And that was all he could do: watch. On his feet now, screaming at the tablet in his hands, helpless. Watching. As Perry himself fell.

And fell.

Then abruptly stopped falling.

And then it all came over him in a rush. The tablet bounced off the deck as Ryan sank to his knees.

Then he kept right on sinking. Flat on his back, staring up from the deck, the pale sky above him felt like a surface he'd left behind, unreachable as oxygen. He felt it in his body like drowning.

CHAPTER 29

In early December 1991, while Cloverhill and his pals were probably ditching class to do whatever white college kids did to keep warm in Minnesota, Kai Keahi's mother had taken third place overall in the Women's All-Age Shortboard Division at the Makaha Revival Open. She'd been nineteen years old.

At twenty, she'd had Kai, become a single mom, and left competitive surfing behind. The inaugural hometown tournament never caught on, and for a long time—at least until Kai learned, at age eleven, that you could make your own Wikipedia entries if you rode a squeaky borrowed bicycle all the way to the Waianae Public Library—you had to work to find any mention of her fiery mother's name anywhere in the world at all.

That's what *Keahi* meant, more or less: "fire." Kai's first name meant "sea." *Makaha* might as well have meant "poorest township in Honolulu County," and none of those meanings had changed in Kai's lifetime.

It probably wasn't completely impossible to imagine a kid from Makaha getting to the mainland on a full-ride STEM scholarship from the Cloverfield Foundation. But it was uncommon enough that Kai had gotten her picture in the local paper when it happened to her. STEM meant "skinny egghead." Her mother had met the news with the fatigued relief of a firefighter collapsing on soft ground, clear of the inferno, the rescued child unharmed.

When Kai turned nineteen herself, her third semester at Cal Poly, Lanikai Keahi died of liver failure back home. Not at Queen's, or Wahiawa General, but in a run-down shack with no running water in the same neighborhood where she'd been born. Her last words to Kai had come in an unpunctuated text from a neighbor's duct-taped flip phone, which had a busted condenser mic and couldn't be used for voice calls anymore:

go get it kk mahalo it's been a ride

KK didn't kid herself. None of what she was doing, here on this other island now, was anything close to what her mom had in mind. Not in this or any lifetime. Not even if it cured stage four hepatic cirrhosis.

But she also believed that some part of her would have understood. The big wave—the One—didn't come for everybody. Her mother, for example. Ever since she was small, Kai always had faith that she'd know hers when she saw it, and when she saw it, nothing was keeping her down on the board. That was the Keahi Creed: *No dick-dragging allowed.*

And she'd been right. She *had* seen it coming, her first week at the Village. The moment the boss had come down to rally the new interns: the one and only Ryan Cloverhill. Undeniable as the moon.

"I'd trade all the tech on this island for a stapler," Jud said.

"Be quiet," she told him, closing the last suture in his forehead.

She'd never actually done this before, but it wasn't so hard. While Jud had been delivering Rollins back to the big house and rounding up the tall one, she'd practiced on a banana from the kitchen with Gulliver, their VR prototype's development code name.

It was odd to think back from here. Early on—already planning ahead to the eventual strategic press leak—Kai had argued that Ryan's *Gulliver's Travels* reference didn't actually make sense. In her mind, the device was clearly the ship, and the person wearing it was the traveler, not the other way around. She'd suggested Antelope, like in the original story. *The* Antelope *sank*, Ryan said. What about Adventure? *Attacked by pirates.*

Gulliver it was, then. The whole conversation had seemed critically important at the time. Now it didn't matter what the hell they called it; the whole fleet was sunk, and she was one of the pirates. Ironically, the alpha versions of MedLink's interactive training classrooms were just what the doctor ordered for this too.

"We're burning time," Jud said. "He'll know something's up."

"I'm going as fast as I can. And he already knows."

"Which is why we need to shag ass." Jud checked his watch again. Every time he did that, he seemed to remember all over again that he wasn't wearing his watch anymore. Kai couldn't stop thinking about why. "You stay here, get packed up. I'll get that tablet and get us our thumbprints. Then I'll come back with Brutus and we'll head to the chopper. Thirty minutes max."

"I still say we go now."

"We can do this."

She finished her knot, snipped the silk, said nothing.

Jud said, "What?"

"It's murdering people," Kai said. "Okay? That was never the plan."

"I won't hurt them any more than I have to," Jud said. "Cross my heart."

"We're still talking about blowing up his boat with him on it. And everybody else. Don't think we're not."

"Red clover," he said. "They do it themselves, or we do it for 'em; it's all the same. Don't think our hands are clean just because somebody else pushes the button."

Except that it wasn't the same. Maybe she *had* bought into a fairy tale. When Ryan Cloverhill served Kool-Aid, it tasted pretty good, okay? Did it matter? All that was over now.

The tall guy. That was the difference. It helped if she didn't think of him by name, but it didn't help enough. "They won't pick red. He knows that."

"Do you?"

"I said be quiet." Kai could feel him watching her face while she worked. She pinched the corner of the bleeding gash on his arm and ran the needle in. He didn't flinch. Jud never flinched. It was one of the things that drew her to him in the first place: no dick-dragging.

After the stitch was in, he said, "Tell me what you're thinking."

"I'm thinking that dev build in there is still worth a fortune if we play it right."

Jud nodded. "That sounds like way too much 'if' for me."

"So little faith."

"No offense, but you just came up with this," he said. "*He's* been planning for months. I'd rather hijack the plane than fly by our asses. And anyway: without Link behind it, is that gear even going to be worth the plastic?"

Ultra-lightweight carbotanium nanofiber and proprietary flexiglass, technically…but he wasn't totally wrong. Kai still couldn't decide if it seemed like a blessing or an agonizing shame. Ten years from now, anyone who could afford a new phone would be able to afford one of these. Beyond the obvious entertainment possibilities, the ADA and learning applications alone were practically limitless. Or pair Gulliver with a smart treadmill system; the average suburbanite could live inside an interface that made going to the DMV, or even the grocery store, a hell of a lot more fun. Next time a bug quarantined the world? Pick a destination from a menu and meet all your friends there without leaving home.

Kai Keahi might not be an angel, and she might not be living up to her mother's dream, but she was not, by nature, a bitch-ass company spy. It had never occurred to her to steal the one-and-only working prototype from Ryan's office until she'd done it yesterday, on her way out the doors of Link Village for the very last time. After all this buildup, she just couldn't resist giving the thing a test-drive before the whole division went *kapow*.

"Somebody will pay," she insisted, realizing it didn't really matter to her if it turned out to be true. They had go-bags and new identities already waiting. They both had a little cash in savings, and if that ran out, they both knew how to live poor. They could do it together. "The hardware spec alone is worth plenty. Let somebody retrofit it to *their* system. You and me? We cut our losses and go underground. Now, in front of the weather. This is his ride now."

"Underground," he said. "Funny. That's right where that tunnel is."

She took a little extra meat with the next stitch.

Still no flinching.

"You are one stubborn asshole."

"I'm stubborn." He nodded slowly. "Sure."

She was just finishing the last knot when the satphone on the table finally rang.

She looked at Jud. He looked back.

The phone rang again. Eyes still locked on Jud's, she put down her needle and thread on a sterile pad, stripped off one bloody glove, and reached for the handset.

She let her hand hover there.

Jud's eyes glinted with the challenge. He held her stare, now grinning slightly. "Boss calling," he said. "Maybe you should pick it up."

The phone rang again.

CHAPTER 30

THE FIRST TIME Emma Grant met Stephen Rollins, he'd been sitting cross-legged on the floor of 205 Anders with Ryan, arguing the merits of their respective CD collections relative to the limited square footage of the room. As soon as she'd seen the size of the "yes" pile compared to the "maybe" and "what's wrong with you" piles, she'd known her main worry about college life was already over: Ryan Cloverhill had made a new friend.

It had not been among his strengths, historically. The only child of university research professors who had divorced before he was born, yet continued their cohabitation out of financial convenience until he'd reached driving age, Ryan had grown up in possibly the quietest, least-sociable upper-middle-class household in Tangletown. On the first day of sixth grade, Emma's mother had spotted him: the only other middle schooler on their street, hoofing it past the first corner alone. He'd been carrying his supplies in a brown paper grocery sack—not because his family couldn't afford better, but because his folks had gotten their wires crossed about which of them was taking him backpack shopping. Connie Grant invited him to walk the seven twisty blocks to Morningside Middle with her and Emma, an only child herself. He'd stayed pretty quiet those first couple of days. But by Friday, he'd already begun to emerge from his shell.

After the first week, her mother peeled away, leaving Emma and the Cloverhill kid to carry on alone, as long as they promised to always stick together. Despite the unkind ribbing from her spoiled friends at school, Emma had genuinely liked her goofy new pal; he was funny, weird, blindingly intelligent, and he knew the teleportation cheat code to *Frogger* even though she was the lucky duck with the Atari at home.

But he'd never been quick to fit in with new people. Once they got to school, he seemed to shrink just walking through the doors. Every day, like clockwork, this process reversed itself on the walk back home—at least until they got to the Cloverhills' big drafty Tudor, at which point an invisible weight seemed to settle on his bony shoulders as he bade her goodbye for the afternoon. *See ya tomorrow, Em.*

By high school, her own parents had more or less adopted him ad hoc, designating one of their two available guest rooms "Cloverville" and setting an extra place at the dinner table as a standing routine. He once stayed for three straight days, under false pretense, before his mother finally called on the phone, apologized for the intrusion, and said: "I was wondering if by chance anyone there had seen Ryan at your home. This is Victoria Cloverhill."

When, the winter before they'd graduated, Emma's own father passed away unexpectedly at fifty—undetected aneurysm, shovel full of snow, even younger than Emma was now—she'd spent nearly as much time consoling Ryan as the other way around. He still sent her mother a handwritten card at Christmastime.

She'd truly, sincerely, utterly believed, in her head and heart and everywhere else, that they'd come to Bardsley thinking of each other as something like stepsiblings. In fact, that was exactly how he'd introduced her to his new roommate, that day in 205: *This is Emma. She's my sister from another mister.*

Sometimes she'd wondered if it had been the simple *fact* of her and Stephen—more than any true sense of romantic betrayal—that had activated in Ryan Cloverhill some yearning even Ryan Cloverhill hadn't known he'd had. As if the processors in his high-powered brain simply couldn't compute the equation of two people he loved finding a love that didn't include him.

———

They found a basic toolbox in a utility closet off Ryan's kitchen. Will spent ten minutes pounding on one of the big windows with a hammer. Emma could see that it was pointless after the first couple of swings, but Will seemed to need to hit something a bunch of times with a hammer, and nobody could think of a good reason to stop him. So they plugged their ears against the booming noise and watched until he finally gave up.

"Must be bulletproof glass," he said.

"It doesn't matter," Stephen told him. "We'd still have to get through the outer barricade."

Will tossed the hammer back into the toolbox with a heavy clatter. "Beau could have been on to something earlier. I'll see if I can find a breaker panel. Maybe we can reboot the place."

Emma doubted very much that Ryan had left them an easy button. But they'd already agreed as a group to put Stephen's blood sugar gambit on hold until Lainie reappeared with the tablet, and the truth was, she was worried about Perry too. If it helped Will to keep busy, so much the better.

So he buttoned up the toolbox and took it with him downstairs to see what he could do about hot-wiring a high-tech smart home. Meanwhile, Emma, Stephen, and Beau split up to check the whole place again for chinks in its armor.

From the main entrance, you entered Ryan's house more or less at the inside angle of the L. The open plan centered the kitchen area and main living space in this central junction, with the floating staircase connecting the levels from basement to rooftop. One leg of the main floor led to a spacious home gym, the other to a library and screening room.

Beau started in the library, pulling books from shelves and putting them back, one after another. On her way past, Emma poked her head in and said, "What are you looking for?"

"The trigger."

"What trigger is that?"

"The one that opens the secret passage."

"Ah." She thought of what Stephen had told them earlier, over lunch— Perry's attempt at more or less the exact same strategy with the exterior light fixtures when they'd been outside the house, trying to get back in. Everybody had laughed, even Will. "I think what you're looking for is an Agatha Christie novel."

Beau pulled the next book, put it back, moved to the next. "Agatha Christie would have made this shit believable."

A fair enough point. "Good luck."

"Em?"

"Yep."

"Whatever Lainie said to you earlier," Beau said, still looking for the magic button that sprang open their mousetrap, "you know she didn't mean it. Right?"

"I know," Emma assured him, privately understanding the truth: On some level, of course she'd meant it. Every word. They both had. It just wasn't the level that truly mattered. "Me either."

Upstairs, the legs of the L housed the guest bedrooms and master suite, while Ryan's home office occupied the main junction. She headed up and went right, past Will and Perry's room, to Lainie's closed door. She waited there for several moments. Listening.

Finally, she knocked. "Lainie? It's me. Can we talk?"

How she wished she'd known earlier what she knew now. It wasn't bad enough that upmarket real estate in Laguna Beach had been soft for half a decade, or that they'd spent themselves silly building what Blainey insisted on calling "our brand." It wasn't bad enough that after it worked, and real money started coming in, they'd made a string of bad investments and signed a series of terrible contracts with sponsorship partners.

According to Beau, the Netflix deal they'd been telling everybody about for months would have plugged a few holes. But the truth was, the proposed reality series for *(I)n (R)eal (L)ife* had died on the vine—along with their agent's enthusiasm for the project. But that wasn't the worst part.

The worst part was discovering, after IRS auditors came calling earlier this year, that they'd been systematically cleaned out by their business manager, whereabouts currently unknown.

"Lainie?" She knocked again. "Honey, come on. Say something. I'm not leaving until I know you're okay in there."

After another long moment she finally heard rustling, followed by Lainie's muffled voice: "Em?"

"Still here."

"Fuck off."

Okay, then.

Maybe later.

Or maybe she'd get lucky and wake up in a psych ward back in Minneapolis. Wrists and ankles strapped to the bed rails. A doctor saying, *Ms. Grant, we've checked, and there is no such island in the location you've described.*

Or she was in her own bed, and the rattling sounds she heard coming from Ryan's office down the hall would turn out to be Kyle, home for the holidays, rummaging around in the kitchen. God, what a relief that would be.

Either scenario, really.

After half-heartedly trying to find some other way up to the roof, Stephen found himself sitting in Ryan's home office chair, jiggling all the drawers of the big, old, 1950s-era Leopold desk.

Everthing was locked. He thought of going downstairs to borrow a screwdriver from Will, see if he could pry something open. Maybe he'd find the Wi-Fi password on a sticky note.

Instead he just sat there, facing the big corner windows. Staring at a picture of the ocean on giant video screens.

So this was how Ryan Cloverhill spent his downtime: alone, on an island, in his fortress of solitude. The lacquered walnut desktop had a computer monitor and docking brick, a wireless keyboard and mouse, but no computer. The only other item occupied the far left-hand corner: a digital photo frame.

As he sat there, watching the images change, Stephen realized that every picture in the slideshow somehow involved the Stillwater Seven. A carousel of scanned old prints from the Bardsley era, intermixed with the very occasional digital snap of more recent vintage:

Ryan with Will and Perry in front of the bank of Jumbotrons at One Times Square.

Ryan with Blainey under a palm tree, all sunglasses and smiles.

Ryan and Stephen himself at a Cubs game, well over ten years ago now—the last time Stephen had seen him in person before this weekend. Ryan had been in town for a speaking engagement at Chicago University, or maybe DePaul, Stephen couldn't remember now. Mostly he remembered that the visit had started out great and ended in some argument, per usual. He couldn't remember what they'd fought about either.

Of the entire batch, one photo had been set to display for a longer interval than the others: Ryan and Emma raising wineglasses at a restaurant table for two. It was the most recent photo in the feed, by the look. Stephen couldn't pinpoint the year, but Emma's left hand was already missing the wedding ring.

He reached out, picked up the frame, and sat back with it. As he studied their faces, the photograph spoke to him: "Giving up already?"

Stephen jumped. He turned to find Emma standing in the doorway behind him. "Oops," she said. "Sorry about that."

He held out the frame. "When was this taken?"

Emma came in, took the frame from his hand. She leaned against the desk with it, spent a moment looking at the photo. Stephen couldn't read her face. "About a year after the divorce, I guess. He hadn't been back home in years. I tried to get him to go visit his mother. He wouldn't do it."

"That surprised you?"

"Not really." Suddenly she beamed. "Oh my God. Look at this."

She turned the frame to show him. The image had finally changed. Another golden oldie: the Stillwater Seven Take Seattle, Part I. They were all crowded around a vertical display case inside Ye Olde Curiosity Shop on Pier 54: Beau, Lainie, and Will on one side; Stephen, Perry, and Emma on the other.

In their midst, inside the case, was Sylvester, the shop's infamous mascot: a balding man with a full mustache, skeletal arms folded across his dessicated torso, frozen in position for eternity as if carved from a man-sized block of wood.

Sylvester Was Once a Real Human Being, read the handwritten placard next to Sylvester's cadaverous, peaceful face, *and Was Mummified by a Phenomenon of Nature.*

Stephen had forgotten all about this one. Seeing it now, it occurred to him that in this snapshot, this moment in time, Sylvester actually served as their seventh member. Ryan wasn't in the photo. He'd been taking the picture.

"Jesus, Em," he said. "What the hell are we *doing* back here?"

Emma sighed. "Not what any of us imagined, that's for sure."

"What did we imagine? No, scratch that. What did *he* imagine?" He gestured toward the frame in her hands. "Do you know every single picture on there is of us? Keep watching."

"I'm getting the gist." She shook her head. "Sometimes I forget how much history this crew has."

"Ancient history," Stephen said. "Exactly my point. We're not part of each other's lives anymore. Not really. We haven't been for years. Whatever idea about us he's built up in his mind, it might as well be Sylvester."

"Don't say that."

"We're locked under glass, aren't we?" He spread his hands toward the big windows. "And who's not in the picture?"

Emma put the frame facedown on the desk. She crossed her arms and looked down toward the floor. It was the classic Emma Grant posture when taking her time to formulate a thought. He waited. It took her a while.

"Sometimes I ask myself," she finally said, "why I still think about you so often."

Stephen didn't know what he'd expected her to say, but that wasn't it. All at once he became extremely aware of how close they were to touching. A couple of inches between his leg, where he sat in the chair, and hers, where she leaned against the desk.

She looked at him. "Do you ever think about me?"

Not more than a hundred times a week, he thought. But he only said, "Yes."

"Why? We're ancient history. Some of it we'd both rather forget."

Now she wasn't playing fair.

"We're not part of each other's lives anymore," she said. "Haven't been for years. But yesterday, on the plane? For me? It felt like no time had passed between us at all." She puffed out a breath. "After all we've been through, how is that even possible?"

"Okay," he said. "I get it."

"You do? Because I sure don't. You might as well ask me to understand Hydrozel."

"Never heard of it."

Hydrozel, she explained, was a polymeric bioadhesive manufactured by the company she represented. They'd developed it in part by studying the adhesive proteins of marine mussels, whose secretions bound and held in harsh, saline conditions. In other words, conditions not unlike those found in the human body.

Hydrozel closed wounds, held tissue to bone, and could withstand load-bearing applications in the joints and spine, all with an industry-low rate of immunore-jection. To activate it, you mixed one bunch of stuff with another bunch of stuff. Chemical reactions ensued. Catalysts catalyzed. For the patient—or to an intel-lectual property attorney—it might as well have been magic. In some recipients, the bond could last a lifetime.

Stephen couldn't help smiling. "So we're stuck together like barnacles, is what you're saying."

"Something like that." Emma smiled back. "But my point..."

"...is that nobody ever solved a Trolley Problem by wasting half the class period wanting to know how they ended up on the damn trolley in the first place," Beau Hemford said from the doorway. "Do you guys seriously not even remember Dr. Mendota?"

Stephen and Emma both jumped together this time. Beau waggled his fin-gers at them. How long had he been standing there?

"Come on, happy clams." He jerked a thumb over his shoulder. "Will needs our help downstairs."

CHAPTER 31

Kᴀɪ ʜᴇᴀʀᴅ ᴛʜᴇ first spits of new rain pattering on the kitchen windows as she followed Jud into the pantry, then down the creaking stairs into the cellar. They hurried across the gritty concrete floor, dead insects crunching underfoot. Roaches and cedar beetles, mostly. She wondered: How did they make it onto the island in the first place? Did they fly? Hitch a ride with the construction crews? Swim?

You're not supposed to be here, she thought.

At the tunnel door, Jud checked the chamber of his sidearm. "Back in fifteen," he said.

She didn't like how fast the weather had come in. Through the kitchen window, she'd seen whitecaps on the water. The cloudbank looked like an approaching spaceship, blotting out the western sky. By the time they made it to the helipad, the rain would be hammering.

Jud saw it all over her face. "Don't worry. I can fly in anything."

There was no point in arguing now. So she took a breath. Nodded. "Go."

He punched in the code. When the locks disengaged, he pulled the door open. The overhead lights snapped on in front of them, illuminating the way.

He leaned over, planted a kiss on her cheek. "Fifteen minutes. Don't forget the gizmo."

Ryan jerked awake with the sound of alarm bells, needles of cold rain stinging his face.

He was sprawled where he'd passed out, slumped against the forward bulkhead, ass planted on the deck. The sky above him had gone hard as wet concrete. Beneath him, the VanDutch rose and fell on choppy water, buffeted by the rapidly cooling breeze.

He coughed, tried to sit up. His mouth and throat were lined in cotton. His guts were on fire. When he turned his head, his stiffened neck sent bolts of electricity into the base of his skull.

To the immediate west, Ryan saw the flashing cloudbank nearly upon them, black and writhing, sizzling from within. It would be directly overhead soon.

The drone had returned to the boat while he'd been out. It now sat on the deck a few feet away like an obedient pet, silently waiting for a treat. Seeing it brought flashes of memory:

Of yellow nylon against a weathered gray piling.

Of tapping the button that called the drone home.

Of desperately calling Kai's phone, again and again, until the pain swamped him.

As these memories returned, reorienting him, the alarm bells he was still hearing gradually resolved into a sound he recognized:

Security alert.

Ryan sat bolt upright, groaning with pain. The tablet fell from his lap and banged against the deck. He scooped it up, wiped water from the screen, and tapped the tunnel cams.

The screen immediately filled with a grid of video tiles. Each tile on-screen represented a camera feed, covering the length of the tunnel from the cottage to the house.

In the first tile, upper left corner, he saw Jud limp into the tunnel alone. Ryan's instinctive first thought was: *Where the hell is Perry now?*

Then yellow fabric flashed across his mind again, drifting away on a breeze.

His thoughts drifted with it. Back in '93, after he'd blown the last of his scholarship payout on IPO shares in an early search engine start-up that failed, it had been none other than Perry Therkle who'd covered Ryan's share of the rent at the duplex for the rest of that semester. The others had no idea. Perry hadn't told anyone about it, not even Will. As far as Ryan knew, that remained true to this day.

Motion on the cameras recentered him. He saw Jud moving with purpose: jerking the recharging plug out of the golf cart, now hopping in behind the wheel. As he pulled away from the wall and out of the frame, Ryan thought, *What is he doing?*

And all at once, in a blinding flash of perfect clarity, the answer came to him.

It wasn't until Jud pulled the door shut behind him, and she heard the heavy *thunks* of the locks reengaging, that it occurred to Kai to wonder:

Why hadn't he changed the code?

Ryan Cloverhill had remote access to the entire system. If he had the capability to upload Jud's thumbprint to the authentication routine for the tunnel on the fly, surely he had the ability to delete it. Change the access code itself. Anything he wanted.

Surely he'd gathered by now that they were ignoring his calls for a reason. That under the circumstances, Jud might be spooked enough to feel like they needed an insurance policy. That under the same circumstances, he himself was now vulnerable.

And surely it would have occurred to him—being Ryan Cloverhill—that the code to the tunnel was the only thing standing between his friends, a man whose loyalty came at a price, and the red-clover recovery plan already in progress.

So why hadn't he changed it?

Just then, as if reading her thoughts, the satphone in her hand sounded off again. Not an incoming call, this time. A simple text message:

If you ever want to see him again stop him now

The wind had kicked up. The rain was coming. While he waited for a response, Ryan placed another call.

Back at the Village, Einhorn answered after the first ring. "Here."

Finally. Somebody who remembered how to use a telephone. "Status report."

"On schedule," Einhorn said. "But I could use Jud back. Any ETA on that?"

"Unfortunately, Jud Bernal has elected to pursue opportunities outside the organization."

Silence from the other end. Then: "He what?"

"I need you to answer one question," Ryan said, raising his voice as the raindrops grew fatter, pelting his waterproof hood. He hunched against them, eyes locked on the tunnel feeds, pressing the phone to his ear with one hand. He used his other hand to hold open a coat flap, shielding the tablet screen as best he could. "And I need you to be honest."

"Copy, Boss. Go ahead."

"Is it within your capabilities to assume command of this operation?"

"I...There's noise on the line. Say again?"

"Can you finish this yourself, or not? I need your answer now."

The tablet popped another security alert. Somebody had entered the passcode on keypad unit 4.

Which meant that his message had been received. Ryan wedged the mobile with his shoulder, swiped the alert away. Jud, alone in the golf cart, had already reached the end of the first row of tiles on-screen.

"I...Yeah," Einhorn said in his ear. "Affirmative. Over."

Back at the first tile, upper left corner, Ryan saw the tunnel door opening again.

"Good," he told Einhorn as his former director of communications entered the tunnel. "Consider yourself in charge."

Then he ended the call and tapped the red-clover icon pulsing at the bottom of the tablet screen.

———

All at once she felt it: The big wave—the One—collapsing and crashing over her. Panic. Swirling darkness. No sense of direction, no air to breathe.

Heart pounding, Kai lunged for the door. She pressed her thumb against the glass, cursing the ridiculous extra second it took to open the stupid shield. The moment she could reach the keypad, she stabbed in the code Jud had given her. Another pause while the locks tumbled, then she gripped the pull handle with both hands and reared back, hauling the heavy door open...

...just in time to see Jud, in the golf cart, disappearing around the bend.

She raced five steps into the tunnel, screaming his name down the echoing corridor: "*Jay!*"

Then the whole world went white, and the big wave hit her with a force that rattled her bones. It lifted her off her feet, driving her back into a floating, ringing silence. Then nothing.

CHAPTER 32

THE MECHANICAL ROOM is down that way," Will told them, pointing down a slate-tiled utility hall off the basement game room. "But it's caged."

"What do you mean, caged?" Beau said.

"I mean locked inside a heavy-duty steel cage."

"Come on. Like an armory?"

"Or a data center," Will said. "What I'm saying is, unless one of you found a plasma torch upstairs, we're not getting to the breaker panels anytime soon."

Beau said, "What about a hacksaw?"

Will brightened immediately. "Do we have one?"

Beau's suntan darkened. "Sorry. I don't know why I said that."

Stephen nodded toward the impressive tangle of electrical wiring currently hanging out of the wall where the keypad had been. "And this?"

"Is as far as I've gotten," Will said. "No idea what I'm doing."

Emma said, "I can't believe you got this far."

"He had a Torx set in the toolbox." Will shrugged. "Couldn't find a computer hardware degree."

Using the tools at hand, he'd managed to break out the glass shield and remove the keypad from its receptacle. They were now standing in the debris of tempered glass nuggets, broken plastic connectors, bits of wiring insulation, and tiny screws scattered about the low-pile carpeting. The keypad itself lay face-down at Will's feet, disconnected, circuit board exposed.

"There were three 10-pin connectors in the back," he told them. "Thirty wires total. I separated everything and tied all the same-color wires together for a start. That takes us back to ten bundles."

"Ten numbers on the keypad," Beau said. "See? I told you you'd be able to figure this out."

"I'm not sure it's that simple."

"What do you need us to do?"

"I just need a few extra hands to help me hold wires," Will said. "And help me keep track of what happens when."

Stephen tried to keep the skepticism off his face as he looked at the bristling shrub of delicate, light-gauge wire. It looked like an unfinished diagram of the human nervous system.

Will sensed his apprehension. "I know," he said. "But listen what happens when I do this."

He carefully took the bundle of red wires in one hand, the yellow bundle in the other. He touched the exposed, twisted ends together.

Everybody waited.

Beau said, "I didn't hear anything."

"Put your ear right up to the door," Will said. "It's really quiet."

Beau complied. Will touched the wires together again. Beau frowned and said, "Emma, you try."

Stephen didn't bother mentioning that even if any of this worked, there was another keypad just like this one at the other end of the tunnel. And on the other side of that keypad were people with guns. Always assuming they didn't run into Jud Bernal before they even got that far. He loved Will Shrader, but this felt like a waste of time.

On the other hand, he saw the way Will kept glancing toward the basement window monitors. It had gone dark and rainy again outside. And where the hell *was* Jud, anyway? More importantly, where was Perry?

So he kept his mouth shut and watched in silence as Emma took Beau's place at the locked tunnel door. Will touched the wires together again. She paused before speaking, narrowing her eyes. "I'm…not sure. Kind of a hum?"

"No, it's a more like a click." Stephen could hear the frustration creeping into Will's voice. "A really faint click when I touch them together. Shit, wait. Hang on." Will flicked away the yellow bundle and grabbed the white bundle instead. "See, this is why I need help keeping track. Okay. Listen close."

Will touched the wires together.

This time, everybody looked up at the same time.

Beau said, "Holy shit."

Emma backed away from the door. "I definitely heard something that time."

Stephen heard it too: distant, percussive, undeniable. It seemed to emanate from somewhere deep in the earth. The lights flickered as the sound grew louder, becoming a sensation: a deep, heavy rumble, quickly intensifying.

Will let go of the wires as if they'd shocked him. He jumped back, eyes wide: *What did I just do?*

Behind them, a painting fell from the wall with a crash. Stephen heard a strange chattering and realized it was the sound of billiard balls vibrating together in the pockets of the nearby table.

He grabbed Emma's hand as everybody backpedaled toward the middle of the room. The window monitors looking out onto the patio began to pixelate as the lights flickered again. Stephen saw dust sifting down from the fixtures.

"What the hell *is* that?" Beau ducked his head, looking toward the ceiling as the rumble grew louder. "Do islands get earthquakes?"

As if on cue, the whole house trembled.

Stephen felt Emma's grip tighten on his. He had just enough time to think of Lainie, still locked upstairs alone, before the rumble suddenly crescendoed to a deafening roar.

CHAPTER 33

Emma was staring at the tunnel door when its smooth steel face suddenly pulped inward with an earsplitting clang, sending Will scrambling. Then a great cloud of dust billowed into the room, blotting out everything.

She coughed and choked on it. She felt arms encircling her, smelled a mixture of sweat and men's deodorant; when she opened her eyes, Emma understood that Stephen had placed himself between her and the tunnel. She smashed her face into his shirt to draw a clean breath.

Still coughing, she craned to see around him through the impossible fog. Track lights and arcade game screens flickered in the murk. Through a brief thin spot in the haze, she glimpsed the tunnel door. It was badly misshapen, hanging from its hinges, as if some hulking thing that lived in the tunnel had tried to pound its way inside the house.

But now, the creature had gone away. The rumbling had stopped. Stephen's dust-caked face inserted itself into her view again; he looked terrified, disoriented, like everything she felt just then. He was mouthing words to her, but she couldn't hear anything over the ringing in her ears.

She nodded to indicate that she was okay. Then she took his face in both hands and moved it aside, out of her way. Through the swirling dust, she glimpsed Beau picking Will up off the floor, checking him over. Will was nodding, too, digging in one ear with an index finger. Then Beau was past them like a shot, disappearing into the cloud.

She caught a flash of Will's shirt, following Beau. Emma followed Will, and Stephen followed her: out of the game room, down the main hall, toward the stairs.

The dust cloud thinned as they went. She still couldn't stop coughing. But little by little, her ears were coming back. She could hear Stephen coughing along with her; she could hear Will sputtering ten feet ahead of them; she could hear Beau calling for Lainie on his way up the stairs. Everything sounded muffled in thick felt.

By the time Emma and Stephen caught up, Lainie was on the main level, embracing Beau tightly. Beau pushed away and touched her all over with his dust-covered hands—arms, shoulders, face, hair—as if he couldn't convince himself that all the pieces were still there.

Lainie looked dazed. She was holding the tablet out in front of her like some otherworldly artifact.

"What *was* that?" Beau shouted.

Stephen said, "Is everybody okay?"

Will said, "It was an explosion. That was an explosion." His voice was ragged. "That was an explosion."

All around the main level, the window monitors had become a patchwork of malfunction. Some of them flickered. Some had gone dead. Others appeared to be working fine. The hammer-proof glass of the window looking out on the balcony, where they'd sipped coffee only just that morning, had developed a long crack from corner to corner. Outside, day had turned to night again.

Lainie shoved the tablet toward Beau. "I didn't touch any clovers. I didn't. I swear!"

Beau took the tablet from her hands. He stared blankly at the screen. Then he looked up at Stephen as if she'd handed him an ancient scroll written in a dead language.

Will said, "That was an explosion."

For a few moments, after the grid of video tiles on the tablet screen went blank, Ryan sat motionless, watching the rain spatter the glass.

He couldn't seem to pull his thoughts together. Everything had changed, and his compass was spinning. He realized that he had absolutely no idea what to do next.

Generally, when attacking a complex problem, the Ryan Cloverhill method was to dive straight in: pick something easy, accomplish it, and move on from there, one step at a time. And somehow, sitting here in the rubble of unspeakable calamity—even as he felt his own planks rotting faster by the moment—he still, God help him, seemed to be Ryan Cloverhill.

So he started with a toast.

In Perry Therkle's honor, he broke out the good stuff. It came in the form of six injector pens in a zippered hard-shell case. Each pen contained a single three-hour dose of an experimental cocktail Mags had procured through the same discreet network she used to fill his daily treatment needs.

Tucking the tablet inside his coat, Ryan took out the first pen, bit off the cap, and jabbed the short, stiff needle straight through the waterproof navigation trousers into his thigh.

Half a minute later, everything felt cottony and calm.

Don't take this until you absolutely need it, Mags had instructed. *It won't be a happy landing.*

But what a hell of a smooth flight.

If Ryan had known it was possible to live like this, he might have tried it before now. His spirit seemed borne upon the forces of the earth, rising and falling with the movement of the sea. The Roxanol was baby aspirin compared to this stuff; even the cold, pounding rain felt like it was falling on somebody else. It wasn't that the pain went away, exactly . . . but it was *so* much easier to not care.

So much easier to think.

So much easier to remember that he still had things to do. And that no matter what had happened—no matter what happened next—he couldn't do them sitting on his ass in the rain.

So he shoved the case back into its waterproof pocket, pulled himself upright, and made his way unsteadily below deck.

It was starting to get ripe down there. Judging from the mess, Amanda Driesen-Briar had lost her battle with seasickness some time ago. Her hair, now stringy and matted, hung in her face as she lolled between Val Cordero and Oliver Chen. Elijah Stanhope seemed to be reciting something to himself in a quiet rasp.

And then there was Tom Carver. Gone was the one-time college wrestling all-American whose interests included hostile takeovers and barking like a dog. In his place was a half-conscious shell of a man who looked like he could use one of Mags's magic pens. He'd had enough rope to move off the couch, a couple of feet away from the others, just inside the open master cabin. He now sat against the foot of the master double bed as if partially deflated. His eyes were clamped shut. Mouth fixed in an agonized grimace.

Bhavna Patel saw Ryan looking at him. She was the only passenger aboard the good ship Cloverhill to comment. "If he doesn't receive attention," she said, "I believe he could eventually lose his hands."

Even from the aft cabin door, Ryan could see what she meant. He'd literally forgotten all about his promise to replace the overtightened zip cuffs. Tom's wrists were now flaked with dried blood. His hands had gone an alarming shade of cyanosis-blue.

Water spattered nearby surfaces as Ryan took down his hood. Seeing his face, Bhavna's eyes widened slightly. Otherwise, her expression remained stoic. "I believe you need attention as well."

"Soon enough," he said. "Trust me."

He tossed the tablet onto the daybed in the aft cabin, next to his go-bag. Using the kitchenette countertop to steady his balance against the increasingly turbulent pitch and roll of the boat, he made his way forward, over to Tom.

From one zippered pocket, he removed a folding hawkbill boating knife. He crouched and locked open the blade. Extending one boot to brace himself against the archway, pinning Tom's hands to his own lap as firmly as he could, he worked the tip of the blade carefully beneath the ligatures. He twisted the back of the blade against Tom's clammy skin to cut his hands free.

Tom groaned but didn't open his eyes. His hands remained limp in his lap. Ryan folded the knife again, stood, and made his way back to Bhavna. From another zippered pocket he removed a .45-caliber Walther handgun.

"Congratulations." He touched her once on each shoulder with the knife's rubberized grip. "I'm appointing you first mate of the Ship of Theseus. Your primary duty, for approximately the next hour, is passenger care."

He handed her the knife.

Elijah stopped muttering. Valeria and Oliver sat up straighter.

Bhavna looked at the gun in Ryan's hand. She looked at the folded knife in hers. She looked up at him.

He pressed the muzzle of the Walther against her forehead and held her gaze. "Do you understand your responsibilities?"

After a long moment, she nodded. "I understand."

"Good. Hand the knife to Oliver."

Without taking her eyes off his, Bhavna extended her bound hands to the left. Oliver Chen suddenly looked like the kid who didn't study getting called on in class.

"Take it," Ryan said.

Oliver took the knife.

"Now, cut her hands free. Just her hands. Be very careful, it's sharp."

His own hands trembling, Oliver did as instructed. He opened the knife, licked his lips nervously, and studied the problem, immediately arriving at the safest solution: he waited for the boat to settle over a particularly high swell, then carefully hooked the knife's downcurved blade over the center locking bracket between the cuff loops. Working slowly at first, then cautiously faster, he used the blade's serrated edge to saw through.

It took a minute. When Bhavna's hands snapped apart, Oliver released a long, wheezing breath.

"Excellent," Ryan said, extending his palm. "Now close the knife and hand it back to me."

Oliver closed the knife and placed it in Ryan's palm.

Ryan lowered the gun. Bhavna never took her eyes off his. From yet another zippered pocket, he removed two spare sets of cuffs and handed them to her. "Water and food in the fridge. Med kit's over there."

"Psychopath," Tom Carver said weakly from his spot against the master bed. His eyes were open now, leaking from the corners. He seemed to be trying to remember how his fingers worked. It didn't appear to be going well. "I swear to God I'm going to find a way to make you pay for this."

"Make sure he's restrained by the time you see me again," Ryan told Bhavna. He looked to the others. "If she needs help accomplishing that task, I advise the same sort of teamwork Oliver just demonstrated." Then he pointed up at the small, black, 360-degree camera dome installed in the saloon's ceiling panels directly over his head. "I'll be watching."

With that, he worked his way back to the aft cabin and closed the door behind him.

Already he could hear the urgent whispers starting up on the other side of the door. Ryan tuned it out for now. He fixed the tablet in its wall mount, tapped the feed for the saloon cam, pulled the satphone from his coat pocket, and unzipped the go-bag. He traded the gun for his laptop. For a brief moment, he considered going for a second magic pen. But he supposed that was probably just the first pen talking.

Work first, he thought. *Then treats.*

He arranged himself on the narrow single bed, opened the laptop, and dug in.

CHAPTER 34

Kᴀɪ ʀᴇɢᴀɪɴᴇᴅ ᴄᴏɴsᴄɪᴏᴜsɴᴇss at the base of a support post, unable to see or hear. At first, she didn't think she could move. She felt encased in a block of pain.

Then she coughed, sending bolts of agony from the base of her skull down her spine, through her ribs, into her hips. She pushed herself up to her hands and knees, coughing until she retched. She produced nothing, each dry spasm of her diaphragm setting off a fresh lightning strike in her brain. She spat a long string of gritty saliva. It pooled in half an inch of dust on the floor between her hands.

The dust was everywhere. Everything around her was blanketed in it, including the air she was trying to breathe. That was why she couldn't see: anything more than a few inches beyond her face was a wall of swirling gray. Kai's scrambled thoughts flashed on the vials of souvenir ash from Mount Saint Helens a tourist could still find at shops around town. The mountain, a hundred miles to the south, had vented from a new lava dome within the past twenty years; longtimers still talked over coffee about whether it would erupt again in their lifetimes. Kai had always privately hoped that it would, and that she'd be here to see it when it did. She'd been born in a land of volcanoes, forty-five minutes by air from the belch and rumble of Kīlauea...and yet she'd never personally witnessed an event firsthand. How was that fair? Her own name meant "fire."

Had she gotten her wish?

But that didn't make sense. Nothing made sense until Jud appeared to her, as if from the cloud itself. Jud, standing in the open door to the tunnel: *Back in fifteen*. It was the last thing she could remember seeing.

Seeing him, she remembered where she was. Then the vision faded back into the cloud, and she remembered how she'd gotten there.

Kai covered her mouth with her T-shirt and tried crawling toward the stairs.

Every movement brought fresh hurt. Her back felt sprung. Her head felt cracked. Anything more than the shallowest breath was a knife in her ribs, and something was wrong with her left arm—a weakness that prevented her from supporting her own weight on that side. She tried standing, but the sharp pain in her back wouldn't allow it; the best she could manage was a stooped, awkward crouch. Even that was nearly more than she could take.

But she needed clean air. She shuffled her feet through the dust, hobbling along like an old woman, feeling her way through the cloud with one outstretched hand. She had no frame of reference and ended up at the tunnel doorway, where her vision of Jud had been standing. Now filled with jagged concrete rubble. The real Jud was still in there. Somewhere underneath all of that.

Gone.

The tunnel door had snapped free of its hinges and lay in the dust to her left. The stairs would be directly to her right. When she found them, she discovered that she couldn't raise her foot even as high as the first tread. So she lowered herself back to her knees and crawled again, tripod-style, dizzy with effort, one impossible tread at a time.

An eternity later, she collapsed on the pantry floor upstairs, among the cans and boxes that had fallen from the shelves, gasping for breath in spite of the pain it caused. Her ribs were surely broken. She knew she was badly concussed; her head was splitting, vision doubled, and the pantry spun around her. Her hearing had been replaced by a ringing emptiness. The weakness and numbness in her left arm suggested some kind of nerve damage; Kai wondered about a fracture somewhere in her spine.

But with three working limbs, she could still crawl. So that's what she did, picking her way through the rubble of dry goods into the dim, shadowy kitchen.

The underground blast had knocked out power to the cottage. How long had she been out herself? She could see the outline of her laptop sitting dark on the table. Had it already run down its battery?

The rain had only been sprinkling when they'd gone down to the cellar; now it pounded the roof and knocked at the windows as if testing for weak spots, looking for a way inside.

Kai crawled to a chair and dragged herself up. Now she saw why the laptop was dark: the keyboard was pulped and shattered, like a mouth missing half its teeth.

Ryan had issued her this unit.

And now he'd pineappled it.

The satellite handset was still downstairs. She was in no condition to go back down and find it, but it didn't matter. If he'd taken out the computer, he'd have zapped the phone too.

Somewhere in her awareness, she understood the basic facts: Ryan had wired the tunnel; he'd brought it down on Jud, intending to bury both of them; but the tunnel door hadn't yet closed behind her, and she'd been blown out backward, like a clown from a circus cannon. And now there was nothing: No power, no phone, no computer. No Jud. Kai herself was injured, stranded, and completely, utterly alone.

She sagged back to the floor, covering her eyes with her useless left arm. In that moment of despair, she did something she hadn't done since giving Lanikai Keahi's ashes to the blowhole at Kepuhi Point: she started leaking tears.

Powerless to stop them, Kai gave in and let them come. A sudden sob hit her like a pineapple charge, racking her all over with pain.

Somewhere in the flash of it, she heard Jud's voice again: *Don't forget the gizmo.*

They drifted among one another like wartime civilians in the aftermath of a bombing raid.

Emma didn't know how much time passed before she could hear properly again. Her ears still rang, but at some point she noticed that somebody had taken the heavy blankets off the world. She could hear the crackle and buzz of fried electronics. She could hear Lainie crying as she wiped at the grime on Beau's face with a wet towel from the kitchen. She could hear Will repeating the same phrase to himself, as if trying to make himself believe it: *That was an explosion.*

Then she heard Stephen say, "Something's happening."

She went to him. He showed her the tablet screen. Two words in white text, on a black background, beneath a pulsing white clover:

Updating Firmware…

She caught movement from the corner of her eye and noticed Will. He'd stumbled over to one of the fully functioning window monitors on the inland side of the house, still hacking dust from his throat.

Emma touched Stephen's hand and broke away, joining Will at this false view of the outside world, looking out at wind-whipped trees in the rain. She laid her palm gently on his shoulder.

"That was an explosion," he said.

Before she could reply, the house interrupted everything.

From silence to sudden fanfare: all around them, a familiar mechanical symphony began to play, a swirling scherzo of clunks and thunks, of invisible motors driving hidden gears. Even as Emma stood there with Will, the heavy panel in front of them began sliding open.

With it, the quality of the light inside the house began to change. The quality of sound changed with it, muted strains of wind and rain seeping in through the reexposed glass like faint strings beneath the percussion. Then came a heavy grinding sound as the panel hitched, lurched, and finally stopped, stuck in its track, leaving them with a confused hybrid view: half digital, half analog.

Around the rest of the house, panels kept sliding. Beau stood with his arms around Lainie. Lainie stood rigidly against him, pressing her hands over her ears. Eyes squeezed shut, she turned her face up toward the high empty space above them, shouting: "Will you *please stop doing that!*"

Then it was over.

They all stood frozen in place. Most of the other security panels had reopened successfully, producing a bewildering, paradoxical effect; the murky natural stormlight, and the sudden absence of giant backlit screens all around them, made the house feel strangely claustrophobic. Somehow less real.

Or maybe that was just a side effect of the faint haze already filtering up from downstairs.

Emma left Will for the moment and went to the front door. It opened with a rush of fresh, bracing air that lifted her hair away from her face, heavy with the scent of evergreens, churning salt water, and damp ground.

A flash of lightning illuminated a long, dark rupture in the earth, snaking away from the house and across the clearing, disappearing into the trees like the world's largest mole track. Wind howled through the swaying treetops. A few cold raindrops speckled the dust on her own cheeks.

They were free again to come and go, it seemed.

Still, nobody moved.

"Guys?" Stephen said. He was looking down at the tablet again.

Emma left the front door open to circulate some air. Everyone moved toward Stephen. Will got there first. Stephen held the tablet so they could all see the screen.

The device had finished its update and rebooted itself.

On-screen, Emma saw one large red clover centered on a charcoal background, with a row of white ovals beneath. She heard Ryan's voice in her head: *As you've already figured out, these are where your thumbprints go.*

Will spoke first: "Why are there only five?"

Beau said, "Huh?"

"There are only five," Will repeated, voice rising. "Why are there only five?"

Emma looked at him. Dust from the explosion had turned his hair gray. His eyes were wild. She looked back at the tablet screen and understood what he meant. Her heart went cold as she counted the ovals.

Before, there had been six, one for each of them. A red clover, a green clover, and spots for six thumbprints: Emma, Stephen, Beau, Lainie, Will, and Perry.

Now there were spots for only five thumbprints.

One red clover, five white ovals.

And Perry was still missing.

"Stephen?" Will pleaded. He grabbed the tablet from Stephen's hand, tapping and swiping at the screen with grime-caked fingers. Nothing changed. The clover pulsed brighter red, and that was all. Will gripped the edges of the tablet so tightly that tendons stood out from his wrists.

No, Emma thought. Her mind raced. She could feel her own heartbeat. *No, no, no.* It couldn't be. She wrapped her arms around Will and squeezed tightly, as if she might hold both of them together until Perry walked in through the open front door. She didn't know what else to do. Will was trembling.

"It doesn't mean anything," Stephen said. He sounded like a person desperately trying to convince himself of what he was saying. He stepped closer, placing his bandaged hand on the back of Will's neck, his other hand on the tablet. "It doesn't mean anything. Give me that stupid goddamn thing."

Then the tablet chimed.

The red clover disappeared, replaced by another live video feed.

As Will's grip melted, Emma glimpsed just enough of the screen to recognize the small aft cabin aboard the VanDutch.

Then Will sagged to the floor, leaving the tablet in Stephen's hands. Emma held him all the way down, kneeling beside him as he curled forward, burying his face in his arms. Beau and Lainie came to them, faces twisted in horror.

From the tablet, she heard Ryan's voice: distant, disembodied, devoid of inflection. Trapped in a flat, rubberized rectangle of circuits and glass.

"I need to see everybody," the voice said.

CHAPTER 35

Back in college, there had been this movie about a rock-and-roll vampire that used to play on late-night cable. It was too ridiculous to resist, and Stephen and Ryan must have seen it two dozen times. Sometimes it was just on in the background. Sometimes they'd get high on the ratty couch and cackle their way through it together. By the end of its run, either one of them could quote it on the fly without looking up from whatever they were studying.

In the movie, part of the vampire's stage garb was an amulet that made it look vibrant and alluring to hot gothy groupies. But in the end, when finally stripped of the charm, the creature shriveled, showing its true form: ancient, ravaged, hideous.

Ryan Cloverhill had been stripped of his charm.

Pinned to the big screen, he looked like a corrupted version of himself: gaunt, yellow, splotchy. Hollowed-out. His eyes were scorched red. His hair lay matted against his scalp. It occurred to Stephen that he actually did resemble Sylvester a little. Was the cancer the only phenomenon of nature that had mummified him?

"What Perry did, he did for you guys," Ryan went on pointlessly, swaying back and forth with the rocking of his boat. He'd muted their end of the connection so that they could hear him, but he couldn't hear them. This was strictly a monologue, closed for comments. "Never forget that, Will. No matter what."

Will sat on the floor, elbows on his knees, head hanging. Every few moments his shoulders quaked. Emma sat at his left, stroking his back. Lainie sat up on the couch on Will's right, a hand on his shoulder. Beau sat next to her, staring at the floor. Stephen stood behind them all, jaw clamped. It was all he could do to remain stationary.

"What my people did, they did for themselves. I won't disrespect Perry by pretending my own reasons mean anything now. It was a catastrophic failure of imagination on my part that brought us to this. And that's supposed to be my department."

Imagination?

A failure of *imagination*?

Stephen was having one of those himself. He failed to imagine how Will Shrader would ever be the same again. He failed to imagine how life for any of them could ever be the same again. He failed to imagine how he could keep standing here, caked in dirt, giving an audience to this travesty.

Clinical diagnoses truly weren't his area, but what would he guess? Some turbocharged strain of narcissistic personality disorder? Straight-up delusional psychosis? How could Ryan Cloverhill continue to pass as himself, yet be so far gone as to believe—truly believe—that locking the six of them inside the most outlandish Trolley Problem ever devised might somehow fix his world? At least the vampire from the movie had an excuse: he was a vampire.

And what would an excuse matter anyway? Would it help Will, or anyone else, to know what the *Diagnostic and Statistical Manual of Mental Disorders* might have to say about Ryan Cloverhill? It still wouldn't change the fact that Perry had stepped outside this morning to sit with Stephen for a few minutes on the stoop. And somehow, unthinkably, he'd never returned.

Outside, the wind seemed to have blown itself out, making way for a steady downpour. Inside, a faint veil of dust still hung in the air. From the balcony windows, you could barely see the ocean for the rain.

"As you can see by the update, the red path is still open," Ryan said. "You don't need the green clover anymore. That's yours, including Perry's share, whatever you decide. You'll be contacted with details. I took the liberty of removing the library and Chamber. At this point there's nothing you need there either, and I had to keep my build time down." He grimaced sharply, drew a hitching breath. "Meanwhile, Jud's second-in-command tells me we're nearly prepped. He's been promoted. The schedule has changed. One way or another, this will all be over by sunrise. Which makes this the last time we'll see each other."

He finally looked at the screen. Stephen hardly recognized the tortured animal he saw in his former friend's inferno-red eyes.

"It was a mistake to involve you," he said. "Believe it or not, in this malfunctioning piece of meat I call my brain, it all played differently. But here's my last promise: I won't let Perry's death come to nothing." Ryan took a long look at them. "I can't tell you how important you've been to me. I love you all."

With that, he reached out and killed the connection. Both screens went black simultaneously: the big television in front of them, the smaller tablet on the coffee table.

In the cavernous silence that followed, only the tablet screen faded back to life: One red clover.

The gizmo.

Unlike her laptop and satphone, the VirtuaLink prototype—aka Gulliver—was designed to be used exclusively over a broadband cloud network. The firmware was stored entirely in flash ROM. Advantage: no Pineapple Drive.

Under normal circumstances, all development and testing for the Gulliver project was conducted in secure, climate-controlled, air-gapped server rooms back at Link Labs. But Ryan sometimes liked to review hardware implementations on his weekends out here on the Rock, so the eggheads had set up an encrypted sandbox he could access via Hermes Junior 1, the new corporate test satellite for the western hemisphere. So while Kai couldn't use Gulliver to access the actual internet from out here, nor emergency services, nor any corporate file shares or source code repositories, she'd discovered that she did have access to something else:

Sham Rock's protected, closed-loop device channel.

Gully's remote access client had yet to make it into a test build, which meant that she had no way of actually overriding control of Ryan's tablet, or the tablet in the house, from the cottage. But she did have a command shell.

And pillows.

With enough of them piled up against one another, Kai found she could lie back on the bed at a cushioned angle that made her pain tolerable. Suffering limited dexterity in her deadened left hand made getting into the haptic fingertips a struggle. Eventually, the wires and sensors would have been sewn into slip-on biometric gloves; she could have used an early pair of those now.

Instead, she used her right hand to rig up her left, one numb finger at a time, then her mouth to help with the rest. Then she ditched the gear she wouldn't need, fitted the headset, and held the power button long enough to boot straight into assistance mode.

The backlighting from inside the goggles was like an ice pick in each retina. Kai squinted her eyes down to slits as she plucked at the air in front of her, calling up the stock visual calibration utility. The first thing she did was select a precision tint filter designed to reduce headaches and eye strain associated with all manner of conditions—including traumatic brain injury.

When she could open her eyes without wanting to vomit, she experimented with her own blurred vision. The eventual goal was to allow users who fell within the correctable visual impairment range to upload their prescription information automatically, enabling them to operate Gulliver without their regular eyeglasses or contact lenses. For demonstration purposes, the manual interface was designed to look like an optometrist's Phoroptor; by manipulating the intuitive, three-dimensional holographic contraption with her fingers, she was able to switch out virtual lenses until she found the optimal settings on her own. "Optimal" was a loose term, but it helped.

Next, under the dexterity menu, she dialed in a movement map to accommodate her weakened left hand. The extrapolation engine allowed her to improve her range of motion virtually, despite her compromised motor control in the outside world.

Then on to SoundStation, where she played with the volume and equalization settings, amplifying and sweetening the audible feedback until it sounded less muffled and garbled to her ringing ears.

Before long, interface-Kai felt close enough to whole that it actually became easier to ignore how much it still hurt real-world-Kai to breathe.

She focused her attention on interface-Kai. To the dim, empty bedroom, she said, "Connect."

Within a few seconds, the unit had located the satellite connection and initialized a user session. There were three rudimentary demo environments currently under development, which Ryan called Facades: the lobby of the Waldorf Astoria Hotel in New York City, the command bridge of the USS *Enterprise*, and the last environment she'd been playing around with earlier that afternoon before Therkle and Rollins had barged in.

Facade number three was a reproduction of the Spanish Colonial street foyer of a historic movie theater: the Castro in San Francisco. Kai swapped out full-body ambulation for a virtual joystick, then proceeded by hand beneath the glowing red-and-gold neon marquee. She crossed the cathedralesque glazed-tile entryway to the ornate, freestanding ticket booth.

As an inside joke among the developers, the avatar behind the window was a video-realistic rendering of real-life Ryan Cloverhill. He grinned as she approached. "Back already?" he said in Ryan's voice. "Good to see you again, Kai. How can I help?"

Kai answered aloud, to nobody: "Nice try, motherfucker. You missed. This is a two-player game now."

Avatar-Ryan cocked his head, portraying a quizzical expression. "Sorry, what was that?" The so-called Uncanny Valley effect—that feeling of eeriness an *almost*-lifelike humanoid figure tended to evoke in real human observers—grew stronger. "I didn't understand."

In real life, rain pounded the shingles of the cottage overhead; Gulliver's external auditory receptors translated the sound to rain inside the interface, tattooing the wet sidewalk with high-definition droplets behind her, beyond the shelter of the marquee. Just to show avatar-Ryan who was boss, Kai pulled down a control panel and tapped the ambient mirror setting to off. The rain beyond the marquee stopped abruptly, as if she'd turned off a showerhead. Who was the wizard now?

"I love the city after a rain," avatar-Ryan observed.

"Eat my ass. I'm here to see *Network*."

The ticket machine whirred and spat out a stub. Avatar-Ryan tore off the ticket and passed it through the window with a toothy smile. "Enjoy!"

"Fuck you." She confirmed her selection by snatching the ticket on her way to the lobby doors.

Kai pulled a door open and stepped, weightless, into a vast, glittering star field. The sensation of motion made her feel dizzy and nauseated all over again. She pulled down the control panel and deactivated the GyroLink feature. The floating sensation disappeared as a glossy black floor appeared beneath her, a vast obsidian plane stretching out to infinity, reflecting the stars.

She waited there a moment, lying very still on the bed. Already she felt leaden, exhausted. Without the motion system, gravity seemed to pull her down. Her head was pounding so severely, the pressure behind her eyes increasing so steadily, that she began to wonder about the possibility of an intercranial bleed.

It took everything she had to keep her eyes open. Kai gazed out into the star field, focusing on the blinking lights and solar wings of the much larger object suspended there. It took eons for the nausea to fade. But finally it passed.

When it did, Kai Keahi reached into the cosmos and grabbed herself a satellite.

Will heaved himself forward and snatched up the tablet. Without hesitating, he pressed his thumb against a white oval and held it there.

Nothing happened.

He growled in his chest and shook the tablet. Then his aptitude for problem-solving kicked in: he sucked dirt off his thumb, wiped his thumb on his shirt, and pressed it to the glass again.

This time, the tablet played a happy chime. From his standing position behind the couch, Stephen watched the white oval turn into a green clover. Thumbprint 1: check.

Four white ovals left.

Will stood to his feet and wheeled on them all, face contorted. Without a word, he extended his trembling hand, offering the tablet to all takers.

Nobody moved. Stephen felt paralyzed. He didn't know what to say or do.

Emma beat him to it. "Oh, God, Will." She started to stand up. "Oh, honey."

The sound of her voice seemed to bring Will back to himself. The mask of rage slipped away, dragging the light in his eyes along with it. He looked down at the tablet in his hands as if he'd just noticed it there.

Stephen finally unglued himself, moving around the couch to join Emma. Will looked back and forth between the two of them. He took two reflexive steps away, retreating, stumbling as he caught his heel against the base of the coffee table behind him. For a moment, Stephen thought he was going down to the floor, but Will managed to catch his balance in time. He looked at the tablet as if it anchored him somehow.

Then he threw back his head and screamed. It was an awful sound. A long, keening wail of simple pain. As Stephen moved past Emma, she reached out and stopped him. Together, they stood and watched Will raise the tablet high over his head, then slam it to the floor.

The tablet merely bounced in its shockproof case, skidding to a rubbery stop on the hardwood a few feet away. Fresh rage seemed to drive Will after it, stooping to snatch the device up again. He looked around, then ran past both of them. At first, Stephen thought he was heading straight for the front door, which Emma had left open to the rain-laden breeze.

Instead, he swung the tablet with both hands, forehand-smashing the screen into one petrified corner of the dining room tabletop, its ancient heartwood long transformed to stone.

Stephen heard the crunch of glass. He felt Emma take his hand as Will slammed the tablet against the table again and again, blow after pulverizing blow. Glittering chips of glass flew. Bits and pieces of circuit board spun away. Will was panting, swept up in a frenzy now, beating the tablet to pieces as if Ryan Cloverhill actually lived somewhere inside.

When the tablet was nothing more than a warped platter of mangled aluminum and crushed circuitry, he threw it down on the table. But it still wasn't enough. He grabbed the table, roaring as he lifted, toppling the massive, heavy piece onto its side with a deafening, floor-cracking *bang*.

Stephen caught movement in his peripheral vision, saw that Beau and Lainie had joined them from the couch. Twenty feet away, Will stood with his back to them all—head down, arms hanging, finally spent. His shoulders rose and fell with each ragged breath.

Without a word, they moved toward him as a group.

But as they approached, Will straightened abruptly, cocking his head. He turned to look at them, confusion on his face. For a moment, he seemed not to know where he was.

Everybody stopped. Emma said, "Will?"

He blinked at her. Did he even recognize her face? Stephen honestly couldn't tell.

Beau raised his palms and said, "It's us, man. We're right here. Let's get a drink and sit down."

Without warning, Will bolted toward the open front door.

Lainie cried after him: "Will!"

Just then, beyond the open door, a column of brilliant white light raked across the pergola, flooding the entire front walkway, throwing crazy shadows against the pouring rain. Once more, the image of the hovering Space Needle flashed in Stephen's mind. Crazily, he thought: *They're finally here.*

Then a new sound emerged above the pounding white noise of the rain. A familiar rhythmic thumping—a version of the same sound he'd heard back in the cottage with Perry, hours ago. Stephen realized he'd been hearing it without even noticing, behind the storm, somewhere in between the low rumble of thunder and the cataclysm of Will Shrader's collapse.

A crackling, modulated announcement boomed toward them from somewhere inside the light. At first, Stephen couldn't make sense of it.

Then the announcement came again, and his heart skipped a beat. Even in his confusion, he felt a swell of melancholy pride. *He did it*, he thought. *The crazy beanpole actually made it happen.*

He wanted to laugh, wanted to cry, wanted to stop feeling what he was feeling. It seemed too horrible to contemplate, too much to accept. But based on what Ryan had told them had happened at the light tower, it might as well have been Perry Therkle himself, calling down to them from above:

"I repeat: This is the United States Coast Guard. If anyone in the house can hear the sound of this voice..."

GREEN FOR GO

CHAPTER 36

EVER SINCE THE diagnosis, Ryan Cloverhill had spent a fair amount of time thinking about time. Not just how much or little of it he might have left, but how much of it had passed. What he'd done with his. And what it had done with him.

He could think of himself as a kid, alone in his room at home. He could think of himself now. Somewhere deep down, he felt the same now, alone in his room at Sham Rock—or at the penthouse in town, or on Red Mountain in Aspen, or in some inarguably excellent hotel on the road, with other people or without them—as he'd felt in that creaky upstairs bedroom of a drafty, affection-free Tudor back in Fuller at nine years of age.

And yet, to find the image of Ryan Cloverhill that looked most like the selfie he carried around in his mind, he'd have to scroll back to Bardsley—the last version of himself he truly recognized.

Prior iterations seemed unfinished, subsequent releases subtly compromised. It was as if each passing year since Stillwater had replaced something old with something new, until eventually, there was no way to clearly identify which parts were original. If, one day, something in the engine room sprang a leak and blew the whole vessel apart, how would you even begin to start putting it all back together again?

Would it even be possible?

"Negative," he said into the handset. "Civic data trends from the past five Labor Day weekends puts minimum traffic density for the area between 3:15 and 4:30 a.m. How long to inspect?"

"Fourteen hours," Einhorn told him. "Seven buildings. Two hours per structure. That's what tomorrow was for, and it was already tight."

He was a good man, Einhorn. But he was no Jud Bernal. "I'm aware of the challenges, Terrance. Would you feel more comfortable with Turner in command?"

A pause.

Then: "We can get by with a spot check. Ready for preliminary detonation by oh-three-oh-five."

"That's top-notch adapting and overcoming," Ryan said. "Now, listen carefully, this is impor—"

But he never got a chance to finish the thought.

A sudden blow rocked him like a brick to the head, knocking him off the bed. Suddenly, he was numb in one hand and deaf in one ear. It was as if he'd lit a firecracker and pressed it against his face until it exploded.

The handset had clattered up against the closed cabin door. Disoriented, Ryan grabbed the phone and immediately felt the heat of its misshapen casing, saw the shattered screen, but he couldn't make sense of it. He smelled the scorched components and knew instantly what had happened, though he couldn't understand why. Within the vast spectrum of natural conditions to be found on planet Earth, the Pineapple Drive was essentially malfunction-proof. What had just occurred should not have been possible.

He dragged himself back up to the bed, still shaking the cobwebs out of his head. Now he felt pain: a skewer in his ear, a hot sting around a numb spot on his cheek, painful tingling in his fingertips.

He reached out and grabbed the tablet from its dock. In the moment before the screen woke up, he caught a glimpse of his own reflection in the glass. It was like glimpsing a stranger. Then the screen popped to life where he'd left it, on the open video chat window, and now he was looking at himself through the onboard camera—essentially a high-definition version of the same reflection.

There was a line of blood trailing from his right ear. A scorch mark already ringed with blisters on his cheekbone. His eyes looked hollow and bloodshot, hair matted with grease. Even to himself, he looked like a man who'd been beaten.

He swiped his own image away and called up the network dashboard.

Before he could say "event log," the screen shattered and went black. The tablet flopped out of his hands and tumbled to the floor.

"What are you *doing?*" he shouted, as if the devices could explain themselves. "You can't be serious!"

He reached back onto the bed and pulled over his go-bag: spare tablet, spare phone, the chunky development laptop he'd used to slam out the update he'd pushed to Sham Rock.

Bang went the spare phone.

Bang went the spare tablet.

Kabang went the high-spec laptop, spitting out keys like teeth.

Each time it happened, it couldn't have happened. With each mini-blast, the gasps and jabbering and general commotion escalated from the cheap seats on the other side of the cabin door, only adding to the clamor in his head. It wasn't the first time today he wished he'd left all their gags in. Ryan hurled a hot pulped handset at the door, shouting at the whole world to shut the hell up, for Christ's sake, and just let him *think*. Because this wasn't possible.

Yet it was happening. And it could only be happening one way:

Somewhere, somehow, *somebody* was hitting each device with a Pineapple command the moment it came online. It was as if his overstressed brain couldn't comprehend the riddle itself, let alone begin to solve it, until the answer suddenly dawned on him, obvious and fully intact. Because there was only one answer possible.

Kai stripped off the headset and finally closed her eyes. She waited for that little voice that sounded a lot like her mother to tell her what to do next.

It was a jolt, returning to the oppressive physics of the real world after the assistive capabilities of the interface. Everything felt so much...heavier. She thought of a LinkStream interview she'd once seen with an American astronaut. He'd just returned to Earth after nearly a year in zero gravity aboard the International Space Station. The man had come back physically taller, only to begin the slow process of shrinking back down to size. He couldn't walk right for a period of time. Everything hurt. His extremities had swollen from the redistribution of his own bodily fluids. *Gravity*, he'd said, *gets you down*.

Gravity and bomb blasts.

She needed a doctor. Even through her jittering eyelids, the light from the bedroom spiked her eyes, intensified the pounding behind them.

What light, KK?

Power's out. Remember?

Her eyes sprang open. The bedroom was still dark, compounding her confusion.

Then the light came again: a brilliant white beam glancing across the rain-speckled windowpanes. As it did, her swollen brain finally caught up to her ears. A new sound resolved itself, emerging from the steady thrum of rain on the roof:

Helicopter rotors.

Somehow, Kai.

As the central communications hub for this operation, she was the only person on the team—the only person on the planet—he'd entrusted with the command syntax a person would need to accomplish what she'd just accomplished. In the event he didn't make it through to the end of this thing, he'd needed to leave somebody he trusted in charge of handling a few small but crucial cleanup routines, beginning with the tablet inside the house.

But how?

How had she managed it? He'd taken out her devices. He'd watched every last one of them go off-line, including Jud's spare in the Sikorsky. Clearly, she'd survived the tunnel. But *how?*

It didn't matter. However she'd done it, Kai had left him dead in the water.

Except for one last life ring:

He dove back into the go-bag, realizing he still had the pile of devices he'd liberated from the gang upon their arrival at the Rock.

Ryan started pulling standard-issue, Dick-and-Jane smartphones from the bottom of the bag, one after another, powering them on one at a time, then tossing them aside. Each one was locked with a passcode...until he got to Stephen's.

Naturally. He mused at the stock, factory-default screen saver. Zero photos saved in the camera roll. Just a crammed-full music library. The model itself was about nine years out-of-date. In short: The phone was Stephen Rollins through and through. A man who had, inexplicably, devoted his entire working career to a widely discredited device that hadn't evolved significantly since the 1950s.

He'd installed the Link app, though. It was hard not to find that sort of touching.

But the outdated piece-of-shit internal antenna was picking up only one bar's worth of signal out here. Roaming.

Ryan pulled up the dialer anyway and punched in a number from memory. Nobody answered. Part of him almost felt glad. He was calling from an unfamiliar number, Chicago area code... There was something vaguely refreshing about somebody following the rules for a change.

But only vaguely. He tried again, then again, letting each call ring all the way through to voice mail until finally, after six more crackling, static-chopped rings, Einhorn finally broke protocol and answered: "Wrong number, asshole. Stop calling it."

"It's me," Ryan said. "Change of plans."

Long pause. "Mr. Clov... Oh."

"Listen carefully."

"I, uh... Is this... Sir, do you mean to be calling me in the clear right now?"

"Exceptional circumstances," Ryan told him. "I'm coming back in. You now have three hours. Be ready."

"Hang on. You're breaking up."

"*Be ready. Three hours,*" Ryan shouted into the phone. "And if you see Kai Keahi before you see me, shoot her."

He ended the call without waiting for a response. He grabbed his coat, shoving Stephen's phone into a pocket. Then he fished around until he found the pocket containing the last thing he needed: his zippered hard-shell pen case.

It hadn't been anywhere near three hours yet, and he could already hear Mags in his head: *If you chain-smoke these, expect your heart to explode somewhere around dose three. Be advised.*

Terms and conditions accepted.

He jabbed the second pen into his leg.

Then he zipped up the case, zipped up the bag, struggled into the coat, and zipped that up too. Then he grabbed the Walther and opened the cabin door to captive pandemonium.

Everybody was standing, shifting around, struggling to maintain their balance with the rocking of the boat, clucking like chickens as they banged against one another. *What was that sound? What's happening? Please tell us what you want. Please think of our families.*

And these were the people who believed themselves qualified to take control of the Linkverse?

Fat chance. He fired three rounds up the open stairwell, into the rain.

Instantly, the clucking changed to yelps and screams. Everything down below got extremely loud for a few seconds. Then extremely quiet.

When he saw that he finally had their attention, he said, "Good news, folks. You caught a break. If you'll return to your seats and prepare for departure, I'll be getting us underway."

A surge of adrenaline drove Kai up from the bed and hobbling to the window. Her first thought was nonsensical: *Jud?*

The sound of the rotors was fading already. She chased it, a lurching hobble through the darkened cottage, out the front door, to the edge of the porch. In the dim light of the storm, through the curtain of rain, she saw the search-and-rescue beam tracking along a truly amazing sight: a long, wide track of plowed earth leading from the edge of the front porch into the timber.

Above the column of light, she recognized the aircraft's silhouette and tail stripe from her mission prep. It was a Coast Guard MH-65 Dolphin. It had scanned the darkened cottage with its powerful spotlight and was now moving across the island, following the track all the way to the big house on the other side.

Help had arrived.

Medical attention had arrived.

Authorities had arrived.

Apprehension, custody, and eventual incarceration had arrived.

Kai tried to think. Her mind felt addled, fuzzy, as if she'd left her core processor back inside the interface. How could she explain this? The trapped houseguests, the collapsed tunnel, her unrestricted presence here...It was her job to know how to spin things. But nobody could possibly spin this.

Anything you could do, you've already done, she heard her mother say. *You can't go back and do any of it over again. Time to rest now, KK. You need help.*

You couldn't exactly argue with that voice.

But you could tune it out, if you tried hard enough. Kai had practiced that a lot recently.

Except this time, she must have tuned herself out in the process. Because the next thing she knew, she was somehow standing in the screen-enclosed porch at the back of the house, go-bag at her feet, holding a wet suit in her hands.

She couldn't remember leaving the front porch. Had no recollection of finding her way back through the darkened cottage. All at once she simply looked up, and... there she was. As if the real world were just another big interface, and she'd stumbled onto a cheat code by accident.

Not a good sign, KK.

Mags and Luna kept a pair of stand-up paddleboards back here. Fourteen-footers for day touring in big water. There were wet suits still hanging on drying racks in the corner.

They'd left it all behind. Kai could hardly blame them. Their job was complete; why travel heavy? When Mags and Luna got where they were going, they'd be able to afford new wet suits. They'd be able to afford to never wear the same wet suit twice for the rest of their lives.

Grinding her teeth through the pain, Kai stripped down and struggled into one of their discarded hand-me-downs. Luna's, she presumed—the two of them were similar enough in height and build to make it work.

You can't even stand up straight.

Yeah, well, she didn't have to stand. She could kneel on the board. She could lie down on her stomach and hang on. She could do anything she needed to do.

Except breathe without crying. Or pick up a sick cat with that arm of yours. Come on, keiki. You really think you're lugging that thing all the way down the bluff in a rainstorm?

Why the hell not? Pain was just the body's way of trying to hold you back in life. Screw pain. Besides, that was what carry straps were for: carrying things. She still had one good arm. She could drag the damn board behind her by the straps if she had to. She could crawl all the way to the dock off the spit if that's what it took. Once she was on the water, she'd be weightless again.

And then what? Seven miles through hard chop. On that thing. Sure.

I can do it.

With a concussion so bad you lost time just now.

Maybe next time I'll wake up onshore.

Maybe next time you wake up, you'll be drowning.

Then I'll drown. *Kai* means "sea." It doesn't mean "prison cell."

Don't tell me what your name means. I'm the one who gave it to you. And this is the last thing you'll do with it?

Kai understood that she was only arguing with herself, no matter how much the voice sounded like her mom. It was pointless. Just a way to stall. Beyond the porch screens, the rain was already letting up.

Or maybe it was raining harder. Who cared? All that mattered was that time was running out. They'd be here soon. And then she'd spend the rest of her life wishing she'd drowned herself when she'd had the chance.

"No dick-dragging," she said, working her arms into the sleeves. She zipped herself in.

This time, the voice didn't have an answer.

CHAPTER 37

It was to have been a long, lazy, device free weekend: a chance for the seven of them to unplug, catch up, and enjoy one another's company for the first time in too many years.

Five of them lifted off the Rock in the rain that Saturday evening, hardly more than twenty-four hours after they'd first touched down.

The big orange helicopter waiting on Ryan Cloverhill's rooftop tennis court—the helipad being currently occupied, and the rain-soaked ground deemed too soft for landing—had capacity for up to twelve passengers. The flight crew consisted of three men and two women—two pilots, a mechanic, one paramedic, and one orange-suited rescue swimmer who hadn't needed to get wet. Even counting them, Stephen couldn't fail to notice how much capacity they had to spare.

At least on paper. "Sorry about the elbow room," Petty Officer Williams called out over the howl of the rotors. "Gets a little cramped in here with this many."

She slid the bay door closed behind her, pounded the back of the copilot's chair, and duckwalked over to help Stephen with his harness, water streaming from her rain gear. She'd replaced the bandage on his wrist with a clear vinyl air splint that went past his fingertips. The sight of his own hand inside the splint made Stephen think of Sylvester in his display case. He imagined the placard: *This was once a real human hand. Through the fateful foolishness of its owner, it caused the sequence of events that led to the death of Perry Wayne Therkle, aged 51 years.*

He stared at it as Williams finished strapping him in. She gave his harness a tug, then seemed finally to hear her own words: *Gets a little cramped in here with this many.*

"Sorry," she said. "Dumb thing to say."

Stephen didn't hold it against her. She was right, after all: It wasn't nearly as comfortable as the helicopter that brought them here. There was no leather upholstery, no sweeping views. Definitely no quiet. He didn't see a cocktail holder anywhere.

What he saw were functional hard surfaces and lots of important-looking equipment tied down with canvas straps. Nobody squabbled over the bare-bones jump seats. This time, Will Shrader had to be sedated just to climb aboard. Not because he'd gone phobic about flying again, but because it was the only way they could get him to leave Perry behind, unrecovered, alone on the island without them. But based on the radio chatter Stephen had picked up, it appeared to be Coast Guard protocol to avoid remaining stationary longer than absolutely necessary on or within any structure that may or may not be wired to explode.

"Where will you take us?" Emma called.

"UWMC," the copilot called back. Ensign somebody.

"University of Washington Medical Center," Petty Officer Williams clarified. "We'll get you there safe. Sit back and save your strength, folks. Long night ahead."

The chopper lifted, creating the sensation of suspended gravity all around them.

In the past hour, Sham Rock had become the most popular law enforcement destination in the Salish Sea. Through the far bay window, Stephen caught the pulsing bleed of red and blue from the waterline somewhere below them, flashing against the bluffs, refracted by the rain. He couldn't pick up everything he overheard, but he'd gathered that a bomb disposal unit out of Port Angeles had finally arrived at the spit. Robots had found the cottage empty so far.

As they ascended, Lainie said, "It's in his brain." It was the first Stephen had heard her speak in an hour; over the rotor noise, and the drumbeat of rain on the hull, he barely heard her at all.

Emma called back: "What?"

"The cancer," Lainie said, raising her voice. Her hair hung around her face in wet tangles. "He put all his medical reports in the library. I read what I could understand. Up in our room."

In the jump seat next to her, Beau took her hand. "He told us pancreas."

"It spread. Meta-neo-something." She looked toward Petty Officer Williams, strapped in against a bulkhead in back. "Do you know what I'm trying to say?"

"Metastatic neoplasm?" Williams answered. "Just a guess. I'm not an oncologist."

"What does that mean?"

"It just means secondary tumor."

"Then that's what I mean," Lainie said. "The case notes said it was rare. Less than one percent."

"Jesus," Emma said. "Ry."

"One doctor was surprised he could still talk," Lainie said. "None of them give him past Christmas."

Stephen heard Ryan's voice in his mind: *Pancreas. For starters.*

And then there was the latest hit, destined to be a classic: *Believe it or not, in this malfunctioning piece of meat I call my brain, it all played differently.*

Beau stared at the puddles of dirty water on the bare sheet-metal floor. Will turned his face and stared into space. Stephen didn't know where to look, so he looked at Emma. She had tears in her eyelashes.

They turned slowly in place, then tilted forward, out over the water, leaving Sham Rock behind. Stephen shifted in his seat, trying to get comfortable, but he couldn't. Some harness buckle poked him every time he moved. He couldn't find anything, then realized that the hard object in his ribs was something pinned beneath the harness, not part of the harness itself.

He forced his good hand awkwardly down inside his jacket and worked to pull out a CD: Jane's Addiction's first album, liner insert faded, jewel case clouded with age.

He stared at it until his eyes blurred. When he felt Emma's hand on his arm, Stephen looked at her again, strapped into her own seat next to him. In a flash, a whole life passed across the screen behind his eyes: a life that might have been . . . had it all played differently.

He saw the wedding at Lake Itasca they'd once imagined. He saw a moving day: from the apartment they'd shared while Emma was in law school to some starter home they'd never ended up purchasing. A cozy little bungalow on a leafy street in Oak Park, maybe. Everybody was there—Lainie and Beau, Will and Perry, even Ryan—pissing and moaning and laughing and pranking each other as they all pitched in to help lug furniture. He saw them coming home to that cozy little bungalow from a hospital, laden with terrifying supplies. The tightly wrapped bundle in Emma's arms was the child who'd had much better timing in the beginning and hadn't miscarried in the end. He saw that child tossing his or her high school mortarboard into the air. He saw another moving day: Into a residence hall, this time. Maybe one of the dorms at Bardsley. Maybe—good God—even a too-small, painted cinder-block room somewhere on the second floor of Anders Hall.

In between, he saw Christmases and birthdays, skinned knees and report cards, a younger brother or sister joining the mix. He saw the Stillwater Seven expanded instead of reduced: normal reunions at normal places, a bunch of little kids running around, raising hell together. Will and Perry had stuck it out and carried through with that adoption they'd pursued once upon a time. One of Ryan's marriages had worked.

Then the movie dissolved, and he was once again looking at a battered old CD in his hand. Honestly, he'd forgotten it was missing from his collection a long time ago. Who bothered with CDs anymore?

And Emma. The sorrow in her face reflected everything he felt, said everything anyone needed to say. She squeezed his arm, appraising him with such a depth of understanding that he couldn't seem to breathe.

I'm not crying, he thought, scraping the backs of his knuckles across his own eyes. *You're crying.*

The best part about piloting an 1,800-horsepower twin-inboard luxury watercraft with a shredded bimini top and overworked bilge pump more than fifty choppy nautical miles from the San Juan Islands, just south of Canadian waters, across the strait and down the Sound, all the way to Link Village, just north of downtown Seattle, doing thirty knots in a pounding rainstorm with burning

coals in your gut, was the relatively light boat traffic one could expect to encoun-
ter at Ballard Locks, which managed the Ship Canal between Shilshole and
Salmon Bays.

Unless, of course, your worst fears came true, and you found the whole operation temporarily shut down due to lightning over the bay.

Plan B.

Or was it plan Q, at this point? Ryan diverted toward the seawall, cut power,
and dropped anchor under Salmon Bay Bridge. The sudden shelter from the
rain felt like heaven. His hands were so numb with cold that they felt lifeless,
like useless blobs of rubber. It took him ages to work the Walther out of its
pocket.

He dragged himself out of the captain's seat and made his way down below
for his go-bag. The combined tang of vomit and body odor hit him in the face
like an open baggie full of warm garbage. He tried not to breathe through his
nose as he addressed his extremely seasick former governing board one last time.

"Congratulations," he told them. "You've survived the retreat."

Back in cuffs, just as instructed, Tom Carver croaked, "What now?"

"Somewhere on this boat is the same knife I used to restore your circulation
earlier," Ryan said. "There's no reason to think you won't find it if you work
together as a unit. You're welcome, by the way."

"Go to hell."

"We'll see."

Bhavna stood and faced him. She looked like she'd been through a wringer
in both directions twice, but she stood and faced him. "What will you do now?"

"Gotta run in to the office," he said. "Shouldn't take long."

"You can still stop." She paused, then added, "The spirit of the battle is still
in the ship."

He smiled. What a bunch of bullshit. "Stopping this was somebody else's job.
Good luck to you, Bhav."

With that, he turned and went back above deck, leaving them all below. He
hustled over to the starboard gunwale, tossed the go-bag atop the seawall, and
climbed up after it, back into the rain.

Ryan scrambled up the slick embankment of grass and mud to a waist-high, galvanized steel safety fence. He tossed the bag over and gritted his teeth, groaning as he flopped over the fence into Commodore Park.

He picked himself up, slung the bag across his body, and hustled up to the footpath. He followed the path through rain-splashed puddles, finding momentary shelter again beneath the rusty steel bridge trusses passing over Commodore Way. He pulled Stephen's phone from its waterproof pocket.

His options from here, he realized, were somewhat limited. Einhorn certainly couldn't spare anybody to come pick him up. Mags and Luna would be halfway to São Tomé by now. Nobody else on the project team was closer than an hour away.

Screw it. Stephen did have the Link app, after all. And Ryde was a partner vendor.

The light of the phone screen threw apocalyptic shadows beneath the side span as he opened the app, which hadn't been updated in who knew how long.

Jesus.

Of course. Whose idea had it been to force people to wait for these things?

At least it wasn't raining on him. He watched the progress wheel spin as the update downloaded and installed itself. Ryan took off his waterlogged ball cap to keep the bill from dripping all over the cracked screen as he booked the nearest driver. He wondered if Rollie would see the humor when he finally discovered he'd paid for this stupid ride.

Within twelve minutes, a silver Nissan SUV rolled into the public parking lot twenty yards from where Ryan waited under the span. Its headlight beams sliced through the rain as the vehicle swung around. He shouldered his bag and hustled out to meet it.

As he approached, the driver rolled down his window a few inches, put his mouth close to the gap, and called, "You gotta be Stephen?"

"That's me," Ryan called back, splashing through puddles. The driver—Jamie, according to the app—saw his bag, sighed, and started opening his door. Even in a rainstorm, he couldn't risk a ding on his star rating.

Ryan waved him off with one hand. "Nope, stay dry. I got it."

"Right on." The door closed. The window went up again.

Ryan hurried around to the passenger side, opened the rear door, tossed in the bag, and piled in after it. It was so warm inside he thought he might cry. The interior smelled pleasantly of vanilla. It made his stomach roll. "You're a lifesaver, thanks."

Jamie laughed. "Great night for ducks, right?" He had a stack of dry towels beside him in the passenger seat. He took one off the top and handed it back. It was a nice touch. "Can't say I've ever picked anybody up exactly right here before."

"Long story. Don't even ask."

"I never do." Jamie chuckled as he put the vehicle in gear. "One Link Lane, South Lake Union?"

"You got it."

"On our way." The man's eyes flashed up to the rearview mirror. "You get in a fight or something?"

"Something." Ryan could see that the gleaming white bow of the VanDutch was just barely visible from where they sat, screened by the rain and a row of young cherry plum trees, still in their trunk protectors. He put his hand in his coat pocket and rested it on the Walther, just in case Jamie noticed the anchored boat, put it with Ryan's seaworthy outerwear, added two and two together, and got too curious.

But Jamie said only, "None of my business. South Lake Union, here we come."

As they pulled out of the lot, hanging a right onto Commodore Way, the eyes came up to the mirror again. "You know, you do kind of almost look a little like that dude."

"Who's that?"

"What's-his-name, Cloverface. The Link guy. When you first walked up, I looked at that address and was like, holy shit, no way."

"Don't I wish." Ryan slipped his finger inside the trigger guard. "Can you imagine? Ryan Cloverhill waiting for a Ryde under a bridge down by the locks?"

Jamie laughed again, accelerating smoothly up the street. "You'd be surprised; I see some crazy shit doing this."

"I bet."

"Maybe not that crazy, though. I mean, you don't look *that* much like him. At a glance is all."

Ryan took his hand off the gun and settled back in the seat. He towel-dried his dripping hair. "You should have seen me thirty years ago."

"What's that?"

"I said I'll take it as a compliment," Ryan answered, thinking, *Five stars for Jamie; would book again.*

CHAPTER 38

POLYGRAPHS," THE MAN in the suit and tie said. "No kidding."

"Nope," Stephen said.

"How'd you get into that line of work?"

"Answered an ad, got hired, got certified, worked for the owner until he retired, bought out the business."

"Kind of an uncommon skill set, isn't it?"

"I guess so."

"So you've worked in law enforcement?"

"Only as a civilian contractor."

"For which agencies?"

"Chicago PD, Cook County Sheriff's Department, Illinois Department of Corrections. Illinois State Fire Marshall's office. I can get you a list, if it's somehow crucially important to making sure Ryan Cloverhill doesn't blow up Seattle before dawn."

The man in the suit had introduced himself as Special Agent Tim Caldwell, Department of Homeland Security, Seattle District Office. With him was Special Agent Valerie Lockhart, Federal Bureau of Investigation, Seattle Division. They'd joined Stephen in an examination room somewhere in the depths of the emergency department at the University of Washington Medical Center. Stephen was the one in the paper gown. He had a trio of fresh stitches beneath the bandage over his eye, more bandages on his various abrasions, a hydration IV line in his arm, and a mild codeine buzz.

"You must have a good reputation," Agent Caldwell said.

"I keep busy."

"Any investigative casework?"

"Occasionally. Not much. Mostly just applicant screenings."

"Polygraphs get a bad rap, don't they?" Caldwell observed. "EPPA keeps you out of the private sector. I've heard it called junk science in my world. Hasn't the whole field pretty much been debunked nowadays?"

"It has its detractors." Stephen glanced between Caldwell and Lockhart. Lockhart, from the FBI, watched him without expression. In fact, since the preliminary introductions, she hadn't said a word. Stephen pointed back and forth between the two of them. "Then again, in your world, you guys both still use 'em."

Caldwell chuckled without smiling. "Would you say you enjoy your work?"

"At one time, probably."

"Not anymore?"

The truth was, Stephen had found the path he'd chosen to be a miserably depressing trudge through emptiness for years. When somebody came up with a lie *prevention* machine, he'd often thought, maybe we'd be onto something. But he'd worked his ass off, and the pump was basically self-priming now, and most days it felt like his best years were behind him anyway. Which felt like a disgraceful complaint, under the circumstances. Starting today, every last one of Perry's years was behind him. And some guy in a suit wanted to know if he enjoyed his *work*? "It's a living."

"Ever worked for Link Labs?"

"No."

"Not even as a contractor?"

"Not in any capacity. As you just said, the Employee Polygraph Protection Act prohibits it."

"Except for qualifying workplace incidents."

"I suppose that's true."

"And Link Labs has offices in Chicago, is that right?"

"Yes," Stephen said. "But I've never worked with them."

"Has Mr. Cloverhill ever *offered* you a job?"

"No."

"Does that surprise you?"

"Not particularly," Stephen said. "Should it surprise me?"

"Oh, I don't know. If my rich best friend had a company like that and didn't at least float it out there at some point, I guess it would probably surprise me."

"Well, he hasn't, and it doesn't," Stephen said. "Like I told you. Complicated history."

"Did it surprise you when he offered Ms. Grant a job?"

This was news to Stephen. It didn't surprise him, no...but at the same time, he'd had no idea. Emma had never mentioned it. "Did he?"

"Not just any job, either. Chief legal officer, according to Ms. Grant."

"No shit," Stephen said. "Wow."

"Any idea why Ms. Grant might turn down a job like that?"

Because she's a senior attorney, not a paid companion, Stephen thought, but he only said, "None. What did she tell you when you asked her that question?"

Agent Caldwell finally smiled. "But Link Labs does have offices in Chicago."

"Jesus Christ, Caldwell. Come on."

"Do you ever see Mr. Cloverhill when he's in town?"

"As I told you. Until this weekend, I hadn't seen Ryan in person since Lou Piniella's first year with the Cubs."

"Yeah, help me understand that." Caldwell leafed back through his notepad—purely for effect, it seemed to Stephen. "Minor perceptions aside, you're all telling the same story. So far, everything fits the intel we're getting from Billionaire Island. What I can't figure out is, why would Mr. Cloverhill go through the trouble of bringing you all the way out here just to lock you in his house? To... what? Cast a group vote, I guess? According to your statements?"

"That seems to be the case, but I can't help you understand it," Stephen said. "Believe me, I wish I could."

It was at this point that Agent Lockhart finally spoke up. "Would you call yourself politically active, Mr. Rollins?"

"Not particularly. Why?"

"Ever donated money to a candidate? Volunteered for a campaign, maybe?"

It was such a strange, abrupt turn in the questioning that it put Stephen instinctively on the defensive. He used a version of the same tactic himself all the time, but being on the receiving end still wrong-footed him. "Not since college. Again: Why?"

Caldwell said, "How about travel?"

"How about it?"

"Do you do much of it?"

"You got me." Stephen put up his hands. Maybe it was more like a medium codeine buzz. "It was the only way to get from my house to here."

"When was the last time you traveled out of the country?"

Before he could answer, there was a brief courtesy knock on the door. The door opened, and the same nurse who'd taken him to radiology stepped in. She saw Caldwell and Lockhart and stopped in her tracks with a rubber-soled squeak. "Oops. Sorry."

"No problem," Caldwell said. "We've got what we need for now. Let us get out of your way."

The nurse smiled and nodded, averting her eyes on her way past the federal agents, as if they were not to be looked upon directly.

"Well, congrats," she told Stephen on her way to a standing computer station. "You've got a fracture in that wrist. I'll pull up your pictures. The doc will be in shortly to discuss."

"Get fixed up, Mr. Rollins," Agent Caldwell said. "We'll speak again when you're finished."

"Already looking forward to it."

Lockhart led the way out of the room. Caldwell followed, then paused at the open door. "Just out of curiosity, could you beat one, do you think? Personally?"

"One what?"

"Polygraph."

Jesus. "You mean debunked junk science test?"

Caldwell grinned. "Like I said. Just curious."

"I don't know," Stephen told him. "It would probably depend on who was giving it."

"Right." Caldwell nodded. "The human element. Sure."

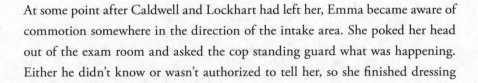

At some point after Caldwell and Lockhart had left her, Emma became aware of commotion somewhere in the direction of the intake area. She poked her head out of the exam room and asked the cop standing guard what was happening. Either he didn't know or wasn't authorized to tell her, so she finished dressing and stepped out to see for herself.

The cop said, "If you could sit tight for now, ma'am. Lots going on."

"Arrest me," she said, following the noise.

So far, she'd heard nothing of the others since they'd been separated for exams and preliminary questioning. Nobody would tell her anything about anything. Physically, the only thing wrong with her was a small perforation in her left eardrum that should, according to the attending doc, heal on its own within a few weeks. He'd prescribed antibiotic drops and told her to keep her ears dry, avoid cotton swabs, and try not to blow her nose too hard. "Piece of cake," he'd said.

Right.

All she had to do for the next few weeks was try not to cry.

In the meantime, Emma couldn't sit still another minute. She'd made it all the way back to the waiting lobby by the time her minder caught up with her.

The place was bustling with activity. A pair of uniformed Seattle PD officers appeared to be holding a group of reporters outside. Two other officers appeared to be taking statements from EMTs. Two others helped medical staff escort a line of new patients toward a cordoned processing station.

Emma counted six newcomers in all: three men, three women. All of them appeared to be her age and older, all of them disheveled in the extreme. Their expressions ranged from open anxiety to blank, thousand-yard stares.

Immediately, Emma understood who they were. She knew it in her bones, even before she glimpsed the Link Labs logo stitched across the yoke of one man's zippered fleece vest:

The same six people she'd last seen on-screen, bound and gagged in the passenger cabin of Ryan's boat.

She felt a warm hand grip her elbow lightly. "Ma'am, I'm sorry. Not supposed to have you wandering around just yet."

In that same moment, one of Ryan's former hostages happened to look up at her. When their eyes met, some immediate connection seemed to pass between them. A stranger recognizing a stranger.

Without a word, Emma pulled her arm free and walked toward the woman. Behind her, the cop said, "Ma'am!"

As Emma approached, the woman stood and faced her. She wore a gray emergency blanket around her shoulders. Above the blanket, her dark hair hung limp around her face. When Emma reached her, the woman said, "Do we know each other?"

Emma tried to speak, but for some reason, just then she couldn't.

She didn't need to. Somehow, this exhausted, preposterously mistreated person in the rescue blanket saw her more clearly than Emma could see herself right now. "You're one of the people he was talking to," the woman said. "Aren't you?"

The tears seemed to come from nowhere, instantly blurring her vision. It was just too much. She hadn't even made it an hour, and she needed to blow her stupid nose already. She took a breath, wiped her eyes roughly, and pulled herself together. Nodded her head. "My name is Emma Grant."

"Bhavna Patel," the woman said. "Hello."

What happened next just happened—simply, calmly, with no perceptible signal of any kind: they embraced. No words seemed necessary. Maybe there weren't any that mattered.

Then a new voice said, "Oh my God. Mom."

A young woman rushed toward them through the crowd. She wore scrubs and a stethoscope, UWMC photo ID badge swinging on a lanyard around her neck. A blue tag affixed to the edge of the young woman's badge holder said MEDICAL STUDENT in white block letters. The resemblance between the two of them was unmistakable.

Emma stepped away voluntarily, letting Bhavna Patel reunite with her daughter in as much peace as she could personally afford them. How much would she give for their roles to be reversed? For Kyle to be a desperately relieved-looking medical student on night rotation at this hospital right now?

She had plenty of time to wonder about that as the cop led her away, gently but firmly, all the way back to her holding pen.

There, she found that DHS Special Agent Caldwell and FBI Special Agent Lockhart had returned. They were standing by the open door, waiting for her.

Caldwell smirked at her uniformed escort, nodding curtly at her. "Getting your steps in?"

"What's happened?" Emma said. "Where did they come from? How did they get here?"

"It would seem your good friend Mr. Cloverhill has returned to the mainland."

"Where is he? Is he alive? Do you have him in custody?"

Caldwell glanced at Lockhart. She was a cold fish, that one. Not a hint of human expression whatsoever. Emma supposed she probably had to be, in her profession. Or did she? Who cared?

"He's dead, isn't he? Please, just tell me."

Caldwell finally sighed. For once, the look on his face seemed genuine, even if Emma couldn't read it.

"About that," he said.

CHAPTER 39

AFTER THE DOCS had finished with him, a uniformed hospital security officer accompanied Stephen from the emergency department to some sort of nearby staff lounge.

Emma was waiting at a central table, sipping flat water from a clear plastic cup. She looked the way Stephen felt: disconnected from reality. When she saw Stephen coming, she glanced at the short cast on his arm, lifted her chin, and said, "Only sprained, huh?"

"Jud did say he was slipping."

"How do you feel?"

"I'll let you know when I feel something." He nodded to his escort and took a seat next to Emma. It seemed that the lounge had been reserved especially for them. "What's going on?"

"I don't know," she said. "But I met one of Ryan's board members twenty minutes ago."

"What?"

"They're all here."

"At the hospital?"

"Just like us."

"Since when? What does that mean?"

"I don't know. Caldwell's coming back to talk to us."

Stephen saw the sleeve of cups like Emma's on the counter. He got up, filled one straight from the tap, and came back. When he sat down again, he said, "When they talked to you, did they ask about your politics?"

Emma nodded. "The whole thing felt pretty weird."

"If I didn't know any better," Stephen said, "I'd think he was already under investigation for something."

"Do we know better?" She shook her head. "I don't feel like I know anything anymore."

"Caldwell seemed interested in your résumé. Something about Ryan offering you a job?"

"We discussed it at length, yes."

"When did this happen?"

"An hour ago? I'm losing track of time."

"I mean the job offer."

"Oh." Emma sighed. "Remember that photo you asked me about?"

He nodded. Wineglasses and a table for two, post–wedding ring.

"It was the main reason he came to town that weekend," she said. "He had a whole pitch prepared. When he asked the owner to take that picture, I hadn't given him my answer yet. He assumed we were celebrating."

"You weren't interested?"

"The salary he was offering? Of course I was interested."

"Why didn't you take it?"

She shrugged. "Didn't feel like the right move."

Emma clearly didn't want to be pressed any further on the topic, so he let it go. "For the record, I told them I had no idea."

"Why would you? Getting you to answer a simple text is like pulling teeth." She glanced over, sighed again, sipped her water. "Sorry. Terrible day."

Understatement of the century. Still, her unvarnished perspective stung. He could hardly dispute it.

Beau and Lainie arrived next, accompanied by a security officer of their own. They both looked like hammered shit. Beau nodded wearily as they took the two chairs on the other side of Emma. Lainie sat next to her. She didn't speak, but she took Emma's hand.

A few minutes later, Will arrived, also under uniformed escort.

Beau immediately hopped up, pulled out a chair for him. Will shambled around the end of the table and sagged into the chair without a word. His eyes were bloodshot and glassy. His expression was vacant.

Beau rubbed Will's back, taking his own seat again. Will stared at the table like a zombie. He hadn't looked at anybody.

Stephen hoped he was tranked out of his mind. He didn't know how he possibly could have faced him anyway. It was easy to feel like a victim in all this when people like Caldwell and Lockhart were in the room, but seeing what was left of the Stillwater Seven gathered together changed everything.

There was no way for him to overlook just how much of what had brought them here—to these chairs, at this table, in this lounge, at this moment—could be traced directly to his own deficiencies as a human being.

It was the simplest of facts: If not for him, Perry would be sitting in the empty chair next to Will right now, where he belonged. If he'd stuck with the others at Sham Rock, Perry would still be here. If not for the contemptible arrogance of his actions on the oystershell path, Perry would still be here. If Stephen had stayed home with his cat in the first place, Perry would still be here. If not for Stephen Rollins, period, Will Shrader would still have a husband.

Was it the whole story? Maybe not, but there was no hiding from the truth of it. Not in the light of this room. Maybe not anywhere. Maybe not ever.

Half a minute after Will, Agent Caldwell arrived, cell phone in hand, a two-way radio now crackling and murmuring on his belt. No sign, for the moment, of his FBI counterpart, Lockhart.

Caldwell nodded to everybody as he squelched the radio. He faced them from a standing position on the other side of the table.

"Our hostages were picked up by responders at Fish Ladder Plaza an hour ago," he said without preamble. "Mr. Cloverhill's vessel was found a quarter-click to the west, give or take, anchored under Salmon Bay Bridge. Bomb techs are processing that site now."

Lainie said, "Where is that?"

"About seven miles by waterway from Link Village," Caldwell said. "Which is where the subject appears to have been heading if the weather hadn't shut down the locks."

Stephen said, "Where did he go instead?"

"Based on your credit and cell records," Caldwell answered, looking directly at Stephen, "we believe that Mr. Cloverhill is, in fact, currently holed up somewhere on campus. Most likely on the fourth floor of the headquarters building, west side, facing the lake."

"That's his office," Beau said. "We saw it on the tour."

"Wait a minute," Stephen said. "What do you mean, my records?"

"It seems Mr. Cloverhill used your phone to book a rideshare to that address."

Stephen would not have been able to put the instant sizzle of rage he felt into words. It was priceless, really; on top of everything else, the son of a bitch had stolen his credit card.

According to Caldwell, from where they now sat, Link Village was three short miles to the southwest, across Portage Bay. You could get there in a rowboat if you took the long way around Eastlake.

"As it stands, we're focusing our primary efforts in three spheres of operation," Caldwell went on. "Evacuation and containment of the immediate neighborhood. Strategic and tactical evaluation of the site itself. And establishing contact with the suspect."

Beau said, "Can't you just go in there and get him? Boots on the ground, guys on ropes, all that stuff?"

"Looks pretty good in the movies, doesn't it?" Caldwell shook his head. "Understand, we're coordinating an effort involving offices from Homeland Security down to public works. We have a barricaded suspect but not a positive location. We don't know his capabilities, his timetable, or his goals. We're positioning to deploy UGVs from multiple agencies for preliminary recon, but as you've seen for yourselves, it's a large complex with multiple structures. Until we have—"

"UGVs?" Beau said.

"Unmanned ground vehicles," Caldwell said. At Beau's blank look, he added, "Bomb robots."

"Oh."

His goals, Stephen thought bitterly. He could have told Caldwell the goal:

Go out with a bang. That was all any of this added up to in the end. A bang so loud nobody would forget it.

Ryan Cloverhill might want them all to believe it went somehow deeper than that. He might want the whole world to believe it went deeper than that. He might even believe it went deeper than that himself. That calling it a "Trolley Problem" made him some kind of Digital Age philosopher.

But it didn't, and he wasn't. He was just the same old pathologically insecure Ryan Cloverhill, and he'd burned his life down before. The only difference was that he had resources now. More resources than anybody in this room, probably in this hospital, possibly including Department of Homeland Security Special Agent Tim Caldwell.

"Establishing contact," Emma said. "Has that happened yet?"

"No," Caldwell answered. He finally pulled a chair from his side of the table and sat down. "Which brings me to why I wanted to see you all together."

CHAPTER 40

AN HOUR BEFORE midnight, Stephen, Emma, Lainie, Beau, and Will arrived, via black Chevy Suburban, at an incident command center set up in unrented office space on the west shore of Lake Union.

The building was tucked in among the restaurants, shops, law offices, and marinas on the Cheshiahud Lake Union Loop, across the water and a mile upshore from Link Village. The location provided clear views of the Link complex, beyond the blast radius for anything short of an ammonium nitrate factory explosion or a suitcase nuke. Under the joint coordination of Homeland Security and the FBI, with the cooperation of the building's property management company, the aptly named "Link Labs Threat Response Task Force" now claimed thirty-five hundred fully wired square feet, with enough surface parking to accommodate a dramatic assemblage of tactical, emergency response, and broadcast news vehicles.

Inside, a bank of flat-panel televisions displayed live breaking news stand-ups, most of which were now being conducted from beneath a massive pop-up shelter in the rain-slick lot directly outside the building. The effect was every bit as surreal to Stephen as watching the scenery outside Ryan's windows on video screens.

A long central table dominated the main space, crowded with people clacking away on laptops and muttering into phones. People in suits and uniforms stood around like war room commanders, which Stephen supposed they were.

Agent Caldwell was there with colleagues from his agency. Agent Lockhart was there with colleagues from hers. Stephen saw leadership from the Seattle Police Department, Washington State Patrol, and United States Coast Guard. There were well-heeled men and women from the Link Labs executive team, along with various aides to the mayor and the governor.

The governor herself had arrived from Olympia by state police chopper shortly after the Stillwater Five. She now sat at the head of the table, dressed as though she'd come straight from a black-tie function at the mansion.

"So he's on his own grid, and we can't jam his signal," she said. "Do I understand at least that much?"

"There's no signal to jam," said a young guy in a T-shirt, hoodie, and jeans. He sat a few chairs down, one of several Link Labs network analysts conscripted into duty. "He's physically connected to the central branch."

"And you can't take down the network somehow? Sniff something or probe something or block whatever needs blocking?"

"He must be running his own conditioning routine off the spine layer," the network guy said. "Right now we're red-teaming the back doors to see if we can—"

"Great. Got it." The governor raised her palm. "Do computers. Faster, if humanly possible. Next." She pointed down the table toward Stephen, Emma, Beau, Lainie, and Will. "Who are you, again?"

"We're his friends," Lainie said.

"Lucky you. Can somebody please restate the concept here?"

Caldwell stepped in. "We're coordinating with the major news outlets to put them on the air, Madam Governer. It may be a long shot, but we're hoping their personal connection to the subject might help us establish contact."

"So the whole plan is predicated on whether or not he's watching TV right now?"

"At the very least, we know he's logged in to his own platform," Caldwell said. "We'll simulcast to Mr. and Mrs. Hemford's LinkStream channel as well. At more than a million subscribers, the Link people tell us their algorithm should get us on his radar at a minimum."

"Well, thank God we've got an algorithm."

"They posted video from Building One yesterday," the network analyst explained—somewhat defensively, it seemed to Stephen. "We're showing engagement on that post three hundred percent over average for their feed, so if yesterday's post was flu season, this should be measles. He'll definitely see it."

"And that's how we stop this madman from blowing a crater in the Great State of Washington. Viral videos."

"As I said, it may be a long shot," Caldwell said. "But we feel it's worth trying."

Stephen couldn't have agreed less. On a borrowed phone, Emma had been texting and calling Ryan's personal mobile for an hour; if he hadn't picked up for her, there was no point to any of this. But what the hell else was there for them to be doing?

"Terrific." The governer looked toward him and Emma. "Are you two Mr. and Mrs. Hemford?"

Emma pointed down the table. Lainie and Beau raised their hands. Lainie's hair was a crazy tangle. Beau looked like he'd spent the night in a steamer trunk. "Nice to meet you," he said.

"Likewise," the governor replied. She looked at Caldwell. "I guess it's your show."

"Okay," said Caldwell. "Let's get these folks on television."

Lights: low and mellow, with a little fill from the vintage Luxo task lamp on the desk.

Camera: stock high-def webcam integrated into an ultrawide LED desktop monitor.

Soundtrack: for his personal apocalypse, Ryan selected an oldie from Link-Blaster Radio. He pushed it up over the audio system in his fourth-floor office at One—a little Gene Autry for the end of the world.

Back in the saddle again.

His desk faced roughly east, with the lake behind him, 183 degrees of ambient smart glass providing crystal clear nighttime views. It would be more befitting a proper Bond villain, Ryan thought, if he could stand at those windows, hands clasped behind his back, imperiously surveying the world spread out below him.

But now it was time to sit down.

And you could still see plenty from an original '60 Eames executive chair in mint condition. For example:

Four stories down, through the steady rain, he could just make out six moving shadows: stealthy figures in wet suits, goggles, and mini dive tanks. He watched them slip undetected into the lake from the boardwalk along the Link Village corporate marina.

Along the south side, he could see the flashing lights and scurrying activity of the neighborhood evacuation currently in progress. Orange safety barricades ran the length of the streetcar line along Valley. Aerial news footage showed I-5 Express traffic blocked from Pike Street to the Portage Bay Viaduct.

Most news agencies appeared to be setting up live shots from the large marina parking lots along Westlake, on the far shoreline, giving them the clearest available wide shots of Link Village across the lake. The way it had played out, Ryan hadn't needed his head of communications to arrange any of this after all; Perry had managed to do her job for her, and with nothing but a windbreaker.

Back to the lake, and a solitary wooden sloop, anchored in the empty water a thousand feet out. Sails lowered, masts bare. Loaded with enough Semtex to kick off the show with a proper bang.

As the ghost of Gene Autry finished his serenade and rode off into an imaginary sunset, Ryan turned his chair back to the desk and rolled into position. He reached out for the zippered pen case waiting for him there. He opened it and removed his four remaining injection pens, lining them up on the desk in a neat row on the left side of the keyboard. He placed the Walther on the desk on the right.

Next, he arranged his virtual workstation across the monitor's ample curve: ignition control console on the left, exterior security feeds on the right, LiveLink interface directly in front of him. He tiled all the available news coverage across the 105-inch screen on the nearest AV wall.

He called up the room control pad and clicked the privacy icon, automatically frosting the windows behind him, shielding the interior of the office—and his position within it—from prying eyes. News choppers, for example. Private drones. High-powered police sniper scopes. Et cetera.

Then he took one last look around the office as he bit the cap off of pen number three. You could have fit both sides of their shitty old Stillwater duplex in the space he had all to himself up here. He missed that place.

Ryan took a deep breath, jabbed the pen into his thigh. He worked to regulate his own breathing until the nerve-jangling initial blast of the injection smoothed out.

Then he fired up a LinkStream and pushed it out systemwide.

Action:

"Greetings, Linkverse," he said to the tiny red light beneath the webcam. "This is your captain speaking."

CHAPTER 41

THEY SET THEM up outside, under the media tent, with the lake in the background. A row of microphones, bright lights on tripods, a crowd of reporters and their camera crews. Lainie and Beau were set to speak first, aiming to gin up maximum viewership within the Linkverse. Then Emma, for maximum viewership with Ryan Cloverhill.

But before they could even take their places, everything lost focus in a hurry. Somewhere in the crowd, a voice yelled, "He's on. He's on right now." Everybody started checking their phones.

Then it was all tumult. The throng of reporters immediately broke apart, scrambling and scurrying in a cacophony of jabber accompanied by the steady patter of rain on the tent overhead.

"Jesus Christ," Agent Caldwell said, mobile phone already pressed to his ear.

FBI Special Agent Valerie Lockhart stepped in and addressed the five of them: "Everybody stay together. We're going to take you back inside." Then she was moving away herself, gesturing toward uniforms with one hand, raising her own mobile phone in the other.

In the midst of all this, Will Shrader finally broke down. He crouched on his heels and buried his head, shoulders heaving.

Lainie said, "We've got him. Go find out what's happening."

But a cop was already moving Stephen and Emma back, saying, "Let's hang tight right here for a minute. Not sure what I'm supposed to do with you."

So they stood there, chaos all around, watching Beau and Lainie try to comfort Will, as a different cop tried to get all three of them to move.

"He doesn't blame you," Emma said beside Stephen. "Will. I hope you know that."

He couldn't look at her. "He should."

"Why? You didn't put us on the trolley."

"Nope. I just pulled all the levers that got Perry killed."

"That's bullshit, and you know it."

"Is it?"

"I'm the one who cracked the code to that tablet," Emma reminded him. "Is it my fault too?"

Stephen sighed heavily, turning away toward the lake. "I don't know if I can take it, Em."

"Take what?"

"Knowing that Perry's dead," he said, pointing toward the water, in the general direction of Link Village, "and that piece of shit still gets what he wants."

Emma stood closer to him, joining him in looking out, into the rain beyond the edge of the tent. "I guess there's nothing we can do now except wait and see."

"I don't know how to do that either."

"What else can we do? I guess I could swim across and chain myself to the front doors." She nudged him. "But I don't think I'd make it. And to tell you the truth, at this point, I'm not sure it would stop him anyway."

No, Stephen thought. In fact, it would make everything exponentially worse. In all of this, Stephen wondered if there was anything that could satisfy the great Ryan Cloverhill more deeply than Emma Grant choosing to die with him in the same pile of rubble.

He glanced back toward Blainey and Will. Beau and Lainie's life was a mess, but they had the boys. Will had already suffered more than any of them, and it didn't matter what Emma tried to say: a month from now, he'd be crawling into bed next to Perry if Stephen had done even one thing differently.

And what would Stephen be doing next month? Or the month after that? Sitting at home with his cat, wishing he could turn back time?

These were his thoughts when he saw the bright flash of light on the lake, far in the distance. A moment later, the sound rumbled over them—a deep, rolling boom, like a towering clap of thunder from the storm.

"Oh, God," he heard Emma say. "That's it. That's the first one. It's happening."

Out on the lake, Stephen saw the same sight as everyone else: a cloud of black smoke boiling up from a column of fire. The chaos under the media tent turned to outright bedlam: gasps, shouting, running, shoving, complete and utter disarray as law enforcement reacted to the explosion on the water and news teams jockeyed to stake out new turf.

Then he couldn't see anything as bodies swarmed all around them, crowding forward, spilling out into the rain.

So it was happening then. Sometime very soon, Ryan Cloverhill would live forever in the annals of history alonside assholes like Ted Kaczynski and Timothy McVeigh. The rest of them would be enshrined in the footnotes as the gang of hapless pals. The people who, in Emma's words, could do nothing. Nothing but wait and see.

What else can we do?

People talked about snapping: *So-and-so did such-and-such, and I just snapped.*

But when Stephen glimpsed his opportunity to answer Emma's question, he actually felt it happen: An actual, physical snap, like something popping loose somewhere deep in his brain. Something that, until today, had always been securely fastened. Immediately, he felt the same kind of tingling, floating sensation he'd felt while pointing a gun at Jud Bernal earlier.

And look where that got everybody, some voice of better judgment tried to advise.

But maybe that was the part of him that had snapped. Not the part that could tell the difference between good judgment and bad judgment. Just the part that cared.

What else can we do?

"Fuck it," he said aloud to himself, already walking, now breaking into a jog.

There will be a small preliminary detonation to establish credibility, Ryan had told them, *before I drop the plunger for real.*

For the rest of her life, Emma Grant would never find a way to fully comprehend how Stephen, in the confused moments following that first explosion on the lake, had managed to slip out from under the media tent, jog out into the rain, steal a KCPQ 13 satellite news van, and drive it away.

Although she supposed that wasn't strictly true. She understood *how* he'd done it. Even if she hadn't been there in person when he did it, anyone who saw the ongoing news reportage in the days to come, or the award-winning Waelder documentary two years later, or the film adaptation the year after that, would have been able to recite the how:

In the mayhem after the anchored sailboat went sky-high, everyone had clambered for a better view... including the production operator behind the wheel of the news van. He'd piled out and skipped a short distance away to see the sight for himself, vehicle still running, door hanging open behind him.

What she'd never be able to understand—what no explanation could ever truly explain—was what, exactly, had possessed Stephen to *do* it.

One moment, he was by her side. The next, she heard him curse. By the time she'd turned to see why, he was already forty feet away, splashing through puddles, now climbing in behind the wheel, now slamming the door.

The van's driver wheeled around and shouted, "Hey!"

Emma shouted Stephen's name and sprinted after him.

But by then he was already gone, in a screech of tires and a hanging cloud of exhaust. The van's former driver—waving his arms in the headlights, trying to blockade Stephen's exit with his own person—wisely dove out of the way as Stephen yowled around a median and banged over a curb. As nearby police began to notice and respond, Emma could only stand dumbfounded, panting in the rain.

The last thing she saw, through the fog of her own heavy breath in the dripping chill, was the van's rooftop satellite dish tilting precariously as Stephen careened onto Westlake Avenue, around a screen of trees, and disappeared.

CHAPTER 42

I WAS WORKING as a government contractor in DC when Flight 77 hit the Pentagon," Ryan said to the monitor. "Before I could reach anyone I knew there, the towers had come down in New York. My oldest friend still talks about nursing her infant son in front of *The Good Morning Show* when the second plane hit the South Tower, live on-screen. Nobody knew what was happening, or what might happen next. Two of our mutual friends were in Manhattan that day; I'll never forget how sick I felt, waiting to hear they were okay.

"Back then, I hadn't even dreamed of Link Labs. Hell: Myspace was still two years away. You couldn't check the locations of the friends in your network at a glance. You couldn't hit up YouTube for person-on-the-street footage from Ground Zero. It seems hard to believe now, but we were past Hurricane Katrina, more than half a decade into a global War on Terror, before anyone had even heard of an iPhone.

"Now, here we are, well into our so-called Social Epoch. We're more Linked, over far greater distances, than at any other time in human history. We have easier access to more information than we've ever had before. We can share our lives with our loved ones in a way that's never been possible; we can organize and mobilize faster than we ever could. Wherever you live, whatever you're into, whatever support you need, you can find your place in the Linkverse, and you can take it with you everywhere you go.

"And yet, poll data suggests we may feel more at odds with each other now than at any other time in the past six decades. Meanwhile, researchers in Australia have hypothesized that the amount of time we spend looking down at our phones may be causing us—literally—to grow horns."

Ryan reached around to the back of his own skull.

"You've heard this one. It's called the external occipital protuberance—a natural anatomical feature we all share. In some people, chronic strain on the trapezius muscle and nuchal ligament—in other words, our necks—can cause this anchor point to add new bone for stability, creating a spur. To put it another way: in less time than it takes to age a good scotch, our devices—if these researchers are correct—may already be making perceptible changes to the human skeleton. So"—Ryan spread his hands—"through all of this, what have we learned?"

According to the intel he could glean from here, the last of the emergency responders had nearly cleared the waterfront since the initial blast. Exterior security cams showed half a dozen continuous-track bomb disposal robots converging on One like hyenas closing in on a carcass. The news banners all read *EXPLOSION AT LINK LABS*.

Almost showtime.

"I can tell you one thing *I've* learned: according to our analytics, outrage, envy, and fear still drive a hell of a lot more engagement than patience and nuance. Link Labs didn't invent human nature, but by God, we've strapped a polygraph to it and handed it a megaphone, and I could show you some real bummer data about how much more amplitude you get from a negative signal than you get from a positive one.

"But I doubt this takes any of you by surprise. Our numbers only show what advertisers have known for decades: the denser the message, the quicker it sinks. I won't insult your intelligence by pretending any of this is new. But I *will* insult your intelligence by asking a question:

"When's the last time you forgot your phone at home and didn't feel itchy all day?"

He could see by the darkened buildings, streetlamps, and traffic signals all along the southeast shore that the city had cut power to the immediate area. He applauded the move as a safety precaution, but it wasn't an operational concern. Link Village employed its own trigeneration plant for each building on campus and had integrated UPS backup for every receptacle on every floor.

"But enough doom and gloom, said the pot to the kettle. I've elaborated on these thoughts at some length in the LinkDrop document pinned at the top of the comments." He made a finger gun and pointed it toward the edge of his screen. "I won't lie, it's a snoozefest. But if you're really interested, act now, while supplies last. In the meantime, what's my point?"

A quick glance at the comments distracted him momentarily, but Ryan couldn't immediately see why. It didn't matter. It was already past time to wrap this up, and he was fading fast.

"I guess it's just this: One of those three friends I mentioned died earlier today. The other two are probably watching this now. The infant has grown up and gone to college. For all I know, he may be watching too. If you're his age, what's about to happen may feel a little bit like your 9/11.

"Or maybe I'm just the self-obsessed asshole another friend of ours always said I was. Either way, someone among you is going to build something new in the spot where the Linkverse once stood. So before I sign off, fellow hornheads, I'd like to leave you with a few words of hard-earned..."

Ryan paused and leaned forward, distracted again by the live comments scrolling like mad along the edge of his screen. Surely his mind was playing tricks on him. It happened more and more frequently these days.

But no: There went another one, sailing past.

Now another.

Three more.

Even as he sat there, staring at the feed, more of these strange new comments began popping up until they were rolling in fast and thick. All tagged with different versions of the same trending cloversign. He looked up at the news reports on the big screen.

He sat there for a moment or two, just staring. Then he punched up the volume.

"You gotta be shitting me," he finally said to the empty room.

***

Brain tumor or no brain tumor, Emma couldn't understand what Ryan thought he was talking about.

Among so many other things: her son, Kyle, hadn't been born yet when the towers came down. There was no reason for Ryan to remember his exact birthday, but he knew full well it was post-9/11.

So she'd never told him any such story about nursing her child while planes hit the World Trade Center. It was an evocative anecdote, rich with meaning, but it just wasn't true. She'd been stuck in meetings when she heard the news, not watching television at home. Even if she *had* been home, and even if Kyle had been born at the time, she wouldn't have been nursing him; the kid bit like a horse and would only take a bottle consistently. She'd stressed over it nonstop for the first six weeks of his life, then gave up and pumped for the next six months straight. She *clearly* remembered what a prick Mark had been about it—critiquing her technique as if she simply weren't momming hard enough, making dairy-cow jokes in front of their friends. But she could not remember ever once discussing the trials of nipple confusion with Ryan Cloverhill.

Had he intentionally told the story like that for dramatic effect? Co-opted someone else's memory because it sounded good in the moment?

Or was it somehow possible that when Ryan looked back, he'd somehow conflated the worst foreign attack on US soil with the birth of her child in his mind? Did he really, truly see himself as some kind of movie villain? Was this the origin story he'd invented for himself?

Whatever the case, he'd invented it.

Emma looked over at Will, who leaned forward in the chair beside her, literally on the edge of his seat. His bloodshot eyes were glued to the television screens on the wall. "Em, what is he doing? What does Rollie think he's *doing*?"

She didn't have an answer. Meanwhile, tucked away in one of the nearby offices, under task force supervision but away from the barking clamor of the war room, Lainie and Beau had logged in and quickly launched a LinkStream of their own.

Still dripping wet from the rain, Emma watched Blainey's and Ryan's dueling feeds play alongside aerial news coverage of Stephen's run toward doom. It was, without question, the most unbelievable moment of her life. Today, that was saying something.

He'd had a clear shot down Westlake, which had been closed to regular traffic for hours. At least until he reached the stop sticks deployed and waiting for him at the Highland Street intersection. Somehow he saw the spikes in time to take evasive action, swerving hard left at the AGC Building, onto the frontage road. Will gasped, and Emma held her heart in her mouth, but Stephen miraculously kept the swaying van on all four wheels, cutting hard back to the right at Eighth Avenue and continuing on, a growing line of Seattle PD units howling on his tail.

"Can somebody tell me how in God's name we let this happen," the governor shouted to whoever was listening, "and how we're going to stop it before this idiot gets himself or somebody else killed?"

But nobody seemed to hear her. It was as if everyone in the room had momentarily frozen, hypnotized by the beaming televisions. They all watched... and watched... until the stolen news van finally, impossibly, careened around the last curve onto Fairview, on the other side of the lake, roaring on.

"So what we've got, Hemsters, is your basic Trolley Problem," Beau babbled anxiously on-screen. Emma could actually hear a muffled version of the real Beau twenty feet away, behind the closed office door—in real life—a beat before LinkStream-Beau echoed himself on the television display in front of them.

Across the table, the city mayor turned to an aide and said, "A what? What's he talking about? Do we need transit in here?"

"Here's how it goes," LinkStream-Beau continued. "Your number two best friend is heading straight for you in a boosted newsmobile. In twenty seconds... shit... in ten seconds he's going to be crashing through the lobby of your building. If you pull the lever, Rollie gets blown to smithereens right along with you, and the Stillwater Seven will be down to four sad assholes. Don't pull the lever, and... uh... dammit, I don't know; help me out, Lainie."

"It's not a Trolley Problem!" Lainie shouted into the laptop camera, leaning farther into the frame beside Beau. She looked flushed and fierce in the light of the screen—eyes wild, hair everywhere. "You know Mendota gave him a C in that class, Ryan; just don't pull the lever! Please! *Enough!*"

And that was all the time they had.

Emma couldn't watch anymore. She closed her eyes.

The KING 5 news chopper picked him up at the Marina Mart, tracking him south along Westlake from above.

By the time Ryan fully accepted what he was seeing, he'd watched Stephen Rollins smash through two patrol cruisers parked nose-to-nose at the intersection of Valley, sending up a silent puff of glittering glass. He watched the flashing convoy behind him screech to a smoky halt, giving up pursuit at the southernmost shore of the lake, allowing the KCPQ van to lurch on into the blast radius alone.

He watched the top-heavy van lean hard to the right as it cornered precariously left, turning the barricades at Fairview and One Link Lane into spinning sticks of safety-orange kindling. He followed it all the way from the big screen on the wall to the monitor on the desk in front of him, as the aerial news footage handed off to the Link Village campus security cams.

He dove into his keyboard, calling up a command shell and typing as fast as his fingers would fly. Then he turned to the ignition console, clicking through the safeguard controls until the mother of all Pineapple commands was armed: a single pulsing clover, ready and waiting. Green for Go.

Meanwhile, the comments kept coming. All tagged with variations on North America's hottest new cloversign:

ROLLIE!

SAVEROLLIE

RollieSavesTheWorld

He held the cursor poised over the Send icon—creator and destroyer, the one being in all the Linkverse with God-mode privileges—but now, at the moment of truth, he couldn't make his finger move. All at once it was as if he could feel the omnipotence draining out of him, like...like whatever was pouring from the undercarriage of that wobbling wreck of a news van Stephen had stolen.

Had he lost his goddamned mind?

Ryan shouted profanity at the screen as he watched the van jounce over a planted median, churning up wood chips and turf. He watched it plow through the security gate, finally tearing away its own grille guards. He watched the van rock and shimmy out of one camera feed and into the next as Stephen bounced up a curb and caromed off a bollard into more landscaping. Then back down onto the granite entryway pavers, leaving a long track of fluid glistening in his wake. Steam billowed from beneath the tented hood. The dangling front bumper threw down a carpet of sparks. He'd be lucky if he didn't blow himself up before he even reached the building.

As the van finally disappeared from the bottom corner of the last available security feed, Ryan took his hand from the mouse and sagged back in the chair, closing his eyes.

A moment later, a god-awful crash rose up from below and surrounded him. The whole building trembled.

He felt numb. There was a sensation of floating. All at once, his chills and sweats and pounding skull and racing heart seemed to belong to someone else; even the searing pain in his gut felt distant, a flutter of sense memory somewhere deep—something that had once tormented somebody he knew at some point in the recent past.

One of Beau's lines from earlier kept looping through his mind: *Couldn't you just unplug everything?*

He didn't realize he was smiling until he opened his eyes and saw himself on-screen. It wasn't until that moment that he remembered he was still broadcasting live.

Ryan winced and sat up.

He reached out and grabbed his three remaining injection pens in one hand. He picked up the Walther in the other.

"If you'll excuse me one moment," he said to the camera.

CHAPTER 43

Emma stood next to Will, watching the soaring glass front entry of One Link Village disappear in a shimmering cascade as Stephen plowed the Channel 13 news van straight through to the front lobby.

Will had leaned so far over his toes that he stumbled forward a step. Emma couldn't breathe. She couldn't even tell if her heart was beating. Beau and Lainie abandoned their feed, bursting out of their temporary office and sprinting over to join.

On the next screen over, Ryan Cloverhill sat alone, slumped in his office chair, arms limp in his lap.

For one beat, the entire conference room fell silent again. Then Agent Caldwell barked, "Can somebody get me a goddamned status report?"

The command center instantly went madhouse, voices talking over voices talking over the chatter of computer keyboards and the ringing of phones. Emma heard somebody yelling into a two-way radio, saying, "No, hold them back, hold them back; I need UGVs at that position..."

And another voice yelling, "...say again, where is that location..."

And then everything blended together until she couldn't separate her own thoughts from the rest of the noise. Will had flopped his arms over the top of his own head as he stared at the screens, tensely waiting for more information. Lainie found a chair and eased herself into it; she sat with one elbow on the table, eyes closed, forehead propped on her fingertips. Beau stood next to her, a hand on her shoulder. Emma found her heartbeat again, pounding below her jaw. Tiny lights danced in the corners of her vision. She had no idea how long she'd been holding her breath.

Ryan stepped off the elevator into a foggy ruin.

Once upon a time, this building he'd been preparing to destroy had been voted #109 on the American Institute of Architects Favorite 150 list. Now look at it.

The lobby smelled like a burning chemical spill. The KCPQ van sat midway through the visitors' lounge in a glinting meadow of broken glass, creaking and hissing, dripping fluid and billowing steam. One of its headlights remained miraculously intact, tinting the haze incandescent. The whole vehicle was draped in mangled aluminum window framing, surrounded by toppled furniture. The rooftop satellite dish hung askew, ripped from its moorings; blood-spattered airbags covered the dash, sprinkled with nuggets of shattered windshield. The passenger door hung open. Somewhere in the swirling smog, he could hear Stephen coughing.

Then he saw him: a hunched silhouette limping around in the murk, crunching through scattered window shards like the walking dead.

"Jesus, Rollie," he called out, already hacking on fumes himself, "I knew Blainey would do just about anything to get their phones back, but you?"

The shape turned slowly, zeroing in on the sound of his voice.

He looked so much like a stranger that for half a second, Ryan almost wondered if the LinkStream had it wrong, and it wasn't really Stephen after all. His face was a patchwork of cuts and abrasions, hair matted and glistening on one side. Streams of blood ran from scalp to chin. His eyes blazed with fury.

And now he was coming—stepping over debris, hobbling around obstacles, doubling over in a coughing fit, kicking more junk out of his way.

"Whoa." Ryan raised the Walther. "Go easy, amigo."

But going easy was not why Stephen Rollins was here. And he was altogether undeterred by the .45 pointed at his heaving chest. For the first time, Ryan noticed the hard cast poking out from Stephen's jacket sleeve. Before he could figure out how to make himself actually shoot the crazy loon, Stephen swung the cast, batting Ryan's gun hand aside...and punted him in the groin hard enough to make him taste acid.

The force of it raised Ryan up onto his toes. He huffed and felt all the strength run out of his legs. The next thing he knew, he was on all fours, head hanging, trying not to vomit. A deep, sickening pain radiated out from his core, mingling with the low, ever-smoldering fire in his gut. His third injection was still doing its thing, but this was truly something special.

"That was for Will," Stephen wheezed. He stooped, pried Ryan's trigger finger back until the knuckle popped. Wrenched the Walther out from beneath his palm.

Somewhere above him, Ryan heard the slide rack and release. The round that had already been loaded in the chamber hit the polished concrete by his hand with a dull click. Fresh new one in the pipe.

"And this is for Perry."

By then, Ryan didn't have the strength to do much more than nod along.

Fine. Not how he'd planned it…but okay.

It was probably better this way, really. Professor Mendota would have called it cheating; shooting the conductor was never a valid answer to the Trolley Problem. It missed the whole point.

But they were past all that. One more for the terrible idea column. And even after such a dreadful day of failure after abysmal failure, he'd still rather it be Stephen than cancer.

So he hung his head and waited for the lights to go out.

Then something shocking happened:

Nothing at all.

As Stephen lowered the gun, he thought:

Today I've smoked two cigarettes, shot a man in the arm, and kicked a cancer patient in the nuts.

It was so absurd he wanted to cry.

Maybe he was already crying. Or it was the blood in his eyes. Or maybe it was the concussion that was blurring his vision.

All Stephen knew in that moment—standing in the middle of his own wreckage, looking down the slide of a handgun at the back of his oldest friend's head—was that no matter what Ryan had done…no matter what else had happened today, or would happen tomorrow…even though Stephen had survived an explosion and driven a news truck into a building within the same twelve-hour period...there was no possible way he could withstand adding, "...*and then executed him*," to his list of accomplishments.

"For what it's worth, you're making the right choice," Ryan said from the floor. He'd rolled over and now lay flat on his back, one arm draped over his face. "She'd never look at you the same way again, even if I did have it coming."

Jesus. "Is that *really* the only thing on your mind right now?" Stephen thought of that photograph again. The one of Emma and Ryan raising glasses, toasting some future Ryan envisioned—a future that, once again, wasn't to be. "Tell me the truth. Did you start planning to tear apart your little kingdom before or after she turned down her room at the palace?"

Beneath his own arm, Ryan chuckled. It sounded more like choking. "I think you have me confused with Jay Gatsby."

Stephen wanted to feel anger. He wanted to feel disgust, or hatred, or anything potent enough to help him somehow hold Ryan Cloverhill accountable for the pain he'd caused. But he couldn't feel anything except exhaustion. The gun in his hand felt like a twenty-pound dumbbell.

"Although I admit there was a time," Ryan added, "when I felt a certain unquenchable desire to make *you* wish you were *me* for a change."

"I don't even know what the hell that means."

"That doesn't surprise me."

Maybe he could feel anger after all. "You stupid asshole. Did it ever occur to you, even briefly, that scorching the earth every time something doesn't go your way isn't a sustainable approach to relationships?"

"Said the man who had it all, and screwed it up just as royally as I ever did." Ryan coughed, then groaned. "She's probably right, you know. We're more alike than we think."

Stephen tossed the gun aside. It clunked against the concrete and scraped across the floor, away from them. "In your place, I'm pretty sure I wouldn't have done this."

"I'm pretty sure that in my place you have no idea what you would or wouldn't do, but there's no point arguing theoreticals." Ryan uncovered his face, struggled up to an elbow. "I'll be gone soon enough. And you, my friend, still need to figure out what you'd do in your place if you were you."

"I don't know what that means either."

"Believe it or not, this weekend wasn't all kidnappings and construction-grade ordnance for me," Ryan said. "I put you two on the same flight for a reason."

For a moment, he caught a glimpse of the old Ryan peeking through: sincere, unsophisticated, all underbelly. Eager to express himself and be understood. Stephen didn't know whether to feel sad or furious. "Wow. I feel so Linked."

Ryan laughed until he coughed again. "You always were a tough room."

Over Ryan's hacking, Stephen heard a ratcheting mechanical sound and turned. He saw two bomb disposal robots climbing up through the jagged, gaping hole in the front of the building. They clacked and wobbled over the wreckage on their rugged track systems, utility arms poised, cameras tracking.

He also saw that a fire had started in a puddle of something beneath the demolished van.

Still coughing, Ryan nodded toward the flames already licking the van's undercarriage. "Another fine mess, Rollie. What now?"

They needed to get away from this spot posthaste, that was what. *Shall I tell you what I think*, he heard Perry say, *so we can go back inside, and I can take my medicine like a man?*

"Now you come outside," Stephen told him. "And take your medicine."

Ryan dropped his chin to his chest in resignation. He took a deep breath. Let it go.

"You win," he said, extending his hand. "Help me up, man. I think you ruptured my testicles."

Stephen barely had enough strength to remain upright himself. He hurt all over. The flames were up to the side panels now; he could actually feel the heat. The first bot through the gap squared its tracks and scurried straight toward them, crunching over glass. It stopped three feet away, camera trained, as he helped Ryan struggle to his feet. It was unnerving.

"Try not to make eye contact," Ryan suggested.

"How do we get out?"

"That way." He pointed toward a fire exit at the far end of the lobby.

Stephen draped Ryan's arm over his shoulders, half propping him up, half leaning on him. The bot's camera turned, tracking them all the way.

Ryan patted it on the camera hood as they hobbled awkwardly past. "Nice doggie. Stay."

Disobediently, it followed along.

Will grabbed Emma's hand as somebody called, "That's fire. I see fire."

Lainie took her other hand, and Beau took Lainie's. They stood together in a line, fingers tightly linked, staring at the newscopter live shot of the punched-in front of One Link Lane. The cockeyed taillights of the competing network's wrecked news van were barely visible, two glowing red eyes in a swirling haze of destruction. Somebody else said, "Something's moving."

A cheer rose up as they watched two figures emerge from a side exit, hobbling slowly into the open. Emma's heart floated away like a balloon. She couldn't believe what she was seeing.

Beau shot his arms into the air and shouted, "Fuck yeah, Rollie!" Lainie grabbed Emma from one side, Will from the other, now Beau filling in, trying to hug them all at the same time. Emma pulled her pinned arms free and grabbed them back. They squeezed each other as if trying to meld into one person. She didn't know quite what the hell had been accomplished just now, but somehow Stephen appeared to have lived through it.

And Ryan.

Helping each other along.

"Okay," said the governor of the Great State of Washington. "This is officially goddamn bananas."

Somewhere in the room, a gruff voice said, "That truck's gonna blow."

"Oh my God," Lainie said. "Come on, guys. Hurry hurry hurry!"

The suspense was nearly unbearable, watching the two of them inching their way across the bottom of the wide aerial shot, until another small cheer rose up from the table.

"I'm in!" the lead network guy called. "Okay. Okay. I think I can…No! No, no. What?"

"I just went down," said the young woman next to him.

"Me too," said the next.

Emma craned her head back around Lainie just as the next tech raised his hands like a rodeo roper. "Dead."

"Wait," another said. "Hey."

From her awkward angle, Emma could just see their blanked laptop screens: half a dozen black rectangles, all in a row.

Now plain white text characters began to appear, joining and building on each other, one line at a time. The lines aggregated from the top down until the same image began to appear on each of their screens, in perfect synchronization. Spiky at the top. Widening as it filled in.

"Oh, shit," Will said as the text art took shape.

The governor said, "What now?"

"I think he booby-trapped us," the lead network guy said.

Agent Caldwell snapped, "Say again?"

"I don't know!" the network guy shouted back. "I don't know. But we definitely just hit some kind of trip..."

...*wire*, Emma finished in her mind.

She didn't know any more about computers than the next person, but you didn't have to be an expert to recognize a picture of a pineapple.

CHAPTER 44

THE LINKVERSE WENT dark just before midnight, the first Saturday of that September, two days before the commencement of Labor Day celebrations nationwide. The buildings came down at Link Village more or less as a connected ring, seven links snapping in concert, crumpling to rubble with bizarrely hypnotic grace. Viewed from the air, in the light of the following days, the site vaguely resembled a child's paper chain trampled flat underfoot.

But the shot that went most viral, reappearing in newspapers and magazines and websites and news broadcasts, spreading across competing social media platforms around the globe, hadn't been taken by a seasoned field photographer, but rather a fifteen-year-old kid with a Samsung smartphone. He'd snuck out of his nearby apartment building and was there on the ground, posting shots to his Linkstamat feed as fast as he could shoot them, when he happened to catch the singular moment:

Two battered friends helping each other over a row of barricades.

Orange blinker lights created an artful flare in the foreground. Searchlight beams crisscrossed over their heads, making long crystal strands of the rain. The soft indigo background provided a quiet glimpse of a four-story glass building in mid-collapse.

It was quite something—one of those happy accidents even the kid himself admitted he didn't know he had until later. At the time, he'd been too distracted by the sudden disappearance of his entire feed, just as his follower count was finally cooking. He hadn't even had a chance to apply any filters to that image.

What the iconic photograph didn't show occurred twenty feet beyond the edge of the frame, perhaps a dozen steps from police custody, when Ryan Cloverhill took his medicine. Within two minutes, he'd gone into cardiac arrest, three portable auto-injectors sticking out of his neck like a bullfighter spiked by his own banderillas.

Later analysis revealed the devices had contained a lead-optimized cocktail of adrenalizing compounds laced with L-49, a Trial Phase 0 analgesic said to deliver twenty times the potency of morphine, with none of the addictive or respiratory-depressive characteristics. Cable news medical correspondents couldn't say with certainty what the recommended dose of such a potion might be, but clearly it was not three 3 mL vials in one go.

Much and little was revealed, in the months to come, about Cloverhill's alleged pet project, conducted entirely behind Link Labs' public-facing veil. Investigators suspected it had been in play ever since the prior presidential election, made historic by allegations of foreign and domestic interference through social media, among other things. Described in the Cloverhill Manifesto as his personal interpretation of "fighting fire with fire," it involved a systematic program of counterinterference involving algorithm manipulation, collusive data sharing, and the exclusionary distribution of targeted analytics, which officials believed could be tied to a dozen midterm congressional elections, half a dozen judicial retention races, and at least three international political scandals. Not to mention the opposition campaign for the presidential contest currently underway, to be decided that coming November.

"The only way to effectively govern a diverse society," Emma mused over coffee, several weeks down the road, as they half watched yet another morning segment on the topic, "is through benevolent dictatorship."

It was nice having coffee with Emma first thing in the morning again. Stephen doubted it would ever get old. He shrugged and said, "It's good to be the king." She took the remote and changed the channel.

Work teams recovered two bodies from Sham Rock: one from the base of the island's automated navigation tower, the other from the collapsed tunnel connecting the site's two dwellings. A third individual—Link Labs Director of Communications Kai Keahi, female, thirty-one years of age—was presumed lost at sea.

The gang from Stillwater saw one another again in Westchester in early October, at Perry's funeral. Beau's footage from their helicopter ride to the Rock comprised the last images anyone had of Perry Therkle and Will Shrader together. Will had framed the clearest shot he could harvest from the video clip and placed it beside the urn.

The twins and Kyle were all there. Lainie caught the three of them getting high in the parking lot before the visitation, but it was only a pretend scandal—at least they'd found a common interest.

The morning after the service, Kyle climbed into his car and headed back to campus upstate to study for exams. Robert and Randy hopped a flight back to Tempe to pull grill duty at their fraternity tailgater on football Saturday. The rest of them, for a change, made it through the weekend together.

L8R

EPILOGUE

She arrived on the island after a few days in Port-Gentil, trying out the breaks off the Cape at Palplanche while she brushed up on her Portuguese and waited for her package to arrive. She'd caught a few nice empties early on, nothing epic, but then the waves went flat for two days straight. So she'd zipped up her bag, gave her board back to the same local kid she'd bought it from, and chartered a ramshackle seaplane from another misplaced character she'd met at one of the beachside taverns in town. They left at dawn and flew west with the sunrise at their backs.

São Tomé was one big volcano, it turned out. She'd learned this fact from her pilot, a Capetonian transplant named VanTonder. How had she managed to miss such a tidbit during prep?

"Part of the Cameroon Line," he'd hollered over the roar of the twin props in his thick South African accent, discovering only after they were airborne that he had only one working headset on board. "The whole island comes right up out of the seafloor, ten thousand feet down. They say the oldest rock on this rock is thirteen million years."

"How old is any rock?" she yelled back.

"Verskoon?"

It didn't matter. From the air, it almost reminded her of home.

December at the equator was a steam bath. But in a settlement of only two hundred people, it didn't take long to find the two *mulheres estrangeiras* who owned the local trekking company.

They had a nice little spot on a rise in a clearing beneath a solitary oil palm. A cute little bungalow with views of the gulf to the east. Five or six clicks to the northwest, you could see the prehistoric spire of Cão Grande rising majestically from the rain-forest mist. Luna had cut her hair short. Mags had grown hers long. When Mags came to the door, she took one look at the gun in her visitor's hand and said, "We heard you were lost."

"Can't believe everything you see on the internet, I guess." It was a pain in the balls, traveling with a pet handgun. But there were plenty of reputable contract couriers for hire if you talked to enough people, and it was the last thing of Jud's she had left. Sig Sauer .380. *Great little gun*, he'd always said. *Not my first choice for stopping power.* But she'd learned how to aim. "Or do you guys have TV here?"

"The island does," Mags said. "But we don't. It's really good to see you, Kai."

"It's June."

"Sorry?"

"I go by June now."

"I see." Mags nodded slowly as Luna joined her at the door.

"Nice to meet you, June," Luna said, eyes fixed on the gun. "I . . . just made a pitcher of iced tea. Can I get you a glass? Or I think we have some palm wine."

"Iced tea sounds nice, but let's play the refreshments by ear. I've come a long way to ask you two a question. Is now a good time?"

Mags said, "What's the question?"

"Did you know he'd rigged the tunnel?"

Mags said nothing. Luna closed her eyes.

"Well," June said. "At least you got paid."

Mags took Luna's hand, took one last look at the gun, and said, "What happens now?"

June Gulliver unshouldered her waterproof duffel and dropped it at their feet. She traveled light: a couple of changes of clothes, a laptop, an e-reader, travel adapters, and some prototype hardware.

"On behalf of myself," she said, "and a few of our more trustworthy former developers at Link, I'd like to speak with you both about an investment opportunity."

They broke ground on Labor Day, two years after the blasts.

Stephen and Emma hopped a connection in Denver and met the others at

Sea-Tac baggage claim. After the hugs, Emma laid a hand on Will Shrader's cheek. "The beard looks good."

Will smiled. "Perry would have hated it."

"Bullshit." She leaned back and appraised him. "Still too skinny, though. How can we get a few more pounds on you?"

"He can have some of mine," Beau said, patting his middle, which had expanded noticeably since they'd seen him last.

"Mine first," Lainie said. "I swear my ass brought its own luggage. Stephen, good of you to join us, darling."

"Huh?" Stephen looked up from his phone. "Oh. Sorry, that was Kyle. He says hello."

Emma glanced over. "Everything okay?"

"No problem. I sent him a pic of the T-shirts they had at the Sub Pop store while you were in the restroom. Remind me to pick up his order on the way home."

Beau stared at him.

"What?"

"Who the hell are you," Beau said, "and what did you do with our friend Rollie?"

"God, tell me about it." Emma rolled her eyes. "That kid texts him more than his own mother. It's not fair."

"We like the same music, what can I say? The young man is corruptible. How are the twins?"

"Aiming for straight C's," Lainie said. "Just like last semester."

Beau nodded proudly. "The C stands for Consistency."

"At least they're back in school," Lainie said, chuckling a little as she sighed. "They're probably not going to light up the world, those two."

Beau shrugged. "Maybe they won't blow it up either."

Stephen and Emma grabbed their bags and followed the others out into a bright blue September day. Beau and Lainie had rented a big white Suburban with enough room for the five of them, the luggage, two elephants, and a marching band. Sunday traffic was light; they made it to the hotel with plenty of time to freshen up and grab a quick drink before it was time to get moving again.

As codirectors of public relations for the Stillwater Foundation, Beau and Lainie had packed their schedules tight, starting with interview segments for each of the local news stations. Then dinner with the mayor and a few municipal types, followed by cocktails somewhere else with some other whoever.

Stephen honestly couldn't keep it all straight. With Beau and Lainie running point, Emma handling the legal stuff, and Will consulting with the architects and civil engineers, his job was mostly to stand around looking pretty anyway. Who needed a technician with a psych degree?

But, strange as it felt to be back in town, he was glad to be along for the ride.

It had taken more than a year before federal investigators released the inheritance funds from the Cloverhill estate, as stipulated in Ryan's will, authenticated following his death by self-proving affidavit: $600 million in cash, divided six ways, with Perry's share transferring to his surviving beneficiary. The foundation had been Will's idea, but everyone had thrown in without reservation.

Now, finally, Stillwater was ready to begin its first big community development project: a thirty-acre public green space on the site where Link Village once stood.

Naturally, Monday dawned gray. It rained off and on throughout the morning.

But that didn't stop an estimated two thousand locals from turning out for the ceremony. There were five gold shovels lined up in a row. Beau and Lainie spoke to the crowd about the importance of thriving community spaces, where people could get out, come together, breathe the same fresh air, and remember what made them all human beings. Emma took Stephen's hand as Will got up to speak about plans for Therkle Station, the new trolley stop on the South Lake Union streetcar line.

Then Stephen got behind his gold shovel and helped his old friends turn up some mud. Several times that morning, he'd have sworn he caught glimpses of Ryan Cloverhill out there, somewhere in the crowd, watching the proceedings with everyone else.

But it was just a trick of the mind, or the light, or maybe just the rain. With umbrellas and ponchos, everyone looked more or less the same anyway. By the time the ceremony was over, the sun was already peeking out from the clouds.

Acknowledgments

As always, a few people have extra gratitude coming. My eternal thanks to Wes Miller for taking a chance on this book, and for the skilled editorial hand. The best editors know exactly when, where, and how to push, and this book improved leaps and bounds under his care.

Additional thanks to Ben Sevier, Karen Kosztolnyik, Deborah Wiseman, Carolyn Kurek, Caitlin Sacks, Albert Tang, and the entire Grand Central team for...well, everything. When publishing a book, that covers a lot, from overall release strategies all the way down to individual punctuation marks. Take the hyphen in "Device-Free Weekend," for example. Grammatically correct to a copy editor? Yes. A splinter in the mouse-clicking finger of a graphic designer laying out a title? Also yes! What to do? (In this case, you have several conversations about the blasted hyphen, confirm that the author barely knows grammar anyway, then file it under "Form follows function, but not always." Admittedly, this is not the sort of anecdote that normally makes it onto an acknowledgments page. But I've been around long enough now to know that these kinds of conversations don't *always* happen, and my appreciation couldn't be more sincere.)

Deep thanks to my longtime agent, David Hale Smith, for his loyalty, belief, and friendship. The dedication on this one is long overdue. Thanks to Naomi Eisenbeiss for keeping the trains on schedule. Thanks to James Watson, Attorney at Law and CPA, for deftly fielding some truly left-field questions, knowing I'd just bend the answers to suit my purposes anyway. Thanks to Ballard Locks for quick info about weather protocol. And big thanks to my small circle of first readers: Victor Gischler, John and Amy Rector, and Jessica and Kate Doolittle. Your reactions were invaluable. I click Like on you all.

About the Author

Sean Doolittle is the critically acclaimed author of eight stand-alone crime and suspense novels. His books have received the Barry Award and the International Thriller Writers Award, among other honors. A native of Nebraska, he lives in western Iowa with his family. You can find him online at www.seandoolittle.com.